THIS GOOD THING

LINDA SHANTZ

eBook edition ISBN: 978-1-990436-02-4

Paperback ISBN: 978-1-990436-04-8

Hardcover ISBN: 978-1-990436-05-5

For Juliet

CHAPTER ONE

The backstretch had a rhythm — to the days, and the seasons — but this morning it was missing a beat, the arrhythmia unsettling. The treatment was obvious, but she wasn't ready for it. She wanted to hold on to this feeling; celebrate the good, weep for the bad. But there could be no resting on laurels, no holding onto sorrow, or she'd be left behind. She'd learned that the hard way. She wouldn't let it happen again.

Eyes drifting over the four stalls, she tried to muster something resembling excitement. Before her was the future. Possibility. Fresh faces pushed over the screens with ears wired forward and nostrils flared, funnelling information from the unfamiliar sights and smells bouncing into their orbit. She would feel it again, despite how hard this year had been. She had to, didn't she?

"Aren't they cute? They're like newly drafted juniors at training camp, vying to make it in the big time."

"How'd that one get the scar? That's nasty."

"You're rubbing that one, Mike."

"And you're getting on him, Miller."

Liv remained silent, a careful smile on her lips as Nate and Michel bantered.

"This is what my career has come to. A barn full of two-year-olds."

She almost laughed at Roger Cloutier's jaded comment because she didn't feel much different from the Triple Stripe trainer. But next to his accomplishments, the short list of the things she'd done in her life so far left her feeling extremely inadequate. Three-quarters of a veterinary degree. Two-thirds of a Canadian Triple Crown. Her plans had been so much bigger than this. She'd expected to achieve so much more. This felt like being back to square one.

Auditions open. Searching for the next big horse. We're not sure what we're looking for, other than raw talent. A brain would only be a bonus. We proved we can deal with crazy.

The trainer's statement wasn't exactly true, mind you. There were still some older horses, but they were all reaching crossroads in their careers — the kind where decisions had to be made because they weren't as competitive as they'd once been, and the fairest thing might be for them to find new jobs. None of them were going to step up to be that next star. It was up to a two-year-old to fill that role. Perhaps one of these young candidates, shipped in yesterday. But if not, what then?

There were no empty stalls on the shedrow, though there was still a hole where Feste should have been, even if another prospect now occupied the physical space. And that filly in the stall next to the office? The stall that had once been Claire's, and most recently, Chique's? That stall was traditionally a place of honour in the barn, those two taking turns holding court there over the past four years. The sleepy chestnut meeting Liv's gaze didn't care about any of that.

The filly was as opposite to Chique as a young Thorough-bred could be. It wasn't just appearance that set them apart —

2

Chique's inky dark coat with merely a spray of white hairs on her forehead, compared to this bright orange chestnut with generous frosting. While this filly was unassuming, Chique was loud. Quirky, cheeky, with a crazy-wild forelock and rude tapping foot. And every annoying bit of her worth it because of her precarious talent.

When she was good, she was very very good. When she was bad... she was that girl.

But, as of two days ago, Chique was retired. Liv accepted that. As the filly's trainer — her only charge, with Feste gone — it had been her decision. It was a relief, she kept telling herself. Chique's wild-child tendencies and bouts of unsoundness made being responsible for her nerve-wracking. In a few years, she could look forward to Chique's foal in that stall. But in the meantime...

Twenty-four hours ago, the chestnut — She Sings, officially — had still been in light training with daily turnout on the Triple Stripe farm. The filly gave off a tranquil energy and was hunter-fat. She would likely spend a few weeks here, then go back to the farm for the winter to grow up a little more. They'd reassess in the spring. There was no rush here, as much as Liv felt the simmering pressure to find something, anything, to fill the vacancy left by Chique's departure.

How long does it take to get a horse to the races? As long as it takes.

"All right, let's get some tack on these brumbies," Roger said with a subtle shake of his head. "Is Emilie coming?"

Emilie, Liv's younger sister by four years, skittered in the end of the barn, helmet dangling from her fingers. She stopped short when she realized her abrupt entrance had startled the languid filly. "I'm here. I'm not missing this for the world. Reba is mine."

"Reba?" Nate raised an eyebrow. "You named a horse after

a country singer? More importantly, you have insider information?"

"Just enough to know who to avoid." She grinned, her eyes flitting to the colt with the scar on his face.

"That's hardly fair. If I break my neck coming off Pacino, won't you feel bad? I just got back from an injury."

It had taken Nate all of two minutes to assign the gargantuan colt a moniker, despite *Solaire* being boldly engraved on his halter plate.

"I have less than a year left in my program." Emilie held her helmet between her knees while she slipped a kerchief over her shoulder-length, dark hair. "I need to finish. I want to offer physiotherapy, not require it. I will help you for free, however, because you're practically family. Deal?"

Nate caught Liv's eye, his grin barely suppressed. *Practically.*

He didn't have to be here. He was done for the morning, and should be on his way home like any other top jock who had spent the last three hours breezing horses for various trainers — even if being sidelined after a dangerous spill had knocked him out of his customary leading rider position at Toronto's Woodbine Racetrack. Yet he was here. With her. Because of her. Ready to help initiate the next generation of hopefuls. Ready to hop on the horse the crew deemed "most likely to earn us a case of beer" — that being the traditional price one paid for parting company with one's mount on the backstretch.

"Do we have enough saddles for four?" Nate asked, following the assistant trainer, Jo St-Laurent. Her response was a quick nod as she headed for the tack room.

"It just means you get the one with the broken tree, Miller." Michel elbowed him.

"There are no saddles with broken trees," Jo grumbled.

"You need a vacation, Jo," Nate said.

"Or a sense of humour," Michel quipped.

"A vacation would help me find it," Jo snarled.

As Jo stacked the riders' arms with saddles and pads and girths, it felt a little like the first day of summer camp, except kids at camp usually chose their mounts by appearance. Once you'd been around the block, you learned to make your choice from body language and conformation. Especially in a barn full of baby racehorses, because though coloured Thoroughbreds were a thing, they were not a thing in this barn. Much of what they'd bred these youngsters for was unseen, waiting to be developed; something much deeper than an unusual coat colour. Things were boring in that department around here. Bay, dark bay, chestnut. Not even a token grey to brighten things up, though Reba was pretty flashy with all that white.

Nate started toward the scar-faced colt. If Nate hadn't been here, Liv wouldn't have balked at getting on him. She and Cory MacDonald had started this group as yearlings a year ago, and the colt had been an agreeable sort. He just hadn't been as humongous.

Cory MacDonald was on a trajectory right now that would see her end the race meet as Canada's leading apprentice jockey. Liv had never achieved that top-bug status. Once she'd gotten over the injury and demons that had interrupted her potential, she'd quietly transitioned to journeyman — woman? She was considered a good rider. She was respected by her peers. But she was nothing more than that. Wasn't that all that she'd asked for, though? Perhaps now was the time to recommit herself to being a rider, with no training side gig. What else was she going to do with herself?

As she prepared the compact bay gelding between Nicole's assignment, the filly Justakiss, and Nate's new friend Pacino, Liv made a mental note to send in a change for the description on the towering dark bay colt's registration papers. The laceration that had given him his distinctive identifier had occurred some time over the summer at the farm. No one actually knew how he'd cut his face that day, which was never an unusual thing. If there was trouble, horses had a way of finding it—especially young, expensive horses.

"Remember this one, Miller?" All tacked up, Liv stood in the doorway of the bay gelding's stall with a hand on the line, while Nate waited for Michel to take Pacino a turn — she already couldn't not call him that. "This is the little horse that dropped Cory that day you came to see Feste last fall when we were starting this group." It still hurt to say the colt's name. It probably always would.

There was a beat before Nate answered; a reminder they shared that ache. "The kid's come a long way. I'm starting to think I should've just retired and offered to be her agent."

"You don't get to quit on me yet. We're not done here. What was it you said? 'We are not yet the good thing we can be.'"

The murkiness left his features, replaced with something brighter, more genuine. "Thanks."

"For what?"

"The pep-talk." A grin emerged, though maybe not full force. They just had to keep telling each other those words.

"Hey, Jo?" Liv called when Michel halted Pacino in the middle of the shed. Her eyes went up and up, taking in the skyscraper of a two-year-old. "I think maybe you should hold this one while Michel legs Nate up."

Nate didn't even joke about vaulting up on his own. He just peered at the rafters, then nodded to Michel. "With feeling Mike."

"Don't forget to duck, Miller," Liv cracked.

He still made it look effortless, though he hunched once he was on top, acutely aware of the minimal clearance. Pacino stood stock-still, and when Michel took over at his head from Jo, he had to encourage the big colt to move forward. Nate reinforced the request with legs that only reached two-thirds of the way around Pacino's generous barrel, like a little kid on a pony.

Liv and Jo exchanged a quick glance at the oversized colt's exaggerated movement before Liv led out the much smaller bay gelding. Trop was his name, one guaranteed to get butchered by the track announcer, because it was French. No need to come up with a nickname for him; they'd just have to teach the anglophones how to pronounce it.

Roger accompanied them on the stable pony, Paz, the juveniles bumping into each other as they shied and snorted at every strange sight. Exercise riders done for the day, riding bicycles with whips stuck out of their back pockets. Laundry on lines drawn from post to post in a barn where they had, for some insane reason, not deemed it cold enough to drop their windows yet. The vet's assistant gathering x-ray equipment out of the back of a black SUV. Going to the track this late overlapped the veterinarians' rounds.

Nate started singing "Opportunity."

The Pet Shop Boys, Miller? The dialogue started in Liv's head.

Don't judge, he'd respond. His musical repertoire was bottomless, as had always been his ability to press through, move forward, though right now she felt he was struggling. This time, she was trying her best to lighten the load. He'd done that job on his own long enough.

He broke from his serenade, peering down at Emilie's chestnut filly from his mountain of a colt. "She's tiny."

"Chique's tiny," Emilie shot back.

"But Chique's fierce. This one's a school pony."

"So? Who cares if she can run?" Emilie said, leaning down

and draping her arms around Reba's neck. The filly's head continued to nod and she let out a happy snort.

"I do," Roger grumbled. "At least a couple of these horses need to be able to run, or I might be out of a job."

That was an exaggeration — the benefit of being a private trainer was he was on salary like the rest of them. But Rog was in a mood this morning. Fair enough. They were all out of sorts right now, the usual feeling of limbo in the weeks leading up to their departure for Florida, amplified by the retirement of a filly whose career had been paying those salaries. It surrounded them with a certain nervousness that only the emergence of a clear equine leader would quell.

Nicole's filly put on the brakes when they reached the gap at the training track. When Roger tried to reach over to help Nicole, the filly ducked sideways, away from him. *Yes, Paz is scary. Really?* Reba came to the rescue, Emilie grasping Kiss's rein to provide direction and confidence. Justakiss sighed, pressing her nose into Reba's neck.

"That's okay, Kiss, you can share a piece of Reba's brain," Emilie cooed. "These two were best friends on the farm."

The training track was more or less deserted — which was the inspiration for taking the neophytes out this late. Few others galloped over the deep sand, dried out and dusty by this time of morning. Some were horses for small trainers at the mercy of freelance exercise help, who left such mounts at the bottom of their list of priorities; others were owned by track workers who had to wait until the ones they got paid to care for were done up before training their own. It was the opposite end of the spectrum from a private stable like Triple Stripe — a dying breed somewhere in between the big public trainers and these small-time stakeholders. They were all connected, though. In the same game. Even if the playing field didn't feel particularly even.

They jogged in pairs, going clockwise along the outside rail, backing up to the half-mile pole. Liv's gelding and Nate's colt led the way in front of the fillies, though Pacino didn't look as if he'd figured out he should care about girls. Roger brought up the rear, assessing his charges.

Trop was a bundle of nervous energy, all flicking ears and bugged-out eyes, while Pacino lumbered along placidly beside him. The bay gelding shied at a Canada goose on the other side of the rail, bumping against his big companion. It was like hitting a brick wall. Pacino didn't bat an eyelash, and Nate looked hilariously disappointed that he was riding the easy one, while it took all Liv's skill to keep her two-year-old from jumping out of his skin.

Just beyond the red and white marker on the backstretch, they slowed. Pacino stumbled over his plate-sized feet, nose-diving.

"Shit!" Only Nate's balance and self-preservation prevented him from toppling to the dirt. He scrambled to gather the colt, then brought Pacino around like he was steering an eighteen-wheeler, joining their little troop facing the infield.

Roger frowned. "Think you'd better stay with me, Nate. You three go ahead. Once around, if they can make it."

Nicole's filly had the biggest spark in her eye, galloping on the tips of her toes with her neck a little too close to the vertical. She was by Just Lucky, like Chique, so maybe no surprise. Trop, also by their stallion, was trying his best to be good on Kiss's outside, staying mostly straight thanks to the brace of Liv's legs. They all rode longer and more defensively than they would with experienced horses. Green two-year-olds were not to be trusted.

Liv glanced over — and back — to Reba on the inside. Emilie sat every few strides to drive with her legs and seat, the filly gamely responding and snorting out a breath before dropping back again. Em finally shook her head and let the chestnut filly fall into a jog. Liv and Nicole pulled up to stay with her. No deserting one of the troop. Even if Reba would have been fine, the verdict was still out on Kiss — and, quite possibly, Trop. They finished the rest of the mile at the slower gait, Roger and Nate watching their progress. Roger continued to look grim as they lined up again.

"The gelding you're on is fine, Liv," Roger said. "And that filly, Nicole. Yours, though, Em, needs more time. We'll keep her around till we head to Florida, then she can go home for the winter. And this one..." Roger paused with the weight of what Liv was certain was about to come out of his mouth, "... is a wobbler."

The trainer said the words like he was passing a sentence, and it introduced another layer of disquiet to an already unstable morning. Two days ago they'd won the richest race in Canada. Today, life was far more ordinary. But there was one thing she knew about the racetrack: hope springs eternal in the heart of an unraced Thoroughbred, and two of them were better than none.

CHAPTER TWO

NATE COULDN'T TAKE Jo's top-forty pop this morning.

"Hey!"

"Just give me one day without Justin Bieber. Please, Jo? I'm in mourning." It seemed wrong to call it grief, but it felt like grief just the same.

Chique had won the Canadian International so easily, and retired with unanswered questions. How would she have fared in the Breeders' Cup? Could she have handled the flight to California and beaten those horses? And with the filly who had defined his career relegated to the Triple Stripe broodmare band, would he ever find that kind of success again?

"Oh, come on, Nate. I bet you love that song." Jo laughed.

"Bite your tongue. If I have to hear it again, I'm gonna cry. I'm sad enough."

"Get over it. There will be other horses. Speaking of which, Michel has Can't Catch Me ready. Why don't you hop on him and go around the shed until I've got this one ready for Liv?"

"Fine. That way, I'll only have to hear this shit when I go past our tack room. Text me when it's time to head out, because

I'm taking long turns. They play a better station at the other end."

He noticed Michel had earbuds when the groom stopped the rangy chestnut two-year-old next to him. Nate wished he could get away with that on the back of a horse.

The backstretch wasn't deserted, but somehow there was an emptiness to it. How that could be, when horses streamed onto the main track under the lights as it opened for training, he didn't know. The routine remained constant, but for Triple Stripe, the players had changed.

He and Liv jogged side-by-side along the outside rail, both of them locked into their mounts. While the silence between them was never truly unexpected, it felt peculiar at the moment. They had a lot to talk about. But since that moment she'd said yes, conversation had been limited to the horses and uncharacteristic small talk.

Maybe it was only him who felt the topic was being avoided. She had asked that they give it time before sharing. And even though she claimed it wasn't because she had any doubt, this was Liv. Her middle name was doubt. He still couldn't believe he'd asked her to marry him, knowing her like he felt he did. He couldn't believe she'd agreed. So maybe he didn't know her at all.

It's only been three days, Miller. Relax.

They pulled up, turning in at the wire. The same notes, the same rhythm, a different octave.

The colts they rode were half-brothers. Elemental, Liv's mount in this year's Plate — off since the middle of the summer — had come in yesterday afternoon after Pacino returned to the farm. Nate calculated in his head. They could probably get Elemental back to the races before the end of the meet, but no one was going to be in any hurry. That was never how Roger did things; never what Triple Stripe's owner — Liv's father, Claude Lachance — demanded.

Sometimes it drove Nate crazy, but the older he got, the more he knew it made sense to slow it all down. There weren't many outfits boasting that kind of no-pressure environment for their horses, and he was lucky, oh so lucky, to have landed himself at this one five years ago. The fact he hadn't ruined it along the way was some kind of miracle. He'd come close.

He'd told himself from day one it would be a bad idea to get involved with the owner's daughter, but Liv had gotten under his skin, with her insistence it would never happen. She'd been so determined to be professional when under that armour of hers was a soft heart that loved these animals above all. Somehow, he'd managed to become one of the few humans who received the same consideration.

In truth, he knew exactly how. Chique. That filly had been a vector, their shared bond, the journey on which she'd taken them what had allowed him in. Maybe that's why Chique's retirement made him so nervous. It was silly, wasn't it? The things they shared were still there. Like Jo said, there were other horses. And this crazy profession gave them a unique connection, a deep understanding of what, ultimately, made each other tick. But his injury, and his less-than-spectacular comeback, had him worried. *What would I do if I couldn't ride?* He hated to think of it ever coming to that, but even if he wasn't there yet, he'd have to face it, eventually.

His stats since returning were merely average, especially when you took Chique's International purse out of the earnings column. He'd better start riding some winners, including Cam here, in the Coronation Futurity. He was grateful to Liv for giving him the mount on the colt — it hadn't been necessary, but it had been kind. A bright light in these past weeks of mediocrity. Sure, the colt was a pain in the ass, but that didn't put Liv off. She'd agreed to marry him, hadn't she?

He'd dubbed Can't Catch Me *Cam* because the colt's full name was way too much of a mouthful. Usually, only vets and officials used actual registered names. Elemental was Eli, so now, the two-year-old out of the same mare, Sea Salt Soul, was Cam. He had the crew onboard. *Nate's back, he's assigning barn names...*

A glance from Liv, his half-nod in response, and they set off.

The colt's confidence had exploded after his maiden win, making him that much tougher to hold. Why were they galloping in company? Thankfully Liv stayed wide, though Cam was still pulling so hard Nate wondered if his back would hold up, despite his careful rehab. If the trauma his spine had suffered in that spill on Feste had been much worse, it would have ended his career. A reminder to be grateful he had one at all.

"Go on, Miller," Liv called. "Let him out a bit."

Cam shot ahead at the mere thought, like he understood her words. Nate glanced over his shoulder and Elemental flicked his ears forward, but didn't seem to mind being left behind. He wasn't like his half-brother. Sharp. Racing fit. A two-year-old colt who didn't want to be told what to do, like a fourteen-year-old kid with attitude.

Even galloping along, the big chestnut was not entirely compliant. It made Nate think of Just Jay, who was by the same stallion, Extra Terra, but totally push-button and professional. Always had been. Was Cam an anomaly, or was Jay? He'd just assumed Jay's tractability came from Extra Terra, as his half-siblings were all a little bit opinionated. But maybe all the agreeable genes had been selected for Jay. Maybe he was an outlier. It was so rare to have all the good bits collected in one horse. Looks. Brains. Talent. *Everything.* It was a shame that since rehabbing from a minor fracture he'd sustained in the spring at Santa Anita, he'd been a pasture ornament on the farm — even though, as far as Nate knew, he'd completely recovered.

While he was pondering the wonder of genetics, Cam was trying to run off. "Tomorrow, dude. You can breeze tomorrow."

He made Cam wait after pulling up, and Liv, not far behind, angled Eli next to the rangy chestnut.

"How'd he feel?" Nate's eyes ran over the more compact bay. Eli had packed on a bit of weight during his brief vacation, and sported a good start on his winter coat. There was a light sweat on his neck, but he'd retained enough fitness he looked otherwise unaffected.

"Good," Liv nodded. "He'll be ready to run at Gulfstream once we get down there, all going well."

They exchanged a look.

They weren't talking about this winter. They weren't talking about the wedding. No date had been set, no ring had been bought, no one had been told. She'd asked, and he'd given. He had to trust her reasons.

It had been a hell of an autumn. A hell of a year. And while part of him wanted the world to know, another part wanted to keep it — and her — to himself. But that wouldn't happen, any more than they could suspend the racing game in time. Everything moved forward, and with Chique retired, and no Feste, they'd have to find their place and purpose.

Leftovers from the spread Nate's agent had brought the morning after Chique's victory on Sunday resurfaced in the tack room. Backstretch tradition, for the winning rider to thank the crew. It had been a good one this time — they wouldn't let Nate get away with anything less. Liv picked at some grapes, but shook her head when Jo held out a wrap. Three days old? That was risky.

"Anyone else see the irony in Pacino turning out to be the most dangerous of those four newbies after all?" Nate said, finally bringing up what they'd all skirted.

Roger's assessment hadn't been a surprise; they'd likely all been coming to the same conclusion. They would get an official diagnosis, but there was no hiding from the symptoms: a big, growthy colt, his lack of coordination suggesting neurological deficits. Not a safe horse to be on top of.

"I'll call OVC," Liv said, adding making an appointment for the colt at the University of Guelph's teaching hospital to her to-do list. With any luck, it would be EPM instead — a treatable disease that could present in a similar fashion. Because wobbler syndrome — cervical vertebral malformation, or cervical stenotic myelopathy — typically had a poor prognosis.

Roger pressed into the room and grabbed the wrap Liv had turned down, sniffing it and shrugging before taking a bite. The possibility of food-borne disease would not deter most race-trackers. Roger's immune system was probably conditioned. "His ataxia's pretty mild. A candidate for surgery, maybe. Why did no one notice it before, though?"

"The new farm manager isn't Geai," Liv said dryly. "It's subtle enough. I suppose it was easy to miss. They probably just thought he was lazy."

"Or like a teenage kid who can't get out of bed before noon because he's growing too much," Nate said.

"Were you that kid, Nate?" Jo questioned with a grin.

"Never. I was a horse guy, remember."

"A unicorn." Emilie laughed.

16

"That, and well, I didn't really grow, did I?"

True enough.

Pacino's exclusion brought them down to four homebreds from the six they'd started last September, if they included Reba. After Feste, Can't Catch Me had been the most physically ready to command a spot in their Woodbine ranks, though his mental state left something to be desired. He was aggravating, as only a two-year-old colt could be. He'd shown brilliance breaking his maiden a couple of weeks ago, enough that Roger had nominated him for the Coronation Futurity, the country's premier race for juveniles. A win there would tag Can't Catch Me as a solid prospect for next year's Plate. He might be the one they'd be hanging their hopes on next.

"Can I talk to you two?" Roger's gaze took in both Liv and Nate. They followed him to the office like a couple of kids being called in to the principal. The trainer planted himself behind the desk and rearranged papers distractedly. "Am I to assume the two of you have made up?"

Nate maintained a perfect poker face, while she had to press her lips firmly together — and even then there was a slight lift to their corners. Though she was sure they could trust Roger with their news, there was an order to who needed to know, with a few others coming before him. And once that happened, all hell would break loose. That was the part she was dreading. Could they just skip past all the congratulations and preparations and get to the part where it was just them again?

"I guess you'd say that." Nate spoke for both of them.

"Good. Glad you finally realized you're better together than apart. We need both of you. Next — we're overdue talking about Florida."

The mutterings about Payson Park typically began as soon as Ontario's temperatures dropped to single digits, which usually happened at least once in September. This year, they'd all been distracted by Nate's injury and Chique's impending retirement. The last big race of the season, the Canadian International — Chique's final start — signaled the fast-approaching end of the meet. It added urgency to winter arrangements.

"I'm assuming you're staying till the end?" Roger directed his question at Nate.

"As much as I hate the idea, yeah, I'd better."

The trainer shifted his attention to Liv. "Do you have a plan?"

She nodded. Nate's answer made hers concrete. "I'll stay too. It's about time you got to go south early, Rog."

"At this rate, there might not be anything staying for you to worry about. I'll book the van." Roger placed his palms flat on the desk, glancing from one hand to the other as if he didn't quite know what to do with himself. Then he looked up. "You know Chique isn't eligible for a Sovereign award? She only has two starts in Canada this year."

It was true, but Liv had accomplished her goal. Gotten the filly back to the races after her laminitis scare last winter. Retired her sound. After that, awards seemed a vain pursuit. "Horse of the Year will go to Ride The Wave." A colt Nate had won the Queen's Plate on, and Liv had taken over for trainer Dean Taylor — neighbour and brother to her best friend, Faye — when Nate had been sidelined.

"They should give it to Chique anyway," Nate said, ever devoted to the filly. "Don't get me wrong, I love The Wave, but Chique deserves to be Horse of the Year for everything she went through."

"You can vote all you want, Miller, but they're not going to give you a ballot. Or change the rules." Not that she didn't agree with him.

Roger rose and shuffled around the desk, glancing at his watch. "I've got to go."

That was it? Why did she feel there were things he wasn't saying?

He paused by the door. "We'll work Can't Catch Me tomorrow. You still want to ride him, Nate?"

"Absolutely. I'm not looking that gift horse in the mouth."

Liv rolled her eyes. She'd let him have the mount on the colt, like a welcome back present after his injury, when she probably should have kept Cam for herself. She'd taken enough flak for it in the jock's room.

"Here's hoping his first race wasn't a fluke." Roger's fingers grasped the door handle. "He's our only solid runner right now." There was that repeated truth, and the vague sense of panic that came with it.

"See you tomorrow, Rog," Nate said, turning back to Liv as the door settled back into its frame. "What's up with him? He's had a bug up his butt all morning."

"We're all a little discombobulated right now," Liv rationalized, letting Nate pull her out of the beaten-up sofa. "Want to go for a run later?"

It had been months since they'd run together. Exercise would aid in a return to routine while they tried to figure out what this new version of normal would look like.

"Sure." He stepped closer, his brief kiss somehow seasoned with heat, sending a current zipping from their lips to where his hand rested lightly on her forearm. It dissipated, slowly, as he moved away. "I'll see you at the farm."

CHAPTER THREE

Chique circled the pen, puffs of dust rising, the breath she expelled visible in the chill air. She pawed with one foot as if trying to conjure grass. When it didn't miraculously appear, she tipped her head between the fence rails, Nate cringing as her teeth scraped slivers of wood from a post that had long ago lost its paint.

"She looks bored," he said, slipping a hand under Liv's jacket and hooking a thumb through one of her belt loops. It tugged her jeans just slightly off one hip, exposing an inch of skin to the cool fall air. She shivered, and he used it as an excuse to pull her closer and kiss her like they hadn't spent the last three months trying to destroy this thing between them.

"That's too bad, because this is her new life," Liv murmured.

"And this is ours."

The small fifty-by-fifty foot paddock next to the training barn was the first step in the post-racing letdown process. Giving up her search for fresh green, Chique crumpled her front legs and, tilting her head, somehow managed not to fall on her shoulder as she nibbled, reaching blades just beyond the lower board. An impressive display of balance and contortion. She totally ignored the flake of second cut hay Liv had set in the middle of the pen.

"What does that look like, exactly?" Liv turned back to watch Chique, which felt to him like withdrawing into herself, as if she could only stay in his arms for so long. She was smiling, but there was uncertainty behind her expression.

"Probably not much different from what it did before we tried to screw it all up."

He should have taken her question as an opening for discussing the practical points of their decision, but he wasn't sure that's what she meant. There would be changes, of course, but for now, he expected things to remain much the same. She would stay at the house, he in his apartment on the farm. Where they would live after that was one of those things they had to talk about. It was the deeper things she was trying to get her head around. The *how does you and me become us?*

Chique let out a long, low exhale, the way her nostrils vibrated giving away her tranquilized state. Liv had dosed her just shy of staggering the first day, dressing the filly in thick polo bandages on all fours and bell boots in front. She'd decreased the dose incrementally since then, but he didn't judge her for maintaining the precautions. An ounce of prevention. Because who wanted to get hurt on their first days of retirement? They'd all heard the tragic stories of well-meaning adopters of Thoroughbreds off the track, turning the horse out in a huge paddock, only to have them run through a fence. A lot of these horses were agoraphobic and needed a gradual reintroduction to normal equine life. They had to learn how to be a horse all over again.

Retirement. He wasn't sure he'd entirely accepted that their big filly, his cheeky little bitch, was done racing.

The filly abandoned her frustrated efforts to graze, casting a hazy glance their way, then meandered to the middle. Still not going for the hay, she pawed again, flopped down, and ground the dust into her still-sleek, inky coat. She was going to need to grow some insulation, fast. Farms rarely indulged broodmares in blankets.

Broodmare. Still couldn't get his head around that, either.

"I don't think she's going to kill herself," Liv admitted, finally.

Over the next few days, Liv would wean Chique off the tranq, have her hind shoes pulled, and in time, move the filly to a larger paddock. Liv ultimately wanted her back out with Claire — closer, in the stalls under Nate's apartment — but that wouldn't happen until Chique had finished her quarantine. Liv wouldn't take chances with an in-foal mare, regardless of the vaccination program in place. The unborn fetus was too vulnerable.

The letdown protocol was the same for all the horses transitioning from racing careers at Triple Stripe, not just those with champion status like Chique. The ones who didn't have the pedigree and race record to join the breeding program would get as much time as they needed to adjust before Emilie and Nicole began teaching them the basic skills they'd need for their next careers. Learning to stand in crossties. Learning to stand at a block to be mounted. Learning to ignore the kissing and clucking that at the track they'd learned meant *go fast.* They'd receive a solid foundation under saddle before being placed in new homes.

No reason Chique couldn't learn some of those things, too. Maybe he'd play with her in his spare time. It'd get his mind off waiting for Liv to be ready to talk.

"Want to go visit the weanlings?" Liv asked.

As they headed to the paddocks where this year's crop lived

22

out, it seemed they'd downgraded their planned run to a walk. Probably not a bad thing, the way they'd been going lately. It was good to take it easy for a change, though it was definitely not the norm for Liv.

Everything was slower on the farm, a contrast to the track where the pace was swift, even if this time of year it was less so. No pressure out here. Mares were incubating next year's foals, weanlings were growing, stallions were enjoying their off-season. Only the yearlings were working, and that was just until the end of October. He hadn't even seen the yearlings this fall. How bad was that? More evidence of how off things had been since his accident. He hadn't been sure he was part of it all anymore. Now he'd signed on for life.

Liv stopped by the fillies' pasture. "That's this year's Sotisse."

He leaned into the rails, arms draped through, and while three curious weanlings sauntered over to investigate, a dark filly with irregular white dripping down her face remained squarely beyond the others, aloof.

"Are you sure she's related to Chique?" He glanced at Liv, grinning. The yearling was a full sister to both the cheeky four-year-old and Feste.

The physical resemblance was there. The filly would be taller than Chique, but was the same charcoal colour; had the same correctness as her siblings. Sotisse had been more generous with the white this time — besides her facial marking, this filly had half-stockings behind. She was striking.

"Does she have a name?" he asked.

"Her barn name is Fleur. We haven't submitted anything official yet."

"That's unimaginative. Who came up with that?" Not that he was one to talk. *Cam. Eli. Pacino.*

"Em, I guess. She thinks that marking looks like a fleur-delis, but that name is on the Jockey Club's permanent list, so we can't register her as that. Too bad. A pretty filly like her needs a pretty name."

Nate stepped away from the fence to avoid causing a squabble among the friendlier babies. "So are you really cool with staying till the end of the meet?"

"Did you think I'd leave you behind?" She raised her eyebrows at him, a droll smile twisting her lips. "As Rog pointed out, we might not even have any horses at the track to worry about. But I might as well keep riding."

"You're a little lost right now, aren't you?" He hoped that's all it was. He would give a lot for a little peek into her mind.

Liv dropped her gaze. "A little. But it'll pass. As long as you're not offended that the whole marriage thing is not the be-all and end-all for me."

He laughed, finding her hands, closing them into a ball beneath his and kissing her knuckles. "Never thought it would be." She'd brought up the subject, but it still didn't seem the right moment to talk dates and houses. He still searched for assurance. "Your answer hasn't changed?"

She lifted her eyes to him, something pure in her smile. "No."

He squeezed her hands gently, then drew out the fingers of the left one, supporting them with his right. "I still need to get you a ring, though."

Her smile dissolved into what he had to call a frown. "How will that work? I can't wear it when I'm riding. What if I break my hand? I'd be horrified if they had to cut it off. Maybe we could get matching tattoos instead."

That was Liv, overthinking things since forever. Tattoos? It was going to take them a while to sort out all the pieces. "Indulge me."

"I'm sorry, I shouldn't give you a hard time about it." Her

grin was sheepish. "I was just never the girl who wanted any of that."

He laughed. "Yeah, I figured that out a long time ago, don't worry. I'll just keep reminding myself what an extraordinary honour it is that you said yes."

Liv pushed him away, but he caught her arm, and pulled her back in. Bit by bit, he'd get her used to this.

She broke away from the kiss, but her arms stayed around his shoulders as her eyes fixed on his. "I know you think I'm avoiding things. It's just this week... it's an adjustment."

"I know. It's okay. This helps."

Too bad the vibration of her phone interrupted. He was enjoying this taking it easy thing. He snatched the device from her back pocket because his hands were there anyway, and handed it to her. It took him a second to pin the twangy notes of the ring tone down to Counting Crows' "Hangin' Around."

Liv snapped it from his fingers. "It's Rog." The trainer was clearly on her limited pickup list. She swiped the screen to accept the call, concern on her face. "What's up?"

He couldn't hear what Roger was saying, but Liv went still, her lips parting slightly before she pressed them together, a crease forming between her brows.

"Say that again?" she asked, quickly putting the call on speaker so Nate heard Roger's response.

"Woodbine asked me to talk you into running Chique once more, so she's eligible for the Sovereign. We just need to tell them what we want, and they'll write the race."

Nate met Liv's eyes. There was no way she'd agree.

Liv's tight expression gave way to a more businesslike visage as she finally seemed to breathe again. "Leave it with me, okay?"

"Take some time to think about it," the trainer said. "A couple of days won't make a difference."

She disconnected and locked onto Nate's eyes again, but didn't speak.

The fillies' heads shot up, swinging to the side in a synchronized motion. Fleur let out a warning whinny. A horse and rider approached, something the reserved filly clearly found concerning. She drew herself up, tail flagging, and snorted. Her companions drifted away from where Liv and Nate stood to get a better view of the stranger.

"Hello Jay!" Nate grinned as he recognized the good-looking chestnut. Emilie sat in a jumping saddle instead of an exercise saddle. Jay wore a quarter sheet over his well-rounded rump, and a track bridle with martingale rings; a hybrid of equine disciplines. The scene solidified his assumption Jay was now retired, even if he hadn't heard an official declaration. "You're turning our stallion prospect into a riding pony?"

"I've been messing about with him all summer," Emilie said. "It seemed such a shame he was hanging out getting fat in a paddock when there's nothing wrong with him. Maybe he wants to be an event horse. He's a pretty good dancer."

"He looks amazing," Nate observed.

"I bet he can jump," Liv said. "But not sure we can justify keeping him as a colt if he's going to do that."

"Why not?" Emilie countered. "You know how much of a gentleman he is. And maybe he could cover some sport horse mares."

"Geai would roll over in his grave if he heard that," Liv said wryly. "Breeding a Thoroughbred stallion to sport horse mares? Blasphemy."

"Not if he's not standing to race-bred mares." Emilie grinned. "I haven't heard any recent plans for that."

"The right offer hasn't come along. He's so well-bred and has a decent race record. He just had terrible luck on the track. Someone will give him a shot as a stallion."

"You can't send him away," Emilie pleaded. "Not Jay."

Liv rolled her eyes at her sister. As if she hadn't been guilty of the same sentimentality. Claire's story came to mind. Possibly the first time Nate had felt he could have feelings for Liv was the day she'd admitted an emotional attachment to Claire, acknowledging that in this business she should know better. But she'd never be that hard-hearted.

"What's the matter with you two?" Nate interjected, being the one to insert common sense for a change. "Look at this horse. He's only four. He's obviously sound. Put him back in training. If he decides he's done with that, he'll tell us. But if he's not? He deserves another shot." He levelled his gaze on Liv.

"So," Liv looked from Nate to Emilie. "That would be fun."

"Damn right," he said. "We need a hero."

Here was their big horse, hiding in plain sight.

In the end they hadn't gone for a run, but there was too much buzzing around in Liv's head; she had to make up for it. She changed into her suit, tucked her hair under a cap, and grabbed her goggles. Nate was probably doing something sensible, like having a nap because this was Wednesday, which meant night racing. If she tried to do the same, she'd only toss and turn.

Some days remained temperate, still beautiful and warm for this time of year, but the nights were cold and often frosty. Today, with the breeze — when the sun ducked behind some distinctly October-like clouds — it was definitely chilly. Thank goodness they'd gotten a heater for the lap pool at the house. When she reached the patio, she slipped her goggles in place, left her hoodie on a lounge chair, and dove straight in.

Swimming was a breathing exercise as much as anything,

and she fell into the rhythm of it: *pull, pull, pull, breathe... pull, pull, pull, breathe.* Her kicks were automatic. Now her mind was quiet enough to think, her pumping heart keeping the blood flowing, feeding her brain as well as her body.

She was second-guessing her big decisions. Oh, not Nate, and her affirmative response to his life-altering question. It was like she'd faced down her fear and leapt over the abyss, landing safely on the other side — when she'd been sure she'd crash to a horrifying end. All the drama seemed so silly now. She'd had two choices: say yes, or lose him. When that's what it came down to, the decision was straightforward. At the track there was a saying: *there's no such thing as a sure thing.* While she might not be sure about the future of Triple Stripe right now, she was sure about Nate Miller.

At some point, they'd have to tell her parents about the engagement. Nate had gone along with her request to keep it just between them for now, but she couldn't put it off forever. Her parents would be happy, but their response would pale compared to Connie Miller's. It was a good thing that announcement would happen over the phone, because Liv loved Connie, but her overt joy was going to be a lot for someone who'd grown up with a comparatively restrained mother. Then, of course, there would be Faye and Emilie. Too bad Connie was in Calgary; she'd get them all in a room together and just be done with it.

Chique, though. Had she been too hasty to retire the filly? There was no real rush to get her to the breeding shed. Liv knew what her own response would be to the question that would come, inevitably, about her own reproductive status.

Sorry, filly.

She couldn't help thinking Chique might be happier with the kind of future Em wanted for Jay. It was Em's passion, the retraining. Sometimes Liv longed for more complexity; missed the precision of dressage, and the finesse of riding a cross-country course. The control of it. But there was only so much time, only so many hours in a day, and what the track didn't eat up, maintaining the level of fitness she needed to keep race riding, did.

But should she bring the filly back for one more race? Chique's brief stint on the farm wouldn't affect her fitness; it would only freshen her. And what Woodbine was proposing was as much an exhibition as anything. Her competitors would be nothing close to the calibre Chique had faced this fall, or would have encountered in California at the Breeders' Cup. But those were famous last words in horse racing: *one more race.*

It wouldn't interfere with her plan to focus on her riding. The filly could run under Roger's name, even. Nate hadn't pushed her to make a decision about the offer any more than Rog had, but she would discuss it further with both of them. She just needed time to bounce the idea around on her own.

And now, Jay. She realized the reason she'd let things sit with the big colt, instead of talking to her father about anything beyond stallion duty, was because of Nate. Because she'd been there that day at Santa Anita, when the colt had toppled over another runner and rider, sending Nate to the dirt. Nate had walked away. Jay too, but they'd needed to euthanize the other horse, his rider succumbing later in hospital to the injuries he'd suffered.

Nate had been the one to bring up putting Jay back into training. Maybe, just maybe, Jay was what Nate needed to get himself back on track. Because she didn't think there was anything wrong with Nate's fitness, or his nerve; just that, like her, since that tragic afternoon in Saratoga when they'd lost Feste, something much deeper was lacking. He'd misplaced the sizzle he'd ridden with before that day. Maybe Jay could fix what had broken with Feste.

She drew herself out onto the deck, snapping up her towel as the breeze roused goosebumps from her skin. When she checked the time, there was a text notification from her father. *Could you meet me in the office?*

Liv tilted her head, perplexed. That was odd. She typed a response. *Just got out of the pool. I can be there in half an hour. Is that okay?*

That's fine. See you then.

CHAPTER FOUR

Liv always acknowledged the painting when she walked into the office. A smile on the good days. A welling of tears, quickly suppressed, on the bad. She wasn't used to being on this side of the desk, looking up at the large oil on canvas instead of sitting under it. It made her feel watched instead of watched over. She studied Geai's face for an explanation for this summons, but he just stood silently with the smile the artist had captured perfectly. Just Lucky on his left, Sotisse on his right.

While that portrait had become a memorial to Geai, of sorts, it also illustrated the legacy of the man presently sitting beneath it. It wasn't a Windfields Farm-sized legacy — far from it — but Claude Lachance had built something... *honourable* was the word that came to mind. He'd kept the outfit small enough to take proper care of the animals and the people who looked after them, a rare thing in the horse world.

Her eyes dropped to him, and she smiled, just a quick flash of the affection she felt but rarely displayed in what had always seemed a cautious father-daughter relationship. Claude wasn't a hundred percent comfortable being a father, and she'd always felt slightly awkward in his presence — except she'd inherited his passion for the Thoroughbred, which somehow made up for the other imbalances.

She perched on the edge of the big chair positioned in front of the desk, scanning the flat surface and wishing she could grab the small stack of foal papers — anything to occupy her hands. Thankfully, not unlike her, Claude wasn't one for small talk. She expected he'd get right to the point.

"There's been a... change of plans... for the winter," he began, his words coming haltingly.

A tremor raked through her, because the last time she'd heard that quaver in his voice was when he'd called her to tell her about Geai's death. Her mind jumped from one scenario to another, trying to prepare herself for whatever blow he was about to deliver.

"Roger is staying home. Hélène has a mass on one of her ovaries, and will be undergoing treatment."

The chill she felt became a numbing cold, freezing her jaw shut when a million questions hurtled through her brain. She wanted to know more, every minute detail so she could help fix it, when she should just nod; agree. Yes, of course Roger must stay to be with her. It explained why the trainer seemed so distracted of late, waiting on news that would cause a shift in the fault lines of his life that would affect them all.

"They've scheduled surgery. They can't biopsy the tumour until then... or really know what they're dealing with. He's suggested you and Jo talk about who will take over. Both of you are capable. For now, of course, you'll just carry on as arranged. Jo will handle things at Payson while you stay here, till the end of the season. In the meantime, the two of you can decide what you'd like to do. If neither of you want the job, we'll have to hire someone... or give the horses to a public trainer."

Which would be a major upheaval. While the news would shake the entire crew, if Jo or Liv took over, they would remain intact. A public trainer would have his or her own employees. Maybe one or two of the grooms would get jobs with the new conditioner, but more than likely, they'd end up unemployed. The ever-loyal Jo. Michel and Sue, who had a baby on the way.

"Does Jo know?" she asked, finally, swallowing away the constriction in her throat so she didn't sound completely strangled.

Her father nodded. "Roger told her. I'll leave the rest up to the two of you."

Thoughts raced as she excused herself and texted Nate. She tromped up the stairs to his apartment, not caring if she woke him. Jo would take over training duties. She had to. It just made sense. And any arrangement they made was temporary, right? Hélène would get treatment. She would get better. That's what had to happen. Hélène, who had always shown her kindness, trying to be a surrogate mother for the daughter of her friends, when said daughter had shunned her own family in her fog of grief and disappointment in the long months following Geai's death.

She let herself in. When there was no sign of Nate in the main room, she pushed the door of his bedroom open. It was dark, blind drawn and bedsheets rumpled, but he was sitting up, phone in hand.

"What is it?"

She crossed the floor and sat next to him, pushing away the self-consciousness that surged, being on his bed.

"The meeting with my father was about Roger. He's going to be taking some time off." She relayed the information she'd received from Claude. It was as if with the words she was sharing the numbness she felt, because Nate went still, his features paralyzed in an expression of shock and dismay.

"You're kidding." His voice was flat, like he was begging her to confirm his mechanical utterance, when it was not something anyone would joke about. "I guess that explains why he's been in such a mood lately."

"Needless to say, they're not coming to Florida."

"I guess not."

"I'll talk to Jo tomorrow. We could always reschedule the van and keep everyone here longer. We don't know for sure yet if Jay will run. All that matters is that Roger knows he doesn't have to worry about anything."

She wanted to be there for Hélène like Hélène had been there for her, but the best way to do that was by helping manage the horses so Roger could devote his full attention to whatever was in store.

"Yeah." Nate reached for her hand; clasped her fingers. "I am so ready for this year to be done."

CHAPTER FIVE

It had been harder than usual to drive back to Woodbine for Wednesday night racing, her father's disclosure still raging in her head. Tonight, there were three of them in the women's room: Cory, runaway hot apprentice, and at the other end of the career spectrum, Luna Russo. What would Luna be now, forty? This game aged a person faster than a kinder lifestyle would. The atmosphere and elements weathered you. The work broke down your body. The mental demands tested your spirit.

Cory was out of the room for the first race and Liv tried to keep her nose deep in a book to avoid conversation. She surfaced as post time drew near. Nate was on a 15-1 shot, and she hoped he could pull one out of a hat here. He needed to ride some winners that weren't Triple Stripe horses. She locked in on the television monitor as the horses leapt out of the gate.

Nate's horse broke on top — there was no faulting him there — settling on the rail once he was clear, in front as the field emerged from the chute. He tried to slow his mount, create a false pace, but there was only so much you could do with a horse like that. Cory stalked on the favourite, creeping up around the turn, hooking Nate at the head of the stretch. He was already into the horse, asking for something Liv didn't think the horse had, but if you don't ask, how can you know? It wasn't to be, though. His horse stuck for a couple of strides before fading, Cory adding another victory to her tally.

"You done messed that boy's head up good."

Liv's head snapped to Luna. So she was to blame for Nate's bad luck? She ignored it, chiding herself for already giving the older rider the satisfaction of a physical reaction. She wished she were riding the second and not stuck in here with Luna for another half hour.

"Nice win, Cory," she said when the apprentice returned. It was getting repetitive, but the kid had worked hard for her success.

"Thanks Liv!" Cory's voice was as chipper as always.

There was no arrogance there. She was keeping her head on her shoulders. Had it really been just a year ago she'd helped Liv start yearlings? Liv grabbed her book, because if she didn't she might find herself going down that path again. If she'd stayed at Woodbine to get her apprentice allowance, would she have been that hot bug? But if that had happened, her course would have been different. How would it all have worked out? Maybe she'd have been the one riding Chique in the Plate. Where would Nate have fit into that story?

"Good luck, Cory," she said as Cory reached for the door, dressed in the next set of silks.

"Thanks Liv!"

And so it went.

Luna flipped through the *Daily Racing Form*, barely raising her head. Chique was on the cover, clear winner of the Canadian International. It seemed like weeks ago now, not days.

"I don't know why you retired that filly," Luna said. "You're too soft to be a real trainer. You can't be all nice and compassionate when you're a woman in that job, if you want to make it. You're better off back in here, riding your pick of your father's horses in your Barbie barn. You don't even know what it's like to survive in the real world. You're pretty much a nobody outside of Triple Stripe, aren't you?"

Tension built in her temples. Whatever. Liv acknowledged it — while Luna had worked her way up the hard way, starting as a hotwalker, Liv, the owner's daughter, benefited from the proverbial silver spoon. She'd never denied it; realized that to someone like Luna, the work she'd put in didn't count. Part of why she'd gone to the States to start her riding career was to get away from that, though the other part, Claire, had probably nullified the credibility of her intent. The whole topic poked at a sore spot — that even in her position of privilege, she'd failed to make a mark. Would she ever shake that?

She would defend her decision to retire Chique, though. "This isn't the nineteen-hundreds anymore," she said, choosing her words, trying to keep her voice level. "It's our responsibility to show compassion. For one, because the horses deserve it; also because the outside world demands it. We can't afford to continue to perpetuate the public's view of racing."

Luna barked with a sardonic laugh. "Come on. She only had three starts this year. What's that, thirteen lifetime? She's only four. If she's sound, why not run her? Why not bring her back next year? *That* would be good for racing. But you're too scared to push her. And that's why you'll never make it as a trainer. No guts, no glory, baby."

Pain radiated from her jaws as she clenched her teeth together. Luna was right. It was true. She'd told herself she was being conservative with Chique, but after Feste, she was terrified. And therein lay the appeal of riding, because she was only responsible to a point for these horses. If a horse she was on was injured in a race, she'd feel terrible, but it wouldn't be because of what she'd induced, or missed, or ignored.

What had happened to Feste, she'd had absolutely no control over, and it haunted her. As the trainer, her charge's health was all on her. It was constant stress, trying to balance the need to challenge a horse to achieve optimum fitness, versus pushing them too far. Making the most of their innate athleticism without exploiting it. Anyone who watched Thoroughbreds grow up saw that will to run. Foals tearing around their mothers. Yearlings racing through pastures, making their caretakers cringe at their antics. Old, retired horses still showing off.

So maybe Luna was right. She wasn't cut out to be a trainer. Which is why she would ride. She'd give Jo whatever support she needed this winter while Roger was on leave, but her place wasn't to be the one in command.

The only time she was completely unaware of Nate's presence was in here, waiting to be sprung from the metal barrier. Happy Together stood square and ready; sweet, sensible filly that she was. If only the filly would exhibit a bit of spark on top of her talent — that mysterious something that differentiated the *can run a bit* from a truly nice horse. They had yet to find it, and Emilie was eager to get her hands on the four-year-old to transform her into a sport prospect if she didn't show something soon.

Calls bounced down the line between gate crew and riders till that moment, a split-second of stillness, when the starter hit his button and set them free. The bell rang in her ears as the doors slammed open and Nate registered on her radar again — but as a rival for the next minute and change.

Sometimes he still rode the favourite, and this was one of

those times. Happy bounced to the lead, free from the same expectations and the turmoil to their outside: the bumps and yells as the rest of the field sorted themselves out. Nate emerged from the fray to contest her lead — just some friendly pressure to keep the pace honest. Not that these fillies and mares were handy enough to play much of a game. This wasn't Elemental and Ride The Wave in the Plate. But Liv played along. *You want the lead? Go ahead.* Knowing he really didn't. *You can't mess with my head out here, Miller.*

He stayed tight to her, buzzing like an annoying insect as they headed into the far turn in the six-furlong race. Was he singing? The rush of air kept words from reaching her ears. *That won't rattle me either, Miller. Does that work on the others? I'm guessing not, because you've been kind of a stranger to the winner's circle lately. Was that mean? Sorry, but I'm not paid to be nice out here.*

Nate's mount had a penchant for bearing out, and though Happy was the soundest horse in the Triple Stripe barn, Liv waved her whip like she was asking the filly to run — with a bit of an open rein to let her drift into his horse. Gently, gently, no impediment. It would just encourage Nate's filly to do what she was already inclined to do. It put Nate in a position. If he tried to keep his filly straight, he'd probably come in on her, and should Happy get out-footed to the wire, well, Liv would have cause to claim foul.

She snuck a peek at him, trying to keep the grin off her face without being fully successful. His jaw, like his posture, was set; his eyes locked ahead. The fillies connected. Just a rub; nothing the stewards would bother with. When they entered the home stretch, Happy straightened, leaving Nate's filly two paths over. Liv started riding, taking advantage of the ground she'd gained — hoping Happy had it in her to get to the wire first.

Nate's filly fought back now that she'd negotiated the difficult-for-her turn. *C'mon Happy.* Liv held off on the whip. *Not yet.* Nate's filly inched forward... to Liv's boot, then Happy's shoulder. Liv cocked her stick, preparing to offer extra encouragement.

She caught it out of the corner of her eye. Something flying. A flash of movement, the flick of the rival filly's ear, a slight bump as she crowded Happy before Nate corrected her. He'd lost his whip. Liv laughed as she cruised through the wire in front.

"Thought your hands were better than that, Miller," she called over as they galloped out.

"You have yet to discover just how good my hands are, honey." There was a little too much pleasure in his grin.

She sputtered, her glare probably not coming off the way she'd hoped, because colour flooded her face and she was frustratingly close to laughter. He had some nerve. Would it be wrong to pull him off his horse? The race was over. They're probably fine her. It would be worth it.

Sue caught Happy when they returned to the front of the grandstand, snapping a paddock shank to the bit and leading her into the winner's circle. Roger nodded, looking satisfied, if not excited, by the win. It might earn Happy a trip to Florida, though. Michel stood at Sue's elbow with a hand on her back for the photo. A good way to end the night; an iota of encouragement after Roger's news.

Riders were already filing from of the jock's room when she returned — she would be the last one out. Luna slipped past her, gym bag looped over her shoulder.

"Miller throwing away his stick to let the Triple Stripe horse win. Not a conflict of interest at all."

Liv stopped dead and turned, but Luna didn't look back. She almost wondered if she'd really heard it. Is that what everyone thought? Or was Luna just in a particularly special mood tonight?

She could take it if people didn't like her. She was used to it. People wondering what Nate saw in her; why he put up with her. She didn't care about that. She cared what they thought of him, though. Luna's comment put Nate's integrity in question. It was insulting. She needed a quick shower to both decompress and refresh herself. The hot water soothed the ache in her overtired muscles, but didn't wash away the disquiet that lingered.

He waited at the car, leaning against the passenger-side door, the glow of his phone's screen casting a faint light on his face as he flipped absentmindedly. He looked up before she reached him, but waited.

When she was close enough, he jammed his phone in a pocket and hooked his hands — those hands — behind her back, the lightness of his touch and the thought of his earlier words sending sparks to her nerve endings. She kissed him, just as lightly, heightening the surge, feeling his steady gaze when he pulled back.

"You want to drive?"

He'd picked up on her frame of mind. Instead of asking what was wrong, he'd offered her a distraction. That wasn't what she wanted, not really. She shook her head and got a raised eyebrow in response.

"I'm just tired," she offered by explanation. It was a legitimate excuse; fatigue would set in quickly now that the evening was done. Did he buy it? Because the bigger reason was, since driving the Porsche home from Saratoga, and during those early weeks of his recovery, she was content to be a passenger in this car. It helped her forget the despair of those days.

And she was... tired...

A touch on her arm woke her, her head wedged against the

window. She pushed herself upright, giving him a sheepish, sleepy smile. They were in front of the house.

Always back to the house. Never his apartment.

All talk, the quip about his hands. It was just that, talk. He had his reasons. She even knew them. It still surprised her he was holding out.

"You okay?" No distraction now. A direct question. "What's wrong? It's more than just Hélène."

It was reflex to brush his concern away; she had years of practice doing it. Not just with him. But that had to change, didn't it? She couldn't continue to keep everything to herself. And this concerned him.

"It was nothing, really..." she began. Luna's comment crackled in her ear, as much as she'd tried to dismiss it.

"But?"

She sighed. "Something Luna said. She suggested you lost your whip intentionally."

He choked on a laugh. "Seriously. If I was riding this bad on purpose, it'd be easier to fix. What did you say?"

"I didn't get the chance to say anything. She literally said it in passing, and just quietly enough, I wasn't sure I'd heard it at all."

"Except you know you did."

"Luna's never liked me, but she's never been that nasty."

"It's not you she was slighting."

"That's exactly it. And it's not going to get better."

"What are you saying?" His eyes narrowed, lips pressed so hard together she thought if she touched his jaw, it would shatter.

"I'm not saying what you think I'm saying. I'm not the one who's going to be hurt by this. I just want to make sure you're prepared for what you'll be giving up. If you're still convinced you want to marry me."

"Right now, what I'm giving up is precious minutes of sleep. I'll do a cost-benefit analysis tomorrow and get back to you." Only weariness remained in his expression. He leaned across the console. "See you in — about five hours?"

She quelled a moan and met his kiss goodbye. "Drive safe."

He laughed, popping the car into gear as she climbed out. She was going to trust he could make it the two hundred metres to his place.

The house was dark and still. Upstairs, she shrugged out of her clothes, pulling on a nightshirt and crawling into bed. But of course she couldn't sleep.

It probably did nothing to help slow the over-firing neurons in her brain, flipping through her phone, scanning stories on Instagram. Images of people she didn't know, mostly. People on vacations. People with kids, playing in the park. People with lives so different from her own. Simpler lives. Marrying Nate wouldn't magically change her into one of them. They would not be those people.

She didn't question why she was the way she was. Her motives were no longer conscious and the thought of delving into them quickly chased everything back to a safer place. She'd never had a reason to change... but he made her want to.

There were times he resented the stairs up to his overhead apartment and this was one of them. He was wiped enough he considered curling up on the big overstuffed chair in the office, except for the number it would do on his back. He couldn't afford anything right now that would put his fitness in jeopardy. Luna Russo wasn't the only one saying things. He needed to be sharper. He needed not to be tossing his stick. What the hell had happened to his grip? Or was his head the problem?

It was inevitable people would make stupid comments. Liv was right. It was only going to get worse when the backstretch learned about the engagement. Maybe Liv's desire to delay the announcement was a good idea.

But it was ridiculous, too. They weren't the first couple to compete against each other out there, though maybe there hadn't been a pair as high profile as they were at Woodbine. It should work in their favour — both of them hated to lose, wasn't that obvious? Apparently not.

Everything was hard right now. Not as much as it had been those two and a half months after the accident, but still. And the hardest thing of all was leaving her at the end of the night. He could tell she questioned it — and that was a good thing, as far as he was concerned, because it convinced him she was overcoming her own issues.

For him now, it had become as much superstition as conviction. He'd waited this long, he could wait a while longer. It would just make one thing in his life easier if he knew how long he had to wait.

He dragged his long-sleeved shirt over his head and made himself brush his teeth. After connecting his phone to the charger by his bed, he tugged off his black jeans and peeled back the covers, landing with a groan. Before he turned off the light, he reached for his phone; the screen brightening at his touch. Passcode entered, keypad tapped. *Hey.*

The ellipsis leapt up almost immediately, chased by her response. *Hey.*

You can't sleep, can you? It's still bugging you, isn't it? he texted.

Yeah.

I could help you sleep, is what he thought, but didn't type it. If he had, he'd bet she'd come. All he had to do was ask. And now he wouldn't sleep. *You have yet to discover just how good my hands are.* No way he'd have gotten away with calling her honey if he'd been on foot. She would've decked him. He grinned. Terms of endearment were a big no-no.

Instead he typed, *You know the answer to this, right?*
What?
Next time, you're gonna have to let me win.

The rolling with laughter emoji came immediately. Then, *Not on your life, Miller. Go to sleep.*

Like it would be that easy.

CHAPTER SIX

THE RAIN TEEMED DOWN, rushing through gutters and filling ditches, the sky a murky slate without definition. This was October in Ontario. At least it wasn't cold. That didn't keep it from feeling miserable.

The text from Roger pinged Liv's phone, the chime on Nate's coming a split-second after. *We'll breeze Can't Catch Me tomorrow. He'll gallop today. The rest of them can stay on the shed. I'll be there in an hour.*

Liv raised her eyes from the screen at the same time Nate glanced her way. "I can get on him. You go do your thing."

"Could my thing be going back to bed?"

"Does that mean I should find my own way home?" She grinned. "Come by when you're finished. We'll tell Rog about Jay." And her decision about Chique. She kissed him quickly and hopped out.

Jo had the same text on her phone and a perplexed look on her face.

"Everything okay?" Liv asked, peeling the hood of her raincoat from her head.

"'Morning, Liv," Jo said, tucking the phone into the back pocket of her jeans. "You got the message from Rog?"

"Yes. I told Nate I'd get on the colt." She left out the part about his little delusion and shut down the twist that threatened to return to her lips.

"Did Roger tell you what's going on?" Jo asked.

"My father did," Liv said. "We'll talk."

Jo nodded. "When do you want to get Cam out?"

Liv glanced out at the dark sky, which was only a shade lighter than it had been when she'd walked in the barn. "No time like the present. Might as well get it over with."

Times like these she wished Woodbine had held out and kept the synthetic surface. The slop splashed up from Cam's hooves and the rain drenched her from above. She could feel it seeping through her gear, finding seams and cracks where the waterproofing had worn out. At least her jacket was breathable; the rain pants not so much. They trapped the heat, her legs damp with sweat. A gross feeling, but better than mud. Only her face remained exposed to that, and it wasn't like a race out here. Not as much traffic, especially on a day like this, when so many just kept their horses in the barn.

The warm front that had brought the weather made it mild enough for a bath, so Michel hosed the colt off while Liv held him. She was already a mess, so no point in the hotwalker standing out here. The groom was SOL. When Michel finished, she passed Cam to Marc, hosed off the bridle, then sprayed the bottoms of her legs and the exposed part of her boots. The rain gear came off, and she and Nicole tacked the shed with the rest of the two-year-olds, then helped do everyone up. Roger arrived somewhere in there, but Liv had only seen him long enough to hear, "If you need me I'll be in the office."

She was wiping off the tack when Nate showed up.

"Looks like you guys are pretty much finished," he said. "I was expecting doughnuts at the very least, after that win last night."

"I promised them cappuccinos and pastries from Triple Shot if they were willing to wait." Liv smiled, hanging up the last of the bridles.

"That's definitely worth waiting for."

"Let's go talk to Rog."

The small room was a quiet little haven, sheltered from the sounds and steady bustle of the barn. Muted whinnies and rattling tubs started out on the shed as Jo began feeding lunch. Roger looked up from whatever he'd been reading.

"Easy morning?" He posed it as a question, though he'd know the answer.

"We heard about Hélène," Nate said. "You'll let us know if there's anything we can do?"

Roger dipped his head slightly. "Yes. Thank you."

"Whatever you need," Liv reiterated. She clenched and unclenched her hands as Nate sank into the cushions next to her. "Can we talk about this race for Chique?"

Both Roger and Nate raised their eyebrows. They knew her well enough to have assumed what her response to the proposition would be. She'd thought she'd known too, until last night.

Nate spoke first, peering at her sideways. "You're actually thinking about it."

Liv restated the facts for herself as much as the men. "She's sound. She's healthy. We were under such pressure with her last race. This would be fun. A celebration."

"No pressure? Fun?" Nate grinned, shifting so he was facing her, arm draped over the back of the sofa. "Did those words just come from your mouth?"

Liv smirked and swatted his leg.

"What changed your mind?" Roger said, his tone more sober.

"I don't recall saying no."

"This isn't about Horse of the Year, is it?" Nate said with a suspicious expression.

She glanced at him. That was true. It wasn't. She tried to tell herself it wasn't exactly because of Luna's digs last night, either, but that had a lot to do with it.

"All right," Roger said. "When, what surface, what distance? Place your order with the racing secretary."

"First of all, they have to call it the Cheeky Little Bitch Stakes." Nate's quip even got a smile out of Roger. "But we barely made it to the International in one piece. I want a special Sovereign — for holding you together."

"You're such an ass," she said, laughing.

"I am. But you love me."

"I do."

He grinned. "That's good. You keep practicing those words."

"Anything else?" Roger interrupted.

"Actually..." she began, eyes flitting back to Nate. "You want to tell him?"

Nate didn't change his casual pose as he addressed Roger. "Jay's coming back. You good with that?"

Liv studied the trainer's face for his reaction, convinced his expression was lighter than it had been. He appeared pleased by the idea.

"It's not the first time the two of you have gone off on your own project, and I seem to recall that working out pretty well for us all. Drive on."

Roger's blessing made it so.

Claire had been their one-rat study, the two of them somehow working together at a time when they were personally at odds. They'd brought her back from what Liv had accepted was a career-ending condition to make the big bay filly better and stronger than ever. That was before, when Liv had only seen Nate as a roadblock, convinced a man would only interfere with her goals. He'd just kept proving, over and over, he could advance them. What could they be once they were totally committed, mind and soul?

Nate sat up, rubbing his hands together. "Jay and Chique both back in training? Things are looking up."

The morning's rain had moved on, leaving an afternoon of clear sky and warm sun. It felt more like September than the middle of October. The only thing that gave the season away was the trees; leaves that a week ago had been vibrant with colour starting to fade and fall, creating slick patches he had to watch for as he ran.

There were two horses on the farm's training track, the way they travelled and the posture of the riders identifying them as yearlings. Nate slowed, stopping to watch the pair, supporting himself with a hand on the outer rail as he stretched his quads. Emilie was one rider — she helped when her packed schedule allowed. The other one was the guy hired to start the babies this year as the usual suspects — Liv, Cory, Nicole, him — were too busy elsewhere.

His name was Chip Evans. It made him sound like a western movie star, or a country singer, and he kind of looked the part with his fringed chaps and moustache. An old exercise rider from the track — okay; he was in his late thirties from what Nate gathered. He'd better stop thinking of that as old when he was only a couple of years away from thirty himself. How did that happen?

Chip had been galloping forever, one of the sought-after freelancers you could put on the tough ones and trust to be good with the nervous ones, too. He'd ridden races a short time when he was younger until he'd given up on making the weight. He worked at the track in the morning, and in the fall, travelled from farm to farm in the afternoon starting yearlings.

Part of Nate missed those days, when starting yearlings had been his job with Triple Stripe, though he didn't miss the stuff he'd been going through. He especially missed the old farm manager, Geai. Having the right person on the ground made all the difference with babies and Geai had been the best. But Geai had become so much more to him than a supervisor and helping hand. It wouldn't be exaggerating to say for that span of time Geai had been his best friend — until he so unexpectedly died.

"Hey, Nate."

He hadn't heard Austin walk up — the latest farm manager who'd started about a month ago. The next one in a stream of Not Geais. Nate had lost track of how many they'd been through in the last three years.

Austin looked like just a kid, though he was probably close to Nate's age. Reedy, average height, his attempt to grow hair on his face not entirely coming off. With Geai's legacy remaining thick in the air and in the very soil beneath his feet, the guy couldn't possibly have the experience or maturity to run a farm like this. It was hard to find a decent manager, and filling Geai's shoes was impossible. It was as if the candidates felt what they would never live up to. Liv's father had yet to hire one who'd stuck around for more than six months.

Nate could never remember Austin's last name; besides, he'd quickly started calling him Austin Powers, and there was no way the kid was going to shake that now. He seemed a decent enough guy, though Nate rarely interacted with him, so he didn't have much to go on. This time of year, it wasn't the hardest of jobs. It was the quiet time. Breeding season was over, hay was done, foals were weaned — and the yearlings were nearing the sixty-day mark of their training, at which point they'd be turned out until the new year. All Austin really had to do was help turn out and bring in, make sure they didn't run out of feed and bedding, and take care of the stallions. The farm staff right now was great and didn't need much direction. He had time to become familiar with Just Lucky and Starway, before he'd get to prove his worth in February, when breeding season started up again. If he lasted that long.

"Chip working out okay?" Nate asked, watching the two riders pull up their mounts, backs to the outside rail as they turned to face the infield.

"I just let him do what he does. Emilie would tell me if he wasn't doing a good job."

"That she would."

Nate didn't know how Em managed all her things: school, the physio internship that accompanied that, helping Faye at the Triple Shot Café, volunteering for the racehorse aftercare organization, schooling horses. Chip hadn't required her help for the early stages — there were only six yearlings this fall, and with Austin on the ground, he would have been able to do the first few weeks on his own. But once it was time to get out of the sand ring — at initially for walkabouts, then the introductory lessons on the track — he'd needed the company.

"She's pretty hot, little Emilie. She's not seeing anyone, is she? I could go for that." Austin's eyes were on Em as she steered her yearling toward the gap.

The hair on the back of Nate's neck prickled, his protectiveness kicking in, and he shot Austin a glare. Was the guy a total idiot, asking him that? "Do you forget who you're talking to? You might want to tread carefully."

"What are you, her father? Does dating her sister give you special status?"

"Yeah. Cause her any grief and you'll regret it." He levelled the threat with a hard stare Austin only managed to hold for a second. He couldn't very well launch into a lecture about not getting involved with the boss's daughter, though, could he? But he could warn the guy to show some respect. Mission accomplished? He'd have to wait and see.

Austin glowered at him and went the other way, toward the stallion barn. *Good.* Nate met the riders as they came off the track.

"What'd Austin want?" Emilie looked from the manager's departing figure back to Nate.

"You don't want to know." He couldn't imagine Em liked the guy. She had better taste than that.

"I can handle it, Nate. Tell me."

Knowledge was power, so might as well. "He just asked if you were seeing anyone."

"Uh-oh!" Chip laughed. "He must be new around here. He's not worthy of Princess Emilie."

Emilie hit Chip on the arm with the butt end of her stick. The two yearlings plodded on, unaffected.

"Who are these two, Em? Good minds." Nate grinned. "Let me know if Austin's harassing you, okay?"

"Thanks, Nate. I can look after myself though."

No doubt she could, but he still felt uneasy about this winter, leaving Emilie with this guy around. Was he over-reacting?

"See you later." He injected some energy into his stride to put distance between him and the youngsters before he broke into a run. Good minds or not, he didn't want to be the reason one of them decided a running human was scary and dropped their rider.

"Wait, Miller! We still have another set to go!" Chip called after him.

"Nice try, Evans," he yelled over his shoulder. Then he stopped dead, spinning to face them again. "Throw the tack on Jay once you're done with the babies, Em."

Emilie's eyebrows arched. "You getting on him?"

"Not today. I'll come watch you. You know what you're doing."

"Do I really want to help you steal my horse?"

"You know you want to see him be his best self."

"Fine," she said, but she didn't look truly upset, because how could she disagree with that?

The aisle lights were on when he made it to the office barn, and he heard a voice over the horses' quiet munching. Instead of heading directly for the stairs to his apartment, he sauntered down the aisle; the voice becoming familiar as he drew closer. Only Liv's legs were visible behind Claire's massive bulk. Claire had always been big, but at eight months in foal, she seemed to take up the entire stall.

"Good run?"

He thought he'd been quiet, but somehow she'd known he was there. "Yep. I stopped to watch Em and Chip on the track with a couple of the yearlings, and shook up Austin a bit. It was fun."

"Why were you giving Austin a hard time?"

"Have to keep him on his toes."

"Please be careful. I really don't want to have to find another manager."

He kept further comments about Austin to himself. He'd give the guy a chance not to screw up regarding Emilie.

"How's the Amazon?" he asked, coming close enough to stroke the length of Claire's elegant neck.

"I'm sorting out her mane. Just because she's a broodmare doesn't mean she needs to look neglected."

"Em's going to get on Jay when she's done with the year-lings. Want to come watch him go?"

Liv barely had to duck to come under Claire's neck, a fistful of fine black hair in one hand. "Sure."

"They've got one set to go. I'm having a shower, then I'll meet you back down here."

Emilie texted him when she was leaving the training barn, and Liv and Nate met her on the walk to the track. This time Jay wore racehorse gear: exercise saddle, martingale, rings hanging off the thick rubber-gripped reins of a track bridle. Em was riding a few holes shorter, too. With a subtle shift of her seat and a gentle *ho,* Jay halted squarely under her.

"You've had him on the track, right?" Nate glanced up at her, a hand resting on Jay's shoulder while the colt wiggled his upper lip against Nate's other, empty, palm.

Emilie nodded. The handsome chestnut's taut abdominals and well-defined hindquarters were a giveaway she'd been doing more than toying with dressage and hacking about the farm.

"Unknot your lines," he said.

"What are you doing?" she asked as he unsnapped the rings from the martingale yoke.

"Let's see where he's at. He looks ready to gallop along a bit. You good with that?"

Emilie shrugged, and unbuckled the reins, her trust in Jay, if not Nate, complete as she gave them up so Nate could slip off the bib. He passed the lines back up to her, and she buckled and re-knotted them before letting Jay walk on.

It was often a tip-off for a racehorse, sending them out without rings — the little leather triangle-shaped piece of equipment used at the track that served the same purpose as a running martingale. Jay, though, consummate professional that he was, strode along serenely; maybe a touch more alert, but chill. It could've been his nature, it could've been the farm setting, or it could have just been that he was far enough away from the backstretch experience not to light up with old routines. Liv was silent as she kept pace, but she'd be assessing each step the colt took; every nuance of rippling muscle.

"What am I doing?" Emilie asked, lips curving up on one side as she paused at the gap in the outer rail.

Nate glanced at Liv, and Liv returned a wry smile very similar to her sister's. "You seem to be playing trainer today, so carry on."

"Just the usual, Em. Back him up. Gallop around, then let him move out a bit in the stretch."

"Yes, boss." She grinned.

When she came past them the first time, Em had shortened her irons still more, Jay bundled underneath her. He wasn't giving her a hard time, but looked like a beast, like the lightbulb was glowing a few watts brighter. Nate pulled the phone from his pocket, ready with the stopwatch while Liv prepared to shoot video with hers.

All Emilie did at the quarter pole was fold her frame into a crouch, and Jay's stride dropped and lengthened with it, RPMs increasing as he rolled into the lane. Nate had only ever been on him when he'd breezed. He'd never had the joy of watching the colt, the impressive beauty of him as his power grew. Jay's ears were up, happy to show off a taste of his talent. It was good that Em was doing this, because Nate would have had a hard time resisting giving him just a little more freedom, asking for just a tiny bit more.

Liv leaned against Nate when Jay and Em flashed past the wire, glancing at the time he'd arrested on his phone.

"He did that easy," she said. "He's pretty damn fit."

"Maybe we should hire a bunch of eventers to leg up our horses." Nate grinned at her.

"That idea has a lot of merit, you know. Think we could come up with a working student model for training off the farm?" Her smile was wry, but Nate could tell the gears in her brain were revolving, pondering the possibility.

In a few minutes Emilie jogged the wrong way around the turn, then slowed Jay to a walk. The colt sauntered off the track and Emilie stopped him in front of them.

"You two look like you're plotting world domination," she said.

"We are," Nate responded. "He looked great. How did he feel?"

"That was nothing for him," Em said, and the fact there was barely a flutter to Jay's nostrils backed her up. "I'm going to hack him home through the woods."

The thought of Jay coming back put a bounce in Nate's step, a cheerier tune in his heart than he'd felt all week — at least since before the reality of Chique's retirement had hit him solidly in the solar plexus; that moment she'd walked on the van to leave Woodbine for the farm. Sure, it looked as if Chique was coming back too — though he wouldn't believe it till it actually happened — but that was a temporary fix. Jay was a longer-term remedy.

"I'll send Roger the video," Liv said, fiddling with her phone as they walked.

The Lachance dwelling loomed ahead behind the privacy fence that contained the backyard. He swore the surrounding trees were barer than they'd been when they'd walked out; a stark reminder of how quickly time was passing. He wanted both to pause it — to hang onto the glorious weather and the optimism of this moment — and to edge it forward.

"So," he ventured, "when are we going to tell people?"

"You still don't believe it, do you? Have a little faith, Miller."

He'd said that to her enough times during Chique's career. Hearing it from her about them made him laugh. "Can I at least tell my mother?"

"No!" she said, but her lips twisted in a crooked smile. "Your mother talks to my mother now, remember?"

"You're not upset because they talk, are you? It's good they like each other. You wouldn't want battling in-laws."

"Of course not. But it would not do for my mother to find out from yours. The timing of who knows when must be carefully choreographed."

"There you go overthinking everything again."

"Better get used to it, Miller."

"You forget I'm not new here. I'm already used to it." He took her hand in his.

Her eyes drifted to their fingers, then back to his face. "You're sure you're ready for it? You know all hell will break loose."

"It'll only be hell for a little while. And you know Em and Faye will totally take over the planning, so you won't have to raise a finger. In no time at all, it'll be old news."

"That's the part I'm looking forward to."

"Yeah. Me too." He slowed her down because her pace was getting a little manic, then drew her in, her ribcage expanding and contracting beneath his palms.

"Soon, okay?" she said, promise in her voice. "But not yet."

"Maybe we should just post it on Facebook, then run for our lives."

"And just have everyone mad at us?"

"Because someone's bound to be, right?"

"Is it too late to elope?"

"Not sure we'd get away with that." He grinned and pulled her closer. "Talk about all hell breaking loose."

She smirked, her hands roaming to his nape, a slight tilt to her head. "Have you compiled that list of pros and cons yet?"

"What?" He was too distracted to think, drifting closer with her touch. He ran a finger across her jaw, to her ear, down her neck. The pendant resting just below her collarbone reminded him to stop.

"That cost-benefit analysis you said you'd come up with last night."

His laugh came out a little too low and ragged. "This is the cost... the benefits come later. Do me a favour. Sit yourself down and map out that choreography."

CHAPTER SEVEN

WOODBINE's handicapper made New York invader Arrested Upstate the morning line favourite in the Grade Two Autumn Stakes, Nate getting the ride on the Don Philips trainee. Silly handicapper. Liv knew things he didn't.

Don had asked her first. She didn't tell Nate that, but the trainer's vote of confidence had bolstered her own. Turning him down was a testament to how strongly she felt about Ride The Wave's chances in the race. The haters probably thought it was another gimme for Nate. This was how she'd prove them wrong and shut them up. Probably not once and for all. Haters didn't give up that easily.

With Liv taking over after Nate's injury, Dean Taylor's colt showcased his versatility — winning the Breeders' Stakes at a mile and a half on the outer turf in August, the Vice Regent Stakes at the beginning of September on the inner turf course at a mile, then switching to the main oval for the Ontario Derby at a mile and an eighth at the end of the month. Now it was time for open company and older horses.

Retaining the mount on Ride The Wave felt moderately

traitorous. Not because he'd been Nate's Plate horse, but because building on the colt's success strengthened his Horse of the Year bid — the inspiration to bring Chique back for one more race. That wasn't public knowledge yet, though it would get out, even though she, Nate and Roger had agreed to train Chique on the farm initially.

Arrested Upstate shipped into the Triple Stripe shed with a familiar face.

"This is my vacation," Jeanne, Don Philips' assistant, said. "Coming to Woodbine with one horse and visiting my Canadian friends."

"At least that's something, when you're not going to win a race," Liv quipped. "I'll take you out to dinner after I do." It was common for horses to come up from the US — Woodbine had a strong purse structure — but if Don thought this was going to be easy for his visiting colt, he was wrong.

"Nate might have something to say about that." Jeanne laughed.

"I intend to leave him speechless." Live grinned.

She purposely avoided him before the race, leaving late from the room when the paddock judge called outside riders and kept her head down as she made her way to Dean in the walking ring. Faye gave her a little wave while Dean shook her hand. Even though they were neighbours and long-time friends — the Taylor's Northwest Farm on the same sideroad as the Lachance's Triple Stripe Stud — pre-race convention reigned.

"What do you know about the New York horse?" Dean asked, the way he hunched as he crossed his arms doing nothing to diminish his height.

"I know we can beat him," was all she said. "You've done an amazing job keeping your colt fit for the entire season. He looks great. I swear he's grown."

Dean laughed. "Yeah. He's going to be seventeen hands

before he's done, I bet. That's all I've got to tell you. It's not like when he was a two-year-old, and he was all over the place, but he has been a bit sleepy lately. Keep him awake out there."

As soon as she was on Ride The Wave, it was obvious he was plenty awake. The only thing wrong with this horse was he wasn't in her barn. She'd loved the big, rangy bay from the first time she'd gotten on him for Dean in the spring, and Dean had begged her to ride him in the Queen's Plate after she'd broken the colt's maiden.

Had Plate favourite Elemental not been her father's horse, she would have given Dean his wish — fulfilling his wishful fantasy about the "girl next door" winning the prestigious classic on his homebred colt. But the rules of racing were clear: if a Triple Stripe horse was in a race, she either rode that horse, or remained in the jock's room. That conflict of interest thing again.

She'd been so dense, not seeing Dean had feelings for her. His fantasy sounded like the good-natured joking of someone she'd always thought of as the older brother she'd never had. It wasn't until the Plate Ball he'd exposed those feelings — the same night Nate had said he loved her. She couldn't give Dean what he really wanted, because Nate had her heart, but she hoped she made up for it with her small part in this talented colt's success.

As the post parade wrapped up, she waved off the pony rider and took Ride The Wave away on his own to warm up. Nate was doing the same with Arrested Upstate — Jeanne must've assured him it would be all right, because it wasn't something he'd normally do with a horse he'd never been on before. Or maybe he had been on the colt last winter, in California. That seemed so far away now.

Turning before Nate did, she galloped back around the turn to where the gate waited at the sixteenth pole, meeting up with her pony escort again until the starter's assistant came for them. The big colt tried to rub his head against the assistant as they waited their turn, knocking the man sideways.

"Ya big goof," he said, pushing back with a grin, then resting a hand on the colt's neck to prevent it from happening again. "Win one for the home side, buddy. Keep those Canadian dollars up here." Like the country's honour was resting on them. He funnelled them into the sixth stall and climbed up next to them. It was only a matter of seconds before they were off.

Beside her, Frequent blasted to the lead and went about setting fractions on the slow side of honest. Liv kept the frontrunner in her sights, The Wave where he liked to be, stalking mid-pack. Close enough to move up if the pace got any slower. He relaxed like a star, loping along with his humongous stride. She didn't know where Nate was. She didn't care at the moment. She'd find out when it was important.

The field coasted along the backstretch like they were on a Sunday hack, with Frequent leading the way. These were mostly veterans; been-there-done-that horses who had contested the stakes for older males all year. Except for Ride The Wave, of course — and Arrested Upstate.

On the final turn, she shook The Wave back up. The pace had slowed, Frequent reaching his limit. Her colt moved steadily past the two horses behind the leader, then eclipsed Frequent at the head of the stretch.

Ride The Wave's ears flipped forward, catching the sound rising from the crowd, but he kept a straight path and an even rhythm to his monstrous stride. He might think he didn't have to put out any more effort than that to win, but Liv couldn't be so complacent. She had to keep him interested. He had a history of loafing in the stretch, and she needed to be prepared for battle.

When the invasion came, it was like Nate took dead aim at her, fast and close, and blew past, leaving her sputtering in his exhaust fumes. Arrested Upstate swooped down to the rail with room to spare.

No way. Not happening.

It startled The Wave out of the lull Liv hadn't been able to keep him from falling into, but he was a big colt, powerful when he had momentum going for him, but not so easy to fire back up. She hissed in his ear.

Now that her colt had something to run at, he was all business again, but time was against them — and he was stuck on the wrong lead. *Damn that growth spurt.* She glanced over her shoulder in case someone else was coming on her right and opened up her outside line. He swapped, not with particular elegance, but the surge that followed made her beam. *Have I told you lately that I love you?*

They mowed Arrested Upstate down, Ride The Wave romping joyfully with this newfound gear. Liv laughed at Nate's face as they rollicked by, hitting the wire a neck up, then opening more distance as they galloped out. *Oh, you wanted to run a mile and a half today? Well, I'll let you go on a little before I pull you up.*

She didn't even see Nate — he'd pulled up and returned Arrested Upstate to the front of the grandstand before the outrider had even met Ride The Wave.

"Please let me take this horse to Florida," she begged as Dean pounded her on the back while she slid off the tack.

"Maybe the Valedictory? I think he'd get the distance."

She would have laughed in agreement, but his suggestion stopped her. Because the Valedictory was supposed to be Just Jay's comeback race, where he would defend his title. If things went according to plan, she wouldn't be allowed to partner Ride The Wave. Jay would beat Dean's colt if they could get him back to his old form. But she couldn't tell Dean where to run his horse.

Nate was still nowhere to be seen when she got back to the room — probably in the shower — and he'd likely taken his share of jibes from the rest of the guys, if the congratulatory comments she received were any indication. Neither of them were riding in the last race, which was convenient, because of her promise to Jeanne.

When she emerged, he was waiting. As she got closer to him, he took half a step back, bowing with a sweep of his arm.

"I'm not worthy."

She laughed and pushed him sideways, heading for the door. He grabbed her arm and kissed her cheek. "Nice ride. I'm still picking kickback out of my teeth. You're on fire right now."

"I'm glad you're being such a good sport about it." He always had been. "Such a nice colt though."

"He is."

"I promised I'd take Jeanne out to dinner after I won," she said, looping her arm through his. "If you agree to be on your best behaviour, you can come too."

They checked in with Dean, and their group for dinner grew to include the Northwest contingent, with Dean and Liv finally settling on splitting the tab. Dean called ahead to get them a table, and they agreed to meet at the restaurant once the horses were taken care of.

Liv's phone distracted her as she climbed out of the Porsche, the first bars of "Don't Threaten Me With A Good Time" pushing her eyebrows closer to her hairline. One of her guilty pleasures — she liked to give important individuals custom ringtones. She hadn't heard that one for a long time. This might be worth picking up. She waved Nate ahead, and he walked to the Triple Stripe shed while she swiped her finger across the screen to accept the call and pressed it to her ear.

"Kenny! How are you, *darlin'?*" she drawled, in her best imitation of her old New York agent's voice.

"Nice win."

"Are you stalking me?"

His laugh reverberated in her ear. "I'm always watching you, darlin'."

The inappropriate endearment barely even registered anymore. When she'd first met him, a comment like that would have made her skin crawl, but in time she'd found that as race-track personalities went, Kenny was benign.

"Now that filly of yours is retired, are you coming back to ride for me?"

She felt what she might almost call affection for that familiar Irish lilt, and didn't point out that, as her agent, he would work for her. "But what about —"

"That didn't work out," he said, his words clipped, but not unfriendly. "And Acosta and I have parted ways."

"What?"

"Oh, it was amicable."

"Acosta can be amicable?"

Ricky Acosta — sometime leading rider in the US, and full-time asshole — had been the bane of her existence when she'd started as an apprentice at Belmont Park. Kenny had handled Acosta's book since the beginning of the journeyman's career and suggested he'd provide guidance. Apparently Acosta's idea of that was to act as headmaster of the school of hard knocks, bouncing her around on the track, and sexually harassing her off of it. Racing was a world where you just shut up and put up with that kind of behaviour. Not a safe sport, on any level.

"Nice to see you haven't lost your sense of humour," Kenny said. "Acosta's riding in California this winter."

"And you're not going with him?"

"Nah. Don't like it out there."

It sounded like there was a story involved — one for another day, though.

"How's that boyfriend of yours?" Kenny continued. "Not sure he's riding at a hundred percent yet. That was a nasty spill in Saratoga."

Fiancé, but she caught herself before correcting him. The last person on earth she wanted to get hold of that information was Kenny O'Connell. "He'll be all right. Just having a bit of a tough time right now is all."

"You're riding good though."

"Girl jocks do well up here." She mimicked the words he'd said as he sized her up for the first time in Don's office at Belmont. Four and a half years — forever — ago.

"I'd keep you busy at Gulfstream. When are you heading south?"

"At the end of the Woodbine meet."

Riding at Gulfstream. That would be okay. That would be fun. Nate wouldn't complain about that. But what would come next left her uneasy. Because after the winter, if all went well, Kenny would want her back in New York. And that would be a harder sell. Because though she had no doubt Nate wasn't expecting an old-fashioned stay-at-home wife, he'd probably appreciate a stay-in-the-same-country, stay-in-the-same-province partner. And both of them riding in New York would be problematic. The NYRA seemed to be the only jurisdiction in North America that considered spouses who were both jockeys a major conflict of interest and required them to be coupled if riding in the same race. That meant they represented a single betting interest to the public. Trainers didn't like that.

She shouldn't even be considering it when she was committed to supporting Jo this winter. But she couldn't help it. She missed being too busy to think and feel anything but extremes. Exhilaration. Exhaustion. The freedom to fly — up and down I-90 every day in her car and on the backs of horses at Payson and Palm Meadows and Gulfstream. Now it was as if she was being asked to sacrifice the last vestiges of her independence. All the big things were steamrolling her toward that new reality.

Did she tell Nate about this? One of Nate's biggest concerns — at least, that she knew about — was she didn't talk. If they were doing this thing, this big, big thing, she had to learn, didn't she? She had to try, when every fibre of her wanted to fold it into herself, see if it festered or if her body assimilated it and came back with the best answer.

She had to talk to him. And she had to tell Kenny the complete story, so he'd understand. But not this second.

"You think about it," Kenny said. "But I'm not going to wait forever, darlin'."

Neither was Nate.

If she opened one more tab, her laptop would probably explode. Research papers, articles, anecdotes. Notes scribbled on the legal pad next to the computer, the printout of the necropsy set to the side. Nothing new. Never anything new. No grand insight to explain how it could have been prevented. Could it have been? *Most intact aneurysms are clinically silent.* She'd scribbled the words on the pad, drawn a box around it, then stabbed it several times with her pen. Such losses were still considered rare, but everyone had a story. There remained more questions than answers when it came to the equine heart.

She fingered the bracelet encircling her wrist, stiff dark hairs tamed into a plait. A daily reminder of her mild-mannered colt. His enormous heart, its tragic flaw — and the sense of helplessness that accompanied his memory. On the clasp was his registered name: *Téméraire.* Reckless. Nothing about the colt had been reckless. Nothing about his raising or training. But all the care she'd taken with him hadn't made a difference.

"What are you doing?"

She didn't look up when Nate approached the desk, but was aware of him peering cautiously at her.

"Thinking about Feste," she said quietly.

His silence didn't surprise her, and a quick glance captured the worry on his face — like he was still afraid his association with the colt's death could tear apart what they'd rebuilt. Like he believed she blamed him when she wanted to blame herself. But there was no one to blame.

"I thought maybe there might be some new research out there. Something that could help prevent it happening to someone else."

"And?" he said carefully, his expression revealing he knew how unlikely that was.

She shook her head in response. It was so frustrating, not having any way of predicting it. It could happen any time, to any horse. A yearling out in the field. Event horses. High-profile Olympic show jumpers like Hickstead. *Bam.*

She dropped her eyes. "A few years ago, there was an exercise rider killed in the sand ring at Woodbine when his horse died under him and sent him into the rail. We — you — were lucky, I guess. All things considered." Silent dangers lurked in this thing they did, riding horses. Yet they did it, despite the risk.

"Do you ever think about it?"

She leaned back in the chair, meeting his gaze directly this time. "What?"

"Going back. Finishing your vet degree."

"I wonder sometimes how things might have been different, if I'd done what I was supposed to do."

She didn't regret dropping out of Ontario Veterinary College when she'd only had a year to go. It would have been the responsible path. A surgical internship, someone else riding Claire while she remained on a more sensible course. Would she have been around to harass Geai about his health; prevented his premature death? Pursued riding once she had the letters after her name?

Or would the veterinary profession have swallowed her up? It had that potential, and she had that propensity. She likely would not be sitting here, engaged to the man across from her. He would have been on her periphery, but the proximity wouldn't have been there. Maybe he'd be marrying Faye.

A hand on her chin tipped it up — she hadn't realized how far she'd zoned out with that cascade of thought; that he'd come around to her side of the desk. He leaned down, kissed her, brought her back to here and now. Would this feeling of wonder ever stop? That this had happened? *They* had happened?

"Obviously you did what you were supposed to do, because you were supposed to end up with me."

His untroubled smile made her smile. "Mission accomplished."

"Nearly, anyway." He stepped back and sat on the edge of the desk.

"I want to ride right now," she said steadily. "Everything's finally clicking. There's always been something to complicate my career. Like Claire, because somehow my confidence was always tied to her performance. Then training Chique. It feels like this is my chance to prove who I am. On my own merits, not because I'm winning with my father's horses." Another reason she didn't want to take over training the horses Roger had developed.

"You're more than who you are on the back of a horse, Liv."

"Like the owner's daughter?" She simmered. "Or your wife? Is that supposed to be enough?"

"I didn't realize being associated with me that way would be a hindrance," he snapped.

She caught herself, made herself breathe. "I'm sorry, Nate. I don't see it like that, not really."

"I hope not."

She didn't want to make excuses for herself. There was still defence in her, the need to stand alone, not depend on anyone else. She'd only shared Luna's comments about him; she'd mentioned nothing about the earlier conversation. "Remember my fun evening hanging out with Luna?"

He mustered a wry grin. "The one where the two of you went out for a girls' night?"

"Yeah, that one. Girls' night with no drinks, sequestered in our little room. She started in on me, saying I was too soft, retiring Chique. Saying I was too soft to be a real trainer and that I only have what I have because of my father."

"You let that influence you about the race for Chique?" He crossed his arms, his vision narrowing. "How, exactly, will it change her opinion? And why do you care about it, anyway"

"I don't know," she said. "It got to me, that's all."

"But Chique's race. Is that a one-off? Or are you considering running her next year now?"

She shook her head. "No. I don't think so."

"I think we should bring her to Florida with us anyway. People take their dogs. It would be like that. It seems wrong to leave her behind."

"You're far too sentimental." But she smiled.

He grinned back. "Don't think you're fooling me. Claire and I talk, you know."

She laughed. There was no comeback for that. Then she sobered, deciding. "I have to tell you something."

Worry creased his features again, and it bothered her she hadn't been able to free him of his doubts about the two of them. About her sincerity. What would it take?

"Kenny called me after the win on Ride The Wave." There. It was out.

He looked perplexed. "Kenny O'Connell? Your fancy New York agent?"

"The very one." She paused, and before Nate could ask, she said, "He wants me to ride at Gulfstream."

He frowned. There was a beat before he spoke. "Do you want to?"

She looked away, then forced her eyes back. "I don't know. Maybe? What if I did?"

"I'm not going to tell you what to do, Liv, but..."

Her mind flashed to last fall, when he'd received the offer to ride in California. She'd pushed him to take it, and later regretted her *career before relationship* stand. This would be different — rather than a continent between them, they'd be based at the same place. And he was as able as she was of supporting Jo at Payson. But she had the feeling he wasn't seeing it the same way.

He reached for her hand, grasping her fingers. "Just give me this winter, please? After this year, I need it. We need it."

There was a familiarity to the campus, and it hit her more like déjà vu than memories. That feeling that she'd been here in a past life, not merely five years ago. The old stone buildings still dominated, facing off against modern structures in a personality clash. Not much had changed. The University of Guelph was beautiful, even as the trees became bare, the palette more monochrome. It had been home to the Ontario Veterinary College for over a hundred and fifty years.

Liv entered large animal reception to check into the teaching hospital, leaving Nate lingering by the truck. She filled out the paperwork, then rejoined him to wait. It wasn't long before the roll-up door opened and a tall young man in scrubs appeared, lead rope in hand.

"I'll grab him," Nate preempted, and he and Liv dropped the ramp.

She analyzed the colt as he descended the ramp, the placement of his hooves exaggerated and cautious. Nate had a steadying hand on his shoulder, but the colt navigated the incline just fine. He stood a moment when all four feet were on the asphalt, head raised high above Nate's, and he let out a melodious call. Announcing himself. He had personality, for sure.

"This way," Scrubs said. He hadn't introduced himself, so Liv deduced he considered himself insignificant. An underling, a barn worker, who may or may not be a vet student, but definitely not a resident or the specialist.

She heaved the ramp up, thinking Scrubs could have at least given her a hand with it, then hopped in the truck's cab and parked somewhere less in the way.

Nate was already on his own with the colt when she joined him. Pacino snuffled and walked through the handful of shavings on the stall floor. The big colt pawed with one of his huge hooves, then dropped to his knees, his massive hindquarters following with a flop. Then he rolled in the ritual of what-a-horse-must-do-in-fresh-shavings. The way he launched his bulk back to his feet was a little scary to watch, but he shook off the bedding without staggering, and cleared his nostrils with a snort that bounced off the high concrete-block walls. He pressed his nose to the grill with an obvious expression of *now, where's the hay?* Liv pressed her palm on the other side. He was the only horse here.

"Did Scrubs say anything?"

Nate shrugged. "Just that they know we're here."

So now they waited. Because this was not an emergency, so there was no rush for the hospital.

"There's a Second Cup just over there." Liv motioned toward an expanse of pristine cinder blocks, more stalls lining the wall.

He grinned. "If you want me to go, you'll have to direct me better than that."

She thought about telling him she'd go instead, because she knew every footfall of the way and would get there faster, weaving through the hallways of OVC. But that would be when the specialist would magically show up. She sent him the easier, if longer, way. He had a sense of direction. He'd be all right.

Being here didn't change her mind. It didn't make her want to return any more than her recent discussion with Nate. She would ride till the end of the meet. She would marry Nate. And she would give him this winter. She owed him, after last winter. After everything. She'd deal with next season when next season came.

As she leaned against the stall front, Pacino nibbled her hair through the bars. The stall was as spartan as a jail cell, so she was as much amusement as the colt was going to find. Chairs. Chairs would be a nice touch. After running out of things to check on her phone, she took a selfie with the colt in the background to post on Instagram.

What to caption it? *Hanging out at OVC with this hand-*

some dude. Then Nate returned, a plastic-capped paper cup in each hand, and she quickly snapped a photo of his suspicious smirk. She re-started her post over with both photos, changing the caption to *dudes* instead of *dude.*

The specialist appeared sooner than she might have thought, and Liv recognized her but struggled to retrieve a name. A professor for one of Liv's courses, way back when. She wasn't much taller than Liv, her red hair in a messy bun.

"Olivia," she said, hand outstretched. "You're somewhat of a celebrity. Erynn Hoffman."

Liv felt Nate's amusement as much as saw it and prayed he wouldn't break out singing *Oh-oh-livia* as she gripped the veterinarian's fingers. She smiled sheepishly. "A famous dropout? If only I could get extra credit for training a Queen's Plate winner. Do you think then they'd give me my degree?" She stepped back as if presenting Nate. "This is Nate Miller. He was the regular rider of said Plate winner."

"So what's going on with this guy?" Dr. Hoffman nodded toward Pacino.

Liv outlined the colt's symptoms without offering a diagnosis and answered the questions that arose. Scrubs materialized, and at the veterinarian's request, brought Pacino from his stall to an adjacent area where there was room to do the neurological tests. Liv tried to see things with fresh eyes, as the vet would — the limited range of motion in Pacino's neck, the slowness in his ability to correct his stance, the way he pivoted as he turned instead of crossing his hind legs, and overcorrected his stride when his tail was pulled to the side as he walked.

"Far from the worst I've seen," Dr Hoffman said. "Next step is to do cervical radiographs and a myelogram and see if there's compression of the spinal cord. We'll test him for EPM and EHV-1 just to rule them out. It's a shame. He's a handsome boy."

"If surgery is indicated, it is an option," Liv said with confidence, feeling it was justified in a colt whose symptoms were relatively subtle. They'd have the results of the diagnostics before the EPM test. And EHV-1 was a stretch, with no fever. "But do whatever diagnostics you have to do." *Before I go running off in my head with all the potential scenarios.*

They admitted the colt, and Liv brushed away a pang in her chest for deserting him. He would be fine, and she needed to leave emotion out of it.

"If they do diagnose Pacino with Wobblers, and he's a candidate for surgery, what's the prognosis?" Back in the truck, Nate selected a playlist for the drive home as Liv shifted the vehicle into drive.

"A year off, probably. Many horses can go back to competitive careers."

"And if surgery wasn't an option?"

She'd read up, of course. Scoured Google Scholar for the latest articles. "He's pretty mild — if that is what it is — so he'd go on strict stall rest and megadoses of Vitamin E, and hopefully his neck would stabilize. There's a slim chance he could have some sort of job if that happened, but racing would probably be too demanding. He's a sweet colt. He might end up being well enough to hack about. Otherwise, a good-looking pasture ornament." They could give him that future at Triple Stripe. Not everyone could.

Nate settled into the seat, angling slightly toward her. "When are you going to tell me who Chique's intended is?"

Liv negotiated the empty rig through the narrow roads. "I don't know. Because I haven't decided yet."

"Really? And I thought you were just being secretive."

"There's just so much to consider."

Conformation. Compatibility. And last, but hardly least: soundness. Chique had enough fragility, they didn't need to introduce more. They were breeding to race, so fashion and popularity didn't get a say. They didn't have to think about what might fetch the highest dollar at the yearling sales.

Then, disposition factored in. Chique's often difficult personality was quite likely inherited from her sire, Just Lucky, who himself was typical of his sire's challenging offspring. They'd been lucky with Feste; he'd inherited his dam's lovely disposition. By breeding to an established stallion, they'd at least give themselves a 50-50 shot of ending up with something reasonably manageable. Not that she didn't love the quirky filly, but a good mind went a long way to the making of a racehorse. That, and a good heart, but clearly that remained a wildcard.

She released a long breath. "I know I should go with Extra Terra. We have a share. And Jay is so wonderful."

"But Can't Catch Me, not so much." Nate gave her a sardonic smile.

"True. But he's not terrible" She shifted in the seat, and threw him a sideways glance. "I'm leaning toward Megalodon."

He laughed nervously.

"What?" She pictured the stallion in her head. A gorgeous liver chestnut with a flaxen mane and tail, the stuff of girlhood dreams. But that was just a bonus. He wasn't a large horse, and his conformation complimented Chique's perfectly. *Breed type to type.*

"You know how hard-headed his babies are," Nate said warily.

"But they can run. And his own race record is just what we're looking for." Chique had enough natural speed that going to a sprinter would result in something sure to burn up in the first half mile of a race. They wanted a horse that could get classic distances. "And you're custodian of the crazy, right? Though his babies aren't crazy, just tough."

"Which, crossed with Chique, gives..."

"Oh, come on, Miller. Don't get old on me already."

"But I'm not supposed to have to ride the crazies anymore." His lips twisted wryly.

"I thought that was the whole reason you wanted to stick around. Your exact words were, I believe, 'Chique's babies are going to be nightmares, and I'm the only one crazy enough to want to deal with that.'"

"I should have known that would come back to haunt me."

He was trying not to laugh, though, she could tell. Or maybe he was on the verge of hysteria.

"He's a complete outcross, too." She built on her case. "His foals are sound. That trumps everything."

"Maybe the Jockey Club would open the stud book up just for her and let you breed to a Morgan," he joked.

"Are you really against it?"

"I actually think it's a brilliant match. I'm just trying to figure out what I want them to engrave on my tombstone." He flashed that old grin. "Breed the best to the best, right?"

"And hope for the best."

The age-old maxim. It wasn't the first time she'd said it. It wouldn't be the last.

CHAPTER EIGHT

HE CURLED his fingers around the cup Faye pressed into his palm, closing his eyes and inhaling the intoxicating scent of espresso. The warm milk had a soothing effect, and he held the first sip in his mouth to let his taste buds bathe in it. The end of the season couldn't come soon enough — but there were still almost eight weeks to go. He was done worrying about calories, and annoyed he'd had to start, like the two-month break mid-season had messed with his metabolism. Maybe he'd solve the alleged conflict of interest issue and retire. He'd go train horses, and Liv could keep riding.

He was only twenty-eight. He didn't want to retire. Some guys rode into their fifties, or longer. He wanted to be one of those guys, but apparently the four or more extra inches he had on them were trying to have their say about that.

"Here, Nate," Emilie said, breaking into his morose thoughts. "You look like you need the extra energy."

The chocolate croissant she handed him was somehow still warm. He didn't hesitate to bite into it, because it would cool quickly. Em was right. He was dragging. If he weighed in a pound over, no one was going to give him a hard time. He wouldn't be the only one, especially this time of year. Motivation and morale took a hit the closer closing day got.

"Maybe I should marry you instead," he said, cracking a crooked grin and looking at Will, creator of the irresistible pastries.

Emilie froze, her eyes widening. Then her mouth fell open. "I knew there was something up. You're getting married!"

Nate glanced at Liv, expecting her to be staring daggers at him, but she managed to look only mildly mortified. She didn't even launch into denial. Impressive.

"Wait, what did I just hear?" Faye wedged herself between Emilie and Will a split second before Emilie plastered herself to Nate and Liv, and it was her *Woop!* that would soon alert the entire backstretch of news that wasn't supposed to be out yet. Oh well. Best laid plans and all that.

"Is it true?" Emilie gasped in her excitement, though she'd obviously decided it was.

"Tell me what I missed!" Faye demanded as Emilie stepped back, leaving Nate laughing and Liv a bright pink.

"They got engaged," Will said off-handedly, like he was talking about the weather.

"Damn it, Will," Nate raised both hands, but one held the cappuccino and the other the half-eaten croissant, so it didn't have quite the effect he was going for. He avoided Liv's eyes.

"You told him?" came her voice at the side of his head.

"Oh. My. Gosh!" Faye leapt for Liv. "I knew you could do it," she said, swinging Liv around, then left Liv standing there looking dizzy before embracing Nate — carefully, so as not to disrupt the pastry and beverage. "Congratulations!"

Dean had come for the coffee and croissants. He stood just behind Will with a resigned smile and only looked slightly defeated as he shook Nate's hand. He hugged Liv, his affection obvious, then turned back to Nate. "Screw this up, Miller, and you have me to answer to. I'm the honorary big brother."

Nate nodded solemnly. That he could live with. He'd said as much to Austin about Emilie with only a fraction as much on the line.

"We have a wedding to plan!" Faye all but squealed, grabbing Emilie's elbows. Then she stopped, and her eyes narrowed on Liv. "We do, right? You're not going to do something crazy and elope, are you? Because you can't. We won't let you."

"That's what I told her," Nate said, leaning in and kissing Liv on the cheek. Had she even said a word?

Faye seemed to notice that too, and scurried over to grab a container of pastries. "We'll have to do something proper, with champagne, but in lieu of that right now... Will made some amazing brioche."

"We need the story," Emilie insisted. "Details! When? How? Have you picked a date?"

When Nate described the scene after the International, completely lacking in any diamond and getting down on one knee — though he had offered — Faye scowled. "You proposed to her on the shedrow? Are you kidding me?"

The more important parts had been there, including his conviction they were better, stronger, together than apart. Not yet the good thing they could be. *Would* be.

He shrugged. "I had to have Chique's blessing."

Faye sighed and rolled her eyes. "Of course you did. But if she's maid of honour, I'm disowning you both."

"It would save me having to choose between you and Em," Liv said.

"Forget that," Faye snapped. "It has to be me, of course. Sorry, Em."

"We are not doing extravagant," Liv warned, nailing Faye

with a stare. "We can have it at the farm. Use the indoor arena. No need to book something two years in advance."

"As much as I'm happy to hear you don't want to wait that long, that's not how it works, sweetie. You need a caterer —"

"If Will can't do that part, why are we even keeping him around?" Liv grinned at Faye's tall, culinary expert of a boyfriend.

"Because maybe it's not fair to ask him to do that and be my best man?" Nate said, nudging her with his elbow.

"How much work does that take, though, really? He stands beside you and hands you a ring. That's about it, right?" Liv said.

"You should probably leave this to the experts." Emilie patted Liv on the arm.

"We need to go dress shopping, pronto." Faye focused on her phone, scrolling rapidly in her hunt for who knew what.

"Sounds perfect," Liv said, taking a step back, her smile too bright, eyes looking a little glazed. "You all go ahead with that. I've got to run." She turned on her heel and headed for the end of the shed.

Faye looked up from her phone and blinked, then exhaled. "Oops. Too much."

Nate laughed and chased after Liv, still with cup and crois-sant in hand. He wasn't giving them up. "I'll see you all later."

He shoved the last bite of pastry in his mouth — worth every unit of energy (calorie was such a hateful word) and sipped the cappuccino more carefully. Liv stood at the end of the barn, just around the corner, staring down the road toward the east gate.

"Not that I wouldn't put running all the way to King City past you," Nate said at her back. She turned slowly to face him. "But, want a ride?"

She closed the space between them before he reached her,

hands slipping to his face, lips engaging his. He didn't want to push her away, savouring the surprise of her initiative. They could stand out here and do this all day, for all he cared. With Emilie's declaration, there was nothing left to hide.

But she broke the kiss, dropping a hand to one of his shoulders, resting her head on the other. He could feel her breath on his neck, but not see her face.

"Sorry," she said.

"No apology needed."

"You still think I'm going to freak out, don't you?"

Didn't you just? But he kept the thought to himself and pulled her closer to him with one arm, still cradling the coffee in the other. "Sometimes. Part of me. Not because of you. More because of me."

She didn't ask; didn't have to. She would smooth over the last fibres of his old scars in time. He wasn't going to judge her on a little wedding-prep anxiety, especially when he wondered about it all himself. Who were they doing it for, anyway? Their families, their friends; not really for themselves. But it felt like a necessary evil.

"Shall we go?" he asked, pressing his lips to her brow.

She pushed away and snatched the cup from him, draining it. "Are we abandoning our own impromptu engagement party?"

"I've had my share of pastry, as much as I hate to admit it. Though I was savouring that cappuccino."

"We can stop at Starbucks on the way home," she said, in motion now. "If you ask me if I want to drive, this time I'll say yes."

He tossed her the keys and started singing, "Follow You."

The last time Liv looked this uncomfortable, Nate had been sitting across from her in Roger and Hélène's dining room in Florida on New Year's Eve — also her birthday. He hadn't exactly been at ease himself. An evening that had started out as awkward developed into nothing less than disaster by the time the sky lit up with the neighbours' fireworks.

This time, though, he was trying to hide his amusement. This night was going to be a lot more fun than that night had been. He'd bet she'd tried to pay Emilie to be here, but Em was not, and there wasn't a fifth place setting to suggest she might appear.

After the backstretch slip-up, Liv's parents had found out. A prompt dinner invitation had ensued, much to Liv's horror. Anne Lachance waved off their apologies for not being among the first to know. She wouldn't be that kind of mother-in-law, even if she and Liv had a somewhat tense relationship. He thought it was only because of Liv's single-mindedness about making a career for herself in horses — at least one not as a veterinarian. That would have been acceptable. Though Nate was pretty sure Anne had come around, Liv retained the residue of that earlier disapproval. Was it a mother and daughter thing? He didn't know. He only had brothers. Well... one brother, now.

So here they were, in the dining room of the Lachance's tastefully decorated home. Liv picked at her food, while Nate made small talk with her parents, who wisely did not ask all the usual questions — the ones Faye and Emilie had fired off within moments of the news leaking out. Leaking out thanks to him.

It had been an unconscious thing. Honest. He could have denied it — Em thought she knew stuff, but that didn't mean she did. Except, most of the time, her gut was dead right.

Have I told you lately how much like your mother you are?

That's what he'd say to Liv right this moment, but she was across from him, not beside.

I'm not sure I want to hear that, she'd respond.

I don't think it's a bad thing, even if you do.

Would you want to hear you're like your father?

That's not fair. Because he wasn't, not one bit.

Likewise, it's not entirely a bad thing, Miller.

Touché.

Funny how he carried on these imaginary conversations in his head. Meanwhile, all she was probably thinking was, *when can I get the hell out of here?*

"When will Just Jay and Chique go into Woodbine?" Claude Lachance topped up Nate's glass.

Better slow down on the wine. Maybe Liv's tension was affecting him. Liv didn't respond, so Nate said, "In a couple of weeks. They'll both need to breeze in there." It wouldn't feel real until then.

They had Jay and Chique to distract them now, at least for part of the stretch of time that often dragged, as Ontario's weather deteriorated into winter. But Liv's disclosure of Kenny's call left a new question mark hanging over what came after that. He'd had this illusion, the two of them taking a break from the usual pace of their lives. Even without Roger around, that's how it would be, the routine always more relaxed in Florida than when they were at Woodbine. He remembered how busy Liv had been when she'd been riding at Gulfstream before, Kenny keeping her hopping from the track to Palm Meadows Training Centre, with only one day a week at Payson. If she did it, that was all he'd see of her. That might make his old-fashioned resolve to hold out for the wedding easier, but it tore at his insides just the same.

A ringing phone — it sounded like a landline — disrupted conversation. Anne excused herself, leaving an awkward silence at the table. He could hear Anne answer the phone softly in French. Claude smiled and passed a bowl to Nate like he needed something to fill in the lapse, but he clearly had an ear to his wife's voice. Liv seemed stuck, no doubt listening as well.

While he'd always gotten along with Liv's parents, Nate found the Lachance family a little strange. They seemed very careful around each other. Maybe it was just his presence that made it all seem so formal and they weren't like that without company, but while Claude had always been friendly toward him and Anne polite, it always felt as if something was being withheld. Only Emilie was freely demonstrative. How had she avoided this odd reticence? Liv had inherited more than enough for both of them, almost as if it had been concentrated in her. Nate had coaxed her out of herself to a degree, but it was slow going.

Anne reappeared. *"Claude, c'est Julien."*

Claude frowned, and Liv glanced quickly at Nate before her eyes dropped back to her plate. The name meant nothing to Nate and Liv wasn't giving him any clues, but the timbre of Claude's voice was solemn, his voice clipped as he took over the telephone conversation. He returned after terminating the call, reassuming his place at the end of the table, meeting his wife's eyes, then sliding to Liv.

"Your grandfather has died."

Claude's tone was clinical, speaking English so Nate would understand. For once he felt a similarity between Liv and her father, because he'd experienced her shift into that mode when he'd been in the hospital after the spill with Feste. Her face showed no emotion. He knew how well she could shut down in the face of death. She was a pro.

"I should probably go," Nate said, pushing away from the table. "I'm sorry for your loss."

"Thank you," Claude responded, with a sincerity that somehow lacked grief.

It was all very confusing. Definitely time to leave.

Anne rose with him, but Liv still hadn't moved; she remained fixated on the remnants of her meal. He wanted to go to her, draw out whatever was necessary to unlock her, because he'd been frozen out before, and the thought of it happening again scared him. They'd so recently taken such a major step in their relationship. This felt like a fresh fissure between them.

"We'll have you back another time, Nate," Anne said, retrieving his coat from the closet in the front foyer as he tied on his shoes.

Liv appeared, hesitating behind her mother before squeezing by. "I'm coming with you." She toed into slip-on shoes and ducked out the door.

He didn't catch up to her until she was down the steps. "Can you tell me what's going on?"

Liv shook her head, loose hair flipping around her shoulders. She hadn't grabbed a jacket, and hugged her arms around her ribcage. Sidling up to her, he slipped an arm around her waist, pulling her closer to share some body heat. She leaned into him and he released a sigh of relief.

Step one: she was here with him, even if she wasn't talking. He could let her be until she was ready.

She broke away from him once they were in the barn, her feet rapid-fire on the steps — leaving Nate behind, leading him to his own apartment. The door wasn't locked, the handle smooth and cool against her palm, opening to her twist. On the other side, she stood in the darkness, shaking.

The room lit up, a shuffle and click behind her, then his

arms encircled her, tightening around her like a thunder shirt, the breath she'd been holding releasing in a shudder. She let herself feel him against her back; let herself lean into him.

"Breathe," he said.

Wasn't it absurd she needed to be reminded? But her heart still pounded, her respiration out of sync, a conscious effort required to keep her from hyperventilating. *Inhale, one, two, three. Exhale, one, two, three.*

"You know my family's secrets," he said, his voice soft in her ear.

They weren't like this, though. He'd suffered a betrayal of trust, sure, and she hated to make it a competition, but hers was next-level.

"I need to know."

She had so perfectly buried it, it should not be disturbed.

But... even if she didn't agree, if he thought he needed to know... he did. What hope was there for them, otherwise?

"Let me be there for you, Liv. Please."

His breath was warm on her neck, and she was aware of the vibration from his throat against her back. Could she allow that? Truly?

She twisted out of his arms, hands clasping her elbows, searching the room as if it would give her a way out. The big picture window was dark, and she took some consolation that she didn't want to leap through it. *You can do this. You can be open with him.* It wasn't the end of the world; in fact, what if it was the start of a new one? Uncovering the past, dusting it off, repacking it and putting it away for good.

When she faced him, he hadn't moved. She pressed her lips together, her chest rising and falling with another breath. Her pulse slowed, the flight response dissipating. "My grandfather was not a good man."

She had never spoken of it. It had only been others: hushed

tones, whispers punctuated with angry bursts. Accusations that had fractured a family. All of it because of her.

"He did things. Inappropriate things." Her tone was dispassionate, as if she were speaking of someone else, a documentary about a stranger. "It started off innocently enough, I suppose. The little things men do that are meant to be harmless." Things that go unnoticed, but make quiet little girls shrink. She didn't want to remember any of it, but there was no stopping the cascade of memories streaming in.

"He had horses. Show jumpers. He rode. Never quite well enough to make the Canadian team, but he had a successful business, training and coaching. And I was the beneficiary of his talent. The horses were my candy. At least when I was riding, he couldn't touch me." Today, despite the risk, the back of a horse was still where she felt safe. It would always be her sanctuary.

"Then it went too far. It was Geai who caught him. Geai who called him out. Who said something when no one else would." Someone had to notice, because she would never tell. "And my father trusted Geai, even if he didn't want to believe it. To his credit, as soon as Geai came to him, he took action. Bought the farm here. Packed us up and left his family behind."

"How old were you?" It was the first thing he'd said, while she raged, all of it coming out in an avalanche. His face was blanched, arms stiff at his sides, like he wanted to do something when there was nothing to be done. History, all of it.

"When we moved, I was fifteen."

They stood apart from each other. Her mind flooded now, bombarded on all sides. "It's why my father is the way he is. He overcompensated by keeping his distance, because he didn't ever want to do anything that might be misconstrued, afraid he'd turn into *his* father. Instead, he said yes to anything I wanted." *Riding your pick of your father's horses in your Barbie barn.*

You don't even know what it's like to survive in the real world. It was true; she'd been sheltered, but there had been a reason for it. "It's why I latched onto Geai. Geai and his wife moved with us. Everyone uprooted. All of it my fault."

"You can't blame yourself."

His words were meant to be a comfort, but only poked further at her guilt. "Don't tell me how I should think or feel, Miller. How could you possibly know?"

The fury and frustration and terror of it was all there, in the assault she released. He didn't deserve to be the target. But he didn't look angry or offended. And she was still here, not a pile of shattered glass on the carpet.

"You're right. I'm sorry," he whispered. "I wish you'd told me."

"I couldn't. I pushed it so deep it became someone else's story. I refuse to let it define me."

"It has, though."

And there it was, the look she'd come to hate — the one she'd been desperate to avoid. *Broken Girl.*

"But it doesn't have to anymore," he added, catching her eyes. His proclamation wasn't a challenge, but a submission. An invitation to grow.

"I'm going," she said, dropping her arms to her sides, squaring her shoulders. "To the funeral."

His eyebrows shot up. "Are you sure you want to? No one would expect that."

"I have to. To put an end to it." Now that the old memories were reawakened, she would properly bury them with the one responsible.

"Then I'll come with you."

"You don't want to do that."

"You came with me. To Calgary."

"This is not the same. My family is not the same."

"I don't care. I can take it. This is it, Liv. This is how it is now. You, and me. This is what we do. I love you, and if you love me, you'll let me help you carry this."

His offer wrapped itself around her heart, massaging the hypoxic parts, reviving them.

"I do," she whispered. "I will. Thank you."

She stepped back into his arms, closing her eyes as she pressed her face to his shoulder.

"Of course, the real reason I have to go is I'm afraid if I don't, some French guy will sweep you off your feet. That accent."

"You realize the flaw in your thinking, Miller?"

"I'm sure you'll tell me."

"If some French guy is going to try and sweep me off my feet, he's probably going to be speaking, you know, French. And not just that, but the same French I grew up speaking. The accent ceases to be an issue."

"Ah, so you liked me for my accent then."

She snorted. "Something like that."

Not the accent. Not the blue eyes that were as warm as a Caribbean sea, or the sandy blonde hair, or the timbre of his voice when he sang. It was the humour, and the heart. A good, good heart.

His lips were strangely tentative when she kissed him.

"Can I stay?" There was a plea in her voice as her eyes searched his.

His head went back, and he pulled her tighter to his chest. Then she felt bad for asking. Her Catholic upbringing was diluted, but he had his own reasons for wanting to wait. It would be wrong to challenge them. He'd never been less than understanding with her; she would meet him there.

"I'll leave," she said, relieving him of coming up with an answer. She kissed him softly, briefly. "I love you."

CHAPTER NINE

"JUST LIKE OLD TIMES, EH CHEEKY?" Nate ruffled the filly's mane with one hand and Chique gave a little shake of her head in reaction; her mane, as crazy as ever, rolling along her crest. Okay, not exactly like old times. As a two-year-old, he wouldn't have dared take a hand off the lines while she was galloping.

Chique was happy, hooves moving lightly over the sandy surface, her stride elastic. She felt amazing, the short-lived retirement refreshing her. Even once her career was over for real, he should make time for this. Who said broodmares needed to be turned out and forgotten about?

Next to him, Liv held Jay quietly, the chestnut colt ever the gentleman. Yes, here they were, after early hours on the backstretch, galloping on the farm before they returned to Woodbine for another Wednesday evening card. Because what did horse people do in their spare time? They rode more horses. They needed this, after last night; something away from the bustle of the track, but with an equine buffer.

Her revelation had both blown him sideways and not surprised him at all. It explained so much. It explained everything. And it left him with an uneasy sense he was in over his head.

Now that it was out in the open, Liv seemed relieved he knew that part of her history. He, on the other hand, felt the weight of responsibility. Like Geai had warned him, very early on: *don't take her loyalty lightly.* Now he knew fully what that meant.

He didn't in any way think she'd been concealing this from him. He truly believed she'd compartmentalized it all. She'd obviously become very proficient at that, and withheld her trust in others for good reason. But if he'd been careful before, what did that mean for him after this? Her confidence was such a fragile thing. They'd come so far, but there was all the more pressure not to take it for granted. There was enough pressure on him right now; he didn't need more.

No. This wasn't about him. It was about being whatever she needed him to be right now. He had to package up his own feelings temporarily. Get through these next few days, and the trip to Montreal. That was going to be interesting. It might have been fun had it been a weekend getaway — like such things existed in their lives — but circumstances being what they were, it was sure to be uncomfortable. He didn't think they'd be touring the city.

"We'll take the Porsche?" he suggested as they walked the horses off the track.

"I don't know, Miller. I'm not trying to impress anyone. I don't want to draw any more attention to myself than I already will be, just by being there."

"It's not about impressing anyone. It's about being confident in who you are now."

"Which is?" Worry lined her brow. "We are going to Montreal. It could snow."

"Because climate change hasn't affected Montreal, and

they get snow earlier instead of later, unlike us here in Ontario?"

"Climate change means weird weather. And... never mind. We'll take it. But if we hit messy driving, it's not my fault."

"You can totally blame it on me." He grinned, but in truth, he was just worrying about himself again. Having the Porsche would let him masquerade as a somebody in a place where he anticipated being a nobody. Was he really attaching his self-esteem to a car?

"How's your French, Miller?"

"Ah... well... inadequate?" He'd taken some in school but had forgotten more than he remembered. It wasn't as if he got to practice, despite spending so much time around a bunch of francophones. They really only ever talked in English. And though French was Canada's official second language, it wasn't mandatory in Alberta schools.

"I'm going to apologize in advance. No one is going to speak English. And I might forget how, within minutes of being in the midst of that." She seemed amused by the possibility.

"Too bad the Babel fish wasn't a real thing."

"Did Em talk you into reading *Hitchhiker's Guide to the Galaxy?*"

"Already had." The thought of a fish in his ear that could seamlessly translate language simultaneously intrigued and crept him out.

She laughed and reached a hand forward to stroke Jay's neck. "We're going to have these two thoroughly checked out," she said, bringing the discussion back to their mounts.

From bow to stern and back again, he imagined. "That heart guy from Guelph, too?"

"Yes. I talked to him. He's going to come out here one day next week."

The farm wasn't beholden to the racetrack regime: after

untacking, Nate simply checked Chique's feet, curried and brushed away the barely damp mark of saddle and girth, and put the filly out in her paddock. Chique immediately rolled, flipping from side to side with abandon before rising and shaking in a cloud of dust.

Liv appeared at his elbow after doing the same with Jay. He leaned on the fence, watching — and being ignored by — Chique.

"It would be kind of nice to train them off the farm like this as long as possible," he said, glancing at her. "Just ship in to breeze them. Bring them back here after."

"No reason we can't. Except, of course, it's a lot more convenient to have them in there."

That was true, if they intended to be the ones galloping the two horses. If Chique was only back in training for a short time, he wanted to be on her every second he could.

He was craving these moments right now. In a year that had made him question everything, the simplicity of this life compared to the track seemed far more attractive. He was just worn out, that was all. And if Liv did decide to ride this winter, it was all the more reason to appreciate these temporary pauses, because they would be few and far between in that version of Florida.

Liv was studying him, and it seemed wrong that her face showed concern for him, when she was the one who'd revealed her past, and tomorrow would probably relive it. He had to do what he'd said he'd do, and be there for her. It wasn't a complicated thing.

"Have you figured out what time we have to leave in the morning?"

She nodded. "At least it's not as if we'll have to get up any earlier than we would on a regular day."

He sighed. "Just once this year I'd like to have a day off with you that wasn't for a funeral."

***

Nate drove the first half of the trip because Liv was in too much of a *let's get this over with* state and would have been in power-driving mode — a dangerous thing in a Porsche. By the time she took over, the miles had eroded the edge from her nerves, though nothing would erase them, or the myriad emotions feeding them.

It was a shame she wasn't bringing him here in a different context. It might have been fun, in a parallel universe, to tour the city, show off the sites; appreciate the history and architecture of this grand *cathédrale* instead of resenting it. Instead, this was an annoyance, an inconvenience. *Go on, judge me for feeling that way about the death of my own grandfather.* But he'd never shown her respect — all she'd ever wanted in this life — so why would she give him hers?

Next to her, Nate seemed uneasy, but understandably so. So much could be uncomfortable for him at this moment. The language, the stiff solemnity of the Catholic funeral mass, the circumstances of the rift in her extended family.

She stared up at the grand arches overhead, tuning out the priest's words as he wafted cloying incense around. It was hard to reconcile the remote God who mystically ruled this ornate structure with the one Nate believed in; the one he'd sung about at his brother and sister-in-law's funeral in Calgary. *You're my only hope. I'm on fire. Love is the answer. Bigger than religion.* Something more relatable than this. So different from what she'd grown up with; what her parents had drifted from. And yet, it still meant so much to the previous generation. It made her think of Geai, and her fingers automatically went to the little pendant at her neck. She'd laughed when he'd given it to her. She hadn't been able to help it; adorned with its delicate painting of a horse who looked remarkably like Claire... and a nun. But she still wore it every day. Not because she felt it offered her any protection from evil, but because it helped her keep his memory close.

She didn't intend to stay long after the formalities — certainly there would be no going to the gathering after the interment, enduring false praise for the man who had clearly fooled so many. A pillar of the community. Untouchable. But that didn't mean she could avoid people entirely after the service.

When they'd moved to Ontario, she'd worked hard to erase any trace of an accent, but immersed back into the language, she gave up, defaulting when she reverted to English with Nate. Her diction took on a different cadence, and she lost her h, and forgot certain English words. He was trying his best to grasp what French he could, but that amounted to greetings and repeated phrases. They wouldn't be here long enough for him to learn much more than that.

After the burial, she looped her arm through Nate's and ushered him away. "Let's go. I'll text Emilie to let her know we're leaving."

She considered letting the GPS navigate to their destination so she could fold back into herself, but she wouldn't. Not yet. There would be time for that later; for absorbing and reflecting. She wanted to be cognizant of this next part; the part that would be easier in some ways and harder in others. So she directed while he drove, with the odd commentary along the way — much like he'd done when they'd driven up to Banff before they'd left Calgary in the spring — heading for mountains that weren't as impressive as the Rockies, but held meaning just the same.

"I came up here. When I lost the mount on Claire? After you tried to rescue me?" She returned her gaze to him after staring out the window, lips lifting at the corners in an attempt to be light when she didn't feel done with the heavy. That had been a dark time, and she'd been in a dark place. The things he'd put up with from her. It was a miracle he'd stuck it out.

"What a waste of gas that was." He smirked. "Do you ski?"

She tipped her head a few degrees sideways, looking at him, though not disappointed at the tangent. "Yes. This is ski country. I grew up close to these mountains."

"Calling them mountains is a stretch."

"They're not the Rockies, no. Snob." She grinned at him.

He looked thoughtful. Maybe in his mind he was back in those mountains. "We should go skiing sometime."

She found herself smiling at the idea. "In another lifetime, where we have normal lives? Sure Miller. I'm up for that."

It made her think of his plea to her about this winter. She'd completely forgotten about Kenny, with all of this, but it reinforced what she needed to tell the agent when her tendency was to do the opposite. To submerge herself in work because it kept the past at bay, even if she realized now she'd never escape it.

There were fresh flowers on the grave, in defiance of the faded leaves that clung with faltering desperation to the trees, the carpet of them composting beneath his feet adding a peaty scent to the fall air. Two names were engraved on the modest headstone.

Jean-Guy Doucet. Marie-France Doucet.

"Jean-Guy?" Nate questioned, hands in the pockets of his dress pants, his gaze lowered to the slab of granite.

"It's a French Catholic tradition, names like that. Very old school. I think my parents' generation did away with the convention."

He'd never known Geai's given name. Never asked how he'd gotten the nickname. "How did he?" he asked.

Liv looked confused, and a wry smile twisted his lips. She'd not been reading his mind, then. Maybe filtering two languages was interfering with the signal.

"How did he what?"

"Get the nickname."

She shrugged, clutching her trench coat more tightly around herself. "No idea. He was always just Geai to me."

The old farm manager had been a very traditional Catholic; no cremation, his final wishes to be buried in his hometown in the Laurentians. After his death, his body had been returned here. They'd held a memorial for him in the small stone church near the farm in King City.

Liv had been in New York with Claire when he'd died. Nate would never forget that day, when she'd come home for the service. It hadn't gone like he'd hoped. She'd lashed out at him, the vivid memory of it making this moment seem all the more poignant. He pulled a hand from his pocket, offering it, and she released the grip on her coat to wrap her fingers around his. *It took a while, Geai. But look at us now.*

"Did you come here, too?"

She shook her head, her hair falling into her face until her free hand reached up to sweep part of it behind one ear. "That would have required talking to someone, to find out where it was. I wasn't capable of talking to anyone at that time, as you might recall. I think just knowing I was close helped. As much as anything helped. It all worked out though, right? Here you are, rescuing me now." She smiled as her face turned to his.

"You don't need rescuing. You just needed a bit of company. Some moral support."

Her grey eyes remained fixed on him with sudden intensity. "You still want to do this thing? The wedding? The *till death do us part?*"

It was fair of her to ask again, after the recent revelations. "Got any more deep, dark secrets you're keeping from me?"

"No."

"Then it's all smooth sailing from here."

"Oh... don't let's jinx us, okay?"

"Can we work on training your brain? Repeat after me: it's all smooth sailing from here."

She laughed, turning into him. "It's all smooth sailing from here. Only good things."

"That's right," He said, pulling her closer. "It might be worth talking to someone, though."

"You mean therapy."

"Just think about it."

To his surprise, she didn't dismiss the suggestion, merely nodded as they returned to the car.

The quiet town probably took on a new life once there was snow, being this close to the slopes. He drove so Liv could refer to notes on her phone to navigate, directing them to a modest bungalow on the outskirts of the village. The small home was nestled amid mature trees, well-tended gardens out front.

Geai's sister was a tiny, frail-looking thing with crepe skin, her gorgeous eyes set above delicately sculpted cheekbones. Liv embraced her without hesitation, and as soon as she stepped back, Marie-Catherine reached for Nate and pulled him in. He didn't understand a word she said, all of it rambling together.

He listened, maybe a tenth of it making sense. Liv's translations came less frequently, immersed in the language she'd been born to. Marie-Catherine asked if they'd like *du thé*. He knew what that was, anyway, and nodded, afraid to utter anything more.

"*Merci, Catherine,*" Liv said, her tone soft.

Here, she was as at ease as he'd seen her since they'd arrived in Quebec. In Montreal, her guard had remained up, a shield of iron to deflect any resurgence of past hurt. He wanted to protect her from it, but knew he couldn't. She'd done admirably, holding her own, like she needed to push through and come clear on the other side. She'd been right to come, and would be stronger for it.

Liv's voice was apologetic when it was time for them to leave.

"I have something for you," Catherine said in English. So she did know some, though it was heavily accented; far more so than Geai's had been. They waited while she scurried to another room and returned with a box. "Some thing he would want you to have," she said, holding it out for Liv.

"*Merci,*" Liv said quietly, receiving it. After Catherine had given him a quick squeeze, he took the box from Liv. The parting embrace between the two women was longer, tighter.

"You want it up with you?" he asked as they walked to the car.

Liv shook her head. "No. There will be a time and a place. It's not now."

She didn't speak again until they reached the highway, zooming back toward Toronto, the music the stereo picked up from his phone shuffling through an eclectic selection of songs.

"We have things to talk about."

He glanced at her, but she was peering out the window at the scenery racing past. "You don't like to talk," he said.

"I'm evolving."

"So?"

"This is the conversation we should have had. Before you asked me to marry you. Before I said yes."

Uh-oh. He waited for her to go on.

She sat straighter, her grey eyes now on him. "People in love make stupid decisions. Let's not be those people."

"Okay?" he sputtered. This was Liv. Don't talk hardly ever, but come at the Big Stuff head on when you do. "Continue."

"You keep asking me if I'm going to back out, but you still can, you know. We haven't discussed some pretty important things. Ones we see very differently. We can't just ignore them."

His vision bounced from her back to the road. "I realized from the beginning of this there would be concessions. That it was part of the deal."

"But you're making assumptions."

"Let's see if I'm right about those assumptions. Do you have a list?"

Was that a nod? She didn't whip out her phone or a piece of paper, at least.

"First, basic stuff," she began. "I'm keeping my name."

"Never dreamed you wouldn't. Next."

"Kids. There are no guarantees on me changing my mind about not wanting them."

"I accept that. I'll just be favourite uncle to Faye and Will's kids." Seeing as he was unlikely to ever play that role for his niece and nephew in Calgary. "You think that'll happen?"

"Faye and Will having kids? Yeah. Faye wants babies. She might not admit it out loud, but she does."

"How do you know?"

"I just know."

"We'll have dogs," he said.

"Of course we'll have dogs." She grinned.

"Next?"

"Where are we going to live?" she asked.

Good question, though he'd live in a tack room with her. Maybe a short-sighted perspective. "Guess we have to figure that out. Kick Austin out of the cottage?"

"I'm not sure how I feel about that."

Which he understood, because it had been Geai's. "In proximity to the farm, though."

"Good enough for now."

As she went through it all, he had to wonder. Had she googled it, or did she really have all those questions rattling around in her head? Not that she was wrong. So far, no deal-breakers. Good sign.

"End of life stuff?" she asked with continued directness.

"You're thorough."

"If I ended up on life support next week after a spill, wouldn't you want to know what I'd want?"

"If you ended up on life support next week, I wouldn't be the one making those decisions."

"You don't think you'd be consulted? Is that how you view my family?"

"No. All right, tell me, and we'll see if my assumptions are right about that, too."

He realized it meant a lot they could talk about this stuff — things no one wanted to think about, but that needed to be documented. It made him think of the other funeral they'd been to this year, for his brother Phil and Phil's wife, Cindy. Cindy had mapped out everything, right down to the songs she wanted at the service. Songs she'd wanted him to sing. Maybe Cindy and Liv weren't quite the exact opposites he'd thought.

"Anything else?" he asked.

"Well... I can't ignore this. I may have been raised loosely Catholic, but I don't share the conviction you do about the existence of God and an afterlife. Is that actually okay?"

Was it? Did he even know? He wanted to believe she'd come to share that conviction, but he couldn't know she ever would, any more than the kid thing. He couldn't believe this was wrong, though, the two of them. "You don't actively oppose my beliefs, or interfere with them. That's about as much as I can ask."

"I promise you can raise Chique's kids however you want," she said.

He laughed, picturing himself as a stay-at-home dad to a herd of bratty foals, with Chique's in the middle of them.

"Anything to add?" she asked.

"Speak now or forever hold my peace?"

"You're very funny."

"Do you want me to sign something?" He didn't know if he was kidding or not.

Her expression was wry. "No, not necessary. I trust you."

And those words, coming from this woman, were all he needed to hear.

It had been a whirlwind of a trip. The drive wasn't especially long — not when you'd made the trip to Florida several times — but the emotional exhaustion was real, even with splitting the driving. Liv did the last leg. When she pulled up in front of the Lachance house, he was out of the car before she was. She actually waited, letting him be the guy who opened the door for her. He followed her up the steps. She didn't make a move to unlock it. The look in her eyes arrested him as she faced him.

"I don't want to wait," she said, the words coming out like a waterfall.

"For what, exactly?" he asked carefully, not trusting his tired brain.

"To get married. I don't want to wait for however long it takes Faye and Emilie to decide they've arranged things to their version of perfection. Let's pick a day, a time and place. And if they want to organize a big party down the road, we'll let them. But this should be about us."

"Okay." He wasn't going to argue.

It took them five minutes to do it — pick that day and place. He kissed her after she said, *à demain* — that much French he knew — and left, finally knowing when his waiting would end.

CHAPTER TEN

LIV ALMOST FELT guilty Nate had to ride Wednesday night. Almost. No one had questioned her not taking mounts the day after her grandfather's funeral, even though she'd fulfilled her weekend riding commitments before it, and galloped the Triple Stripe barn with Nicole the morning after. They didn't need to know it wasn't for the reasons they assumed.

Back at the farm, she and Nate trained Jay and Chique, then while he caught a couple hours' sleep, she caught up with Faye. Faye was home this afternoon, which was rare these days — she'd thrown herself into the café in town since buying it just over a year ago. Liv hadn't seen her friend since her mini-meltdown after the unplanned engagement announcement, though at least she'd had a good excuse. An update was necessary.

The deck outside the old red-brick Victorian was covered in yellow and brown leaves. This time of year, as soon as you swept them away, more appeared, the surrounding trees not done shedding their ageing foliage. Before she even knocked, Faye swung the door open and ushered her in, the Taylor's

Golden Retriever providing the official welcome, swirling around Liv's legs with a drawn-out *a-row-row-rowl*.

"Hello to you too, Gus." Liv laughed, bending to run her hands over his broad head.

We'll have dogs.

Of course we'll have dogs. They would. It wasn't exactly practical right now, but one day. Soon.

"Let's go for a walk," Faye said before Liv had a chance to take her coat off. "Gus has been a little neglected recently. It gets dark so early, by the time I'm home most days he's out of luck."

"Doesn't Dean take him out?"

Faye laughed. "Gus would have me believe he does not. I know he's lying, but pretend otherwise. He's always up for a romp, and it gets me out of my head. Here. I brought cappuccinos from the café." She swept two cups from the counter.

"Of course you did." Liv grinned, accepting gratefully. "Thank you. But who's minding the shop this afternoon?"

"Lucy. She likes to come in every now and then and make sure we haven't totally botched things."

"Does she approve?"

"I think so. It's hard to tell." Faye slipped on her vest. "C'mon Gus!" The Golden bounced and circled at the back door, the sun coming in through the window catching flying long, blond hairs in its rays.

"Em said she'd come when she was done at the clinic." Liv followed Faye out. "Then I'll fill you both in on the whole wedding thing."

Faye raised an eyebrow, only slightly. "So Em and I didn't scare you off last week?"

Liv laughed, softly. "No. But a lot has happened between then and now."

Another twitch of those perfectly shaped eyebrows; part sympathy, part curiosity, but Faye didn't say anything else.

Northwest, the farm Faye and her brother Dean had inherited following their parents' death in a car accident twelve years ago, was more workmanlike than Triple Stripe — converted from a cattle farm, outbuildings clustered behind the century home with paddocks of various sizes around them. One barn was newer, with an upstairs apartment where the farm manager lived. Gus raced ahead, past a pond under weeping willows, and on to the hay fields beyond.

Liv felt content to walk; not compelled to run, as she so often did. Like her brain was more settled. It might be a transient state, and she certainly would not give up exercise, but today, it was strangely pleasant to stroll, take in the muted colours of the farmland, sip the warm froth of the drink. Gus's golden coat fit perfectly with the autumn palette.

"That was the first time you'd been back, wasn't it?"

Liv glanced over, finding Faye's brown eyes on her. She nodded. When they'd met, it had been easy to say the Lachances had moved to Ontario for Claude's work. Faye probably deserved to hear the truth, and it felt as if doing so would free her just a little more.

"There are things I've never told you," she began, and thought she saw a slight curve to Faye's lips — *I bet there's a lot you haven't told me, sweetie* — but Faye waited for her to go on.

It was easier, this time. Not that she planned to share it with the world. Maybe one day, somewhere far down the road, she'd be one of those athletes advocating for women and girls in such situations. Faye was silent a beat when she finished, then slipped an arm around Liv's waist and squeezed.

"I'm sorry you had to go through that, and I'm glad it wasn't worse. I hope you can move forward from here."

"Nate thinks I should talk to someone. Like a professional."

"Can't hurt. I should probably do the same thing myself." Faye gave her a wry grin. "Maybe we need another pact."

"I guess it eventually turned out all right with the last one," Liv responded drolly. Last winter they'd both made stupid decisions about their relationships, though Liv maintained she was more justified in encouraging Nate to go to California to ride — without her — than Faye had been breaking up with Will because he asked her to fly to Calgary with him at Christmas to meet his mother. Not that she could trust herself to be entirely objective.

The hay fields remained lush, the late-season growth in defiance of the trees shutting down around it. Gus's plumed tail trailed him as he rollicked through the sea of green, only his head and topline visible, almost like he was swimming. When they headed back in the direction of the buildings, nearing the pond, he was definitely considering an actual dip.

"Don't you dare," Faye said, laughing as he approached the edge.

He didn't launch in like he would have in summer, instead seeming to contemplate how warm he was from running versus how cold the water might be. In the end, he waded through the reeds, emerging wet up to his belly. The dripping tendrils of his coat and the leaves stuck in his full tail completed the happy dog look. He shook and tore past them at warp speed.

"That should help dry him off a bit, at least," Liv said, grinning at the resigned look on Faye's face.

Liv's phone rang with Sarah McLachlan's "Perfect Girl," her designated ringtone for Emilie. Liv put her on speaker as they reached the house.

"I'm on my way. Wine or cappuccino?" Even through the filter of electronics, Emilie's voice was cheery.

"Wine, definitely," Faye said. "We're celebrating an engagement, right?"

"So that means we haven't scared Nate off, Liv?" Emilie said.

Liv laughed. "Faye was just saying you and she were the scary ones."

"We are. Hurry up, Em, so she can give us the latest scoop." Faye towelled Gus off and picked out what leaves and other refuse she could before letting him inside. "I heard about Hélène. What does that mean for you?"

Liv sobered. "Roger's still coming in, but that won't last forever. He's not going to Florida. I'll keep riding for now. I expect Jo will take over, though."

"So, an adjustment, but not a big one."

"Something like that."

By the time Emilie arrived, Faye had a fire in the hearth and soup warming on the stove. Faye being Faye, a pan of apple crisp waited on standby for dessert.

It wasn't until Em distributed the wine glasses that Faye prompted Liv again. "So?"

"How would you feel about Florida in December? Can you both pull it off?" The plan was a compromise, and all Liv could hope was it would come together. She'd still need their help.

"Come hell or high water, I will make it happen," Faye responded, Emilie nodding in agreement. "Which my life might be by December. I've already got people asking about ordering platters of baked goods for Christmas parties. It's going to be mayhem."

"I'll help!" Emilie chimed in.

"Amid your own mayhem? Though your help is assumed, Em. We'll reward ourselves by going to the royal wedding," Faye said, putting on a posh accent, then laughing with Emilie. "Let's eat. Don't let me forget we have to watch Dean's horse run. Not that I expect you would, because Nate's riding for him." She glanced at Liv and smiled.

Five minutes before post time, Faye brought up the live stream from Woodbine on the computer in the office, and Liv switched back to professional mode, scanning the odds for number four, Sun And Stars. A two-year-old colt, owned by Northwest Stables and Partner, trained by Dean Taylor, ridden by Nate Miller.

"Dean says Nate's still not got his mojo back. Not in those words, of course," Faye commented.

There was enough talk like that around, it seemed a betrayal to agree, so Liv remained silent. The camera followed the bay colt and his red-and-white clad rider as the pony warmed them up.

"It's completely your fault, of course," Faye added.

"My fault?"

"Think about it."

Liv scowled and waved her off, refocusing on the screen. The two-year-olds were behind the gate, being loaded with varying success, the usual scenario in a maiden race for juveniles. Sun And Stars was one of the more experienced starters with three tries so far. He'd always been in the money, earning him co-favourite status in tonight's attempt. Finally all in and settled, the starter turned them loose.

Sun And Stars rated kindly for Nate, finding a spot in the middle of the pack, Nate saving ground on the rail. He slipped the colt out a path approaching the turn, but looked to be stuck in a pocket heading into the stretch. *Find a way out of there, Miller.* The colt was on the bit, ready to run; he just needed a little luck.

There, a hole. Sun And Stars went boldly for it and Nate urged him through. Liv sucked in a breath, wincing when the first-time starter on his right wobbled and swerved out, knocked off stride while Sun And Stars broke free and targeted the leader.

"Come on, Sunny!" Faye cheered, and the three of them watched the bay colt sweep under the wire a length up, but the way Nate put his stick away was all Liv needed to know. He knew how this would turn out.

Disqualified, placed last, because that's where the little horse he'd impeded ended up. In hindsight, the hole wasn't big enough. Races for maiden two-year-olds were like bumper cars, with all those green babies just figuring things out, but that didn't excuse the incident. Oh well. That's the way it went out there. You had to take chances and hope things turned out in your favour.

On the racetrack, there was a confidence in Liv Nate hadn't truly seen since Claire had been in training. Her assurance had always seemed tied to that mare. Somehow, all the elements had fused, the pressure on her creating something new. Coal made into diamonds. Well, there was no diamond yet, but there would be, before the actual wedding, he hoped.

He still wasn't riding at the top of his game; hadn't regained his form from earlier in the season. She, on the other hand, was taking no prisoners out there. He was going to have to marry her for the financial support, at this rate. If he didn't shake this off soon, he was never going to hear the end of it.

Can't Catch Me in the Coronation Futurity was his next best chance to show he still knew what he was doing. The colt wasn't the favourite, because he was facing off against Interconnected, who had stepped into the spot Feste had vacated as leading two-year-old. He wasn't half the horse Feste had been... but he was still more experienced than Cam. The juvenile ranks were volatile this time of year, though. It just took one race to change the picture.

He let Nicole warm them up. He didn't particularly trust Cam. Paz kept his ears pinned and nostrils wrinkled the entire time, eyeballing the good-feeling colt to keep him in line. It was kind of funny, for now. Nate would be on his own once the gates opened, though.

"Say a prayer for me, Nicole," he quipped as she handed him off to the starter's assistant, who Cam immediately tried to bite. "You have my permission to give him a smack."

The handler laughed. Slowly waving the end of the long strip of leather he'd taken over from Nicole seemed to do the trick to keep the colt's attention, though there was a bit of head bobbing happening.

They walked forward — or at least in the general direction of the gate. Cam took two steps, stopped. The assistant pushed him sideways and got another three steps, then they weaved for two more, until at last they poured the big colt into his slot.

"Have fun out there, Miller," the handler said, balanced on the frame between stalls, trying to keep Cam's head straight.

"It's not going to be boring, I don't think," Nate answered between tight lips and hoped the final three starters joined the lineup in the barrier without delay.

Cam's ears were up, catching the sound of the crowd, a gathering that was much larger than the day he'd broken his maiden. Then he plunged, hitting the front doors hard. It broke the magnetic connection, and he burst through the barrier like an Olympian making a false start.

Nate wrestled him back, and the outrider was on them like a shot, helping to get the colt in hand.

"Thanks," Nate grumbled, keeping the choice words he had for Cam in his head.

"He all right?"

The commission vet would have the final say on that, but in Nate's opinion, the faster they got him back in the gate, the better, because he needed to run some of that stupid out and find his brain. Everything was popping on the colt now — veins, nostrils, eyes. It was a total wild man look.

"You good with going ahead?" the vet asked once his inspection was complete.

Because Nate could influence this. The vet's word was the official one, but if Nate said he didn't want to ride this tornado beast, he could get him scratched at the gate. But no way. The horse was sound; he was going back in, and would it be too much to ask for him to behave this time?

Once all the two-year-olds were lined up, the starter didn't waste time sending them off. The bell revved Cam up, which he definitely didn't need. Nate let him think he was having things his way as he joined the cavalry charge with the others.

He was a colt, so it wasn't like Chique. Fillies required sensitivity. With Cam, there were no mind games happening. This was a pissing contest.

Cam: *I'm bigger and stronger than you.*

Nate: *You may be right about that, but I'm older and wiser, so actually, we're going to do things my way.*

He closed his hand and set his weight back. Cam's ears swivelled, but his head only went up slightly before he decided it was too much work to fight. *That's a good baby monster. Promise I'll let you do your thing in a bit, buddy.*

Five wide was not really where he wanted to be going around the clubhouse turn, but what he wanted less was to be jammed on the rail. Cam wasn't handy enough to get out of trouble easily. Again, not like Chique, but there was no point making comparisons. That would just get him in trouble.

Cam seemed to like it out here. He could monitor everyone. Keep the leaders within striking distance. And hopefully not consider heading back to the barn when he saw the tunnel. His first race had been seven furlongs, so they hadn't come this way.

Nate sighed when they were safely into the backstretch. Now Cam seemed to realize this race was different. There was an extra turn. He settled even better, letting Nate take a breather without worrying about the colt trying to run off with him again.

Interconnected was just in front of them, one flight up, and started making up ground as they rounded the final turn. Cam turned on instantly, and Nate let him follow, still keeping him wide in case the stupid came back. Interconnected chipped away at the distance between himself and the leaders until he took over as they turned for home, with Cam in his wake.

Then it was like Cam swapped his ratty jeans and checked shirt for a three-piece suit, because he found more than a new gear, he made a career choice. He took aim at Interconnected, keeping straight like a grown-up racehorse, and closed the gap with each thundering stride, everything in him firing the way it was supposed to. When Nate popped him with the stick to back up his effort, the colt wasn't the least bit bothered. He just dug in harder, throwing kickback in the faces of those left behind.

He hung for a stride when he drew even with Interconnected, and Nate gave him another wake-up smack with the whip. *You're not done yet.* Interconnected was fighting hard, the two colts digging in as they stared each other down in the final furlong.

This one was theirs. Nate could feel it, Cam fully invested in this duel. He was making Nate work, but it was worth it as Cam out-powered his rival in the final strides, inching ahead by a nose, then a head, then a neck when they hit the wire.

It wouldn't knock Interconnected out of his position as likely winner of the Sovereign award for outstanding two-year-old colt, but it would designate Can't Catch Me as one to watch on the trail for next year's Queen's Plate. When Feste had died, so had the barn's hope of having a horse for next year's classic, but Cam had brought it back.

The celebration back at the Triple Stripe barn was more like the low-key gathering they'd had after Chique's win in the Prince of Wales last summer, but it was jubilant just the same. Everyone was happier, and more excited about leaving for Florida. It felt good to have a solid two-year-old star on the shed. Can't Catch Me would never be Feste, but that was just a reminder for Liv not to let her emotions become involved. Easier to do with this tiresome bay terror than it had been with the kind-hearted colt whose woven tail hairs encircled her wrist.

"What a beast. I earned that one," Nate said, Michel pressing a beer into his hand. "I need to up my fitness program. The horse had plenty in the tank, once he went in the right direction, but he almost ran out of rider."

"Set him up, Em," Michel said.

"I'm a physiotherapist, Michel, not a fitness trainer. Or at least I will be, if I ever finish school."

"Same thing, isn't it?" Michel asked with a cocky grin.

"No!" Emilie snapped.

"You looked all right out there, Miller." Liv gave him a coy smile. Pressure off all around. Nate had been putting too much of it on himself lately.

"Maman and Papa should be home by now," Emilie said, wandering over to Reba. She couldn't be there every day, but still came in on weekends to gallop the filly. Reba's status still hadn't changed — she'd winter in Ontario.

Liv followed her. "It's too bad they missed the race."

"Have you and Jo talked yet?"

Liv shook her head, frowning.

"What's up?" Emilie asked.

There were times when Emilie was just the right person to hear her concerns. Em had never felt like her little sister, even though she was younger by four years. Liv glanced toward Nate, out of earshot, talking to Sue and Michel. "Kenny asked me to ride at Gulfstream this winter."

Emilie's eyebrows went up. "Does Nate know?"

Liv nodded, slowly. "He doesn't want me to."

"Why wouldn't both of you ride?"

"Because that would be abandoning Jo."

"She'll have Cory and Nicole. And how many horses?"

"I know. Not as many as other years. But it's about more than that. I think after this year... he just wants the time off."

"A concept that isn't easy for you."

"If I commit to it, I'd have to be in Fort Lauderdale most of the time. And... I admit... it feels selfish."

Emilie, always stable and sensible, met her eyes. "It sounds as if you have your answer."

The sun went down far too early these days, which was harder to take in Ontario than it would be in Florida — because the temperature dropped abruptly with it. It broke up their mini-stake party as a chill settled and the buzz wore off. Jo and Michel tag-teamed the winning colt to get him done up. Roger hadn't even come back to the barn, and was taking tomorrow off for an appointment with Hélène. With her surgery date approaching, Liv expected he'd be around less and less.

Nate tossed her the keys, and she caught them as they walked to the car. They seemed to share the driving more often than not now, and usually with the Porsche, because why would anyone want to be in a Nissan when this was an option?

"Have you decided what you're going to do with your baby

here?" Liv asked, caressing the dash before turning the key in the ignition.

"I could ask Michel to drive it south for me. If I can come to terms with being without it for a month. And trusting him with it," he added with a smirk.

"The alternative is to be without it all winter, because if you don't decide soon you're not going to have much choice except to put it in storage." They were taking the Triple Stripe truck and trailer down at the end of the Woodbine meet, hopefully with Jay aboard.

"I'll talk to Mike," Nate said, his voice muted.

Liv glanced over. His eyes were closed, and he leaned against the headrest. He'd been more worried about coming through with that win than he'd let on. It was mental stress more than a physical deficit that caused his weariness. He wasn't out of shape; he was just worn out.

Before they'd decided to bring Jay back, she'd wondered if it was really worth it to stay until the end of the season. Less than six weeks left. Who would judge them? Why didn't they all just go to Florida? But Jay and Chique gave them a reason to stay.

"Have you decided about Gulfstream?" He rolled his head toward her, his expression serious, searching — for her eyes, for the answer.

"I'll tell him no." She reached for his hand. "Don't worry. We're going to have the best winter." This time, she would do it right.

CHAPTER ELEVEN

"ESPRESSO, PLEASE," he said when Faye asked him what he'd have. He sat adjacent to Will at a table in the café.

Faye set down the tiny cup of rich, dark liquid. Then she took a knife, cut off the end of Will's croissant, and placed it on the plate next to the cup.

"You take such good care of me." Nate grinned wryly.

"You're marrying my best friend. It's an obligation."

He looked at the bite-sized piece of pastry, then took a sip of the espresso. "I got days for that ride on Dean's two-year-old, so I could probably eat a whole one."

"They suspended you?" Faye managed to look sympathetic, despite the fact that the ride had cost Northwest any part of the purse money. "Ouch. Sorry. Maybe you need a butter tart."

Three days. And he wouldn't appeal it. He'd take the punishment, because what was another knock in a year where he'd had so many? He nibbled the croissant, determined to make it last as long as he could, then followed it with another swallow of espresso, letting the flavours mingle.

"How's Liv?" Will asked.

LINDA SHANTZ

"Fine, as far as I know." Was that accurate?

"You're not having doubts, are you?" Will said, leaning forward to rest his forearms on the table, and closing his hands — a little protectively, Nate thought — around his plate and what remained of the pastry. "Like maybe you jumped into this like you always do, instead of letting the two of you just be a couple without the pressure of getting married?"

Nate glared at him. "She said yes."

"Like, without balking at all? That seems suspect."

"Her exact words were, 'Yes, damn it.'"

Faye, who was pretending she wasn't listening when of course she was, began to laugh. A low, victorious kind of laugh.

"What's that about?" Nate asked her, wary.

"That's exactly what I told her to say, should the question come up."

"You've been coaching her?"

"You're welcome."

"So what's the problem?" Will persisted.

"There is no problem," he said with his customary grin, trying to chase his fears away.

The truth was, he was a little freaked out, thinking about everything that had piled up in the last week. This might all be bigger than him. It was great Liv was talking more, and not avoiding the hard discussions — but he hoped she would find a professional.

If only Geai were still here. He would make the old man tell him everything, things the family might conceal. He needed to know it all to understand what was required of him — when all that might be was to keep walking beside her as they negotiated their future together.

"When are we getting together to play again? I'm stuck in Ontario till the second week of December. We could do another unplugged night here." When in doubt, change the subject. The one evening last summer he and Will had set up in the café with guitars had been a big hit. It would be fun to do it again.

His phone rang, avoiding any thoughts Will or Faye might have of bringing the conversation back to Liv. The name on the screen drew his eyebrows together. Kenny O'Connell?

"Sorry, I have to take this," he said, pushing away from the table and heading out the door. "Kenny! How are you?" He hoped he didn't sound too mystified.

It was cool today, and he'd left his coat on the back of his chair inside. He couldn't imagine this would be a long call. He couldn't imagine why Kenny would contact him at all.

"Good, kid. Good."

He'd never spent any time wondering how old Kenny was, but Nate thought probably in his thirties and not late into the decade, so he could lose the kid label. There was an immediate lull, but he waited for Kenny to go on. The New York agent hadn't contacted him to waste time with pleasantries.

"I just talked to Liv. You knew I tried to talk her into riding at Gulfstream, right?"

"Yeah."

Kenny ploughed on. "And you know she turned me down?"

Nate breathed a happy sigh, hearing Kenny confirm Liv wouldn't be gallivanting back and forth from training centre to racetrack this winter. "Yes."

"But what about you?"

The agent's question caught him off guard, but Nate had been obtuse not to think the call had something to do with riding. "So I'm your second choice? Nice."

He was kidding, even though he could easily believe it might be a theme in his life. Second choice for his first girl-friend, who'd turned down his proposal and married his brother. Second choice for Dean Taylor with Ride The Wave, who'd gone back to Liv even though Nate had given him his first Queen's Plate.

"We go way back," Kenny said. "Don't take it personally."

"I'm riding like shit. Why would you want me?"

"You had a nice win the other day."

"On a horse anybody could ride."

"That's not what Liv said."

"Was this her suggestion?" He was confused now, and a little angry. She was honouring his request, but sending him in her stead? Defeated the purpose. Or was this a test? No. She was done with that. She was changing. Getting better at being invested in them.

But what would be the point of him being the one to ride at Gulfstream? Same problem. She wasn't going to follow him. She'd stay at Payson and gallop every day, because that's where she was needed. The only thing he could figure was she'd done it to pacify the agent.

"I hear you two are getting married. Is that why you're riding like shit? Keeping each other up at night? Seems to be working for her."

Nate pressed his forehead into the glass next to the café's door, the insinuation enough to get rid of the chill he'd felt when he'd stepped outdoors. Kenny was taunting him, a couple of little wasp stings hitting home. *That probably is why I'm riding like shit,* but not because she was keeping him up... it was because she wasn't.

"We're not—" He stopped himself.

Kenny howled. "What? Why did it feel like you were going to tell me you're not sleeping with her? Is it because she's Catholic?"

Nate almost snorted, thinking of what Liv would say to that. "No. She's not exactly enamoured of her family history with that religion."

A customer approached the café's door, and he stepped away. He should go sit in the car, because this was not a conversation everyone in King City needed to hear.

"Are you? Because that never stopped—"

"No." He cut Kenny off before the agent launched into some teenage conquest story. "That's not the only reason to... why is it any of your business?" Kenny was an unlikely — and unreliable — confidante. He was telling this guy nothing.

"If you're riding for me, it is."

Nate laughed outright now. "We haven't agreed to anything." If Liv wasn't accepting mounts this winter, neither should he. They'd both take the winter off. That was the idea, wasn't it?

"When's the wedding?" Kenny persisted.

"That information is being given out on a need-to-know basis only."

"Well, I need to know, if you're riding for me." There it was again. "And I expect an invitation, of course."

He tried to picture Kenny at their wedding. Dancing with his mother. Drinking with Michel. Hitting on Faye. It could be amusing, or it could be a complete disaster. But he was Liv's friend, as odd a reality as that was.

"In a month," he admitted.

"We'll talk again once you've been married for a few days. I bet you'll be back to riding like your old Eclipse Award-winning self. Seriously. That can't be healthy. But congratulations on your impending nuptials. And think about it. It would get you out from under their umbrella. Let you prove yourself for you."

He hadn't done that? Besides, it was an umbrella he had absolutely no problem being under.

Drinks on the patio next to the pool with her parents seemed serious and grown-up, like this engagement thing had officially given her adult status. It was warmer today than it had been yesterday, allowing for this outdoor get-together. It made the thought of staying behind next week while the others left for Florida bearable.

Her mother served appetizers, which Liv and Nate both politely declined. For her, it was more about the nervous churn in her stomach than the impact it might have on her weight. Nate continued to be careful. She was aware he was struggling in more than one way right now, professionally. He hadn't talked to her about it. That seemed wrong, when she was doing her best to share; so contrary to her usual inclination. But maybe it was because it was professional, and they were in direct competition. Never reveal your weaknesses to your rival, even if that rival, the rest of the time, was the person you were planning to spend the rest of your life with. Is this the way it would have to be for the two of them? That part of their lives kept behind a door the other didn't have access to? It was an unfortunate consequence of their careers. While it made sense to the logical side of her brain, the emotional part seemed to demand more of a say these days.

"It's our turn for an announcement," her father began.

Liv glanced at Emilie, who made a *no idea* face.

"We've decided to move back to Montreal."

Liv blinked, and Emilie's eyes widened.

"As you know, my mother is not well," he continued.

His mother, not their grandmother; a woman with whom neither of his daughters had any real relationship. Had not seen, before the funeral, since they'd left twelve years ago. Geai's wife, when she'd been alive, had adopted that role. Her mother's parents, though kind, had been just remote enough since the move. Birthday cards and calls at Christmas. They'd never come to Ontario, and Liv's small branch of the family had never gone to Montreal.

"So it's time," Claude said. "I'm needed there."

Liv's heart was racing now, her thoughts not with her ailing, estranged grandparent, but with her home, with the place that had been a gift, her escape from the unwanted memories of her place of birth. "So what does that mean? For the farm?" What if he meant to sell it? He wouldn't do that, would he?

Nate must've noticed her distress, his hand finding hers. Her first instinct was to bat it away, but she caught herself and squeezed back.

"The day has come..." Claude paused.

Liv's stomach was ready to drop out, and she held her breath.

"For you to begin overseeing things. It was always the plan, was it not?"

She exhaled, slowly and silently. Not selling. There had been talk of her assuming that position, but in her mind such a thing was years in the future. No mention had been made since she'd left vet school, though perhaps her being even more involved in the farm decisions since then reinforced the expectation: when Claude retired, Liv would take over.

Claude's role in the farm's management wasn't hands-on. He made sure the bills were paid; the one making the money that kept things running, bridging the gaps between expenses and income — from boarding and training, breeders' awards and purse money. Would he still be providing that security?

"And I expect Emilie might want to be a part of it?" Claude shifted his gaze to his younger daughter.

Liv and Em exchanged another look. "I guess we have lots to talk about." Liv turned back to her father. "Do you have a timeline?"

"Do you have a wedding date?"

Nate ducked his head, smothering a laugh as her mouth opened, but no words came out. She didn't know why she was stuck; she'd expected to share the decision sometime this afternoon and was moderately surprised they didn't know already.

"Yes," she answered finally.

"You can have the house, of course. Perhaps renovate; make Emilie an apartment if she plans to live here too."

Again, Liv's jaw opened. The house? This house? This huge house? "That's incredible," she said at last.

"That's very generous, thank you," Nate said quietly.

His hand moved under hers, and she realized just how hard she was gripping it. She eased off and threw him a small, apologetic smile.

"So the three of you are willing to do this?"

"Let them have time to process it, Claude," Anne interjected. "We'll talk again."

But Emilie's eyes were shining with excitement, Liv already seeing big ideas in them. They flowed freely in her sister. Em was the entrepreneur in the family. She'd want to get together soon to discuss this, but there was no question she was on board. But Nate? The track was his thing, even though he cherished the ability to retreat to this place. What role would he play, beyond moral support?

"There's another thing," Claude said. "Your grandfather left each of you money, and not an insignificant sum."

Liv went from jumbled thoughts to unwavering decisiveness. "I don't want it. Give it all to Emilie." She snapped her hand from Nate's as she scrambled to her feet, mumbling, "Excuse me," and dove through the sliding doors.

It was a knee-jerk reaction. The old her wasn't dead quite yet.

Maiden and barren mares dotted the rolling pasture, claiming the last of the green blades of grass. Claire spotted her and sauntered over, her belly swaying with each step. It was hard to believe she still had over two months to go; she already looked so enormous. Spending most of her time at the track among the tucked up racehorses, it still caught Liv by surprise when she saw an in-foal mare at this stage of her pregnancy. Claire would get larger still, making this current shape seem svelte in comparison by the time she was ready to pop.

So much for progress. She'd bolted, leaving her parents and Emilie and Nate — poor Nate — sitting there. But she didn't want the money. It felt like she was being paid off, not like an indication of remorse for her grandfather's behaviour. A reminder to stay quiet after he was gone. Nothing could change that part of her past; she just had to learn how to prevent it from hindering her future. Maybe she should take Nate's name, shed the association of the one she'd been born with. Liv Miller. She'd try it on, imagine writing it on the cover of a note-book like a teen crush. See if it fit. See if it helped.

Her parents' news was just one more thing on top of all of it. Of course she wanted to be part of the farm, to preserve the legacy her father had created. But why did it all have to happen now, when she finally felt as if she was riding with some authority? At least no one could claim this would be a conflict of interest. She could oversee the farm and still ride. There was a manager to manage. He wasn't Geai, but Austin seemed capable enough. Life wouldn't be that much different from right now with this change. She and Em had their roles, and it wasn't as if their father wouldn't be accessible if they needed his input. He just wouldn't be living here.

Claire stuck her head over the top rail and made her best

peppermint face, and Liv didn't disappoint, digging deep into the pocket of her jeans for a candy. A couple of the other mares wandered over, hoping to cash in, but Claire gave a slow swing of her head, ears pinned and nostrils pinched, and they kept their distance. Not a dramatic show like Chique would give, just a quiet boss mare reminder. Claire lipped up the white disc, tongue carrying it to her molars, grinding it with a minty release. Liv squeezed through the boards of the four-rail fence, winding her arms around the mare's neck, sliding hands under Claire's mane to her withers and letting her nails dig into the flesh there. Claire grunted and distorted her upper lip in pleasure as Liv scratched, rubbing off crusted mud, winter coat growth well started. When Claire curled her head, trying to reciprocate the gesture, Liv let her, trusting her, the mare using the edge of her teeth against Liv's shoulder blade. Through the sweatshirt she wore, the pressure was pleasant. Claire's massages were almost as good as Nate's.

The mare stopped abruptly, lifting her head, stilling her body. Liv glanced over her shoulder, following Claire's wall-eyed gaze.

It wasn't a surprise to see Nate there, standing just the other side of the fence, hands in the pockets of his jacket. She pressed a kiss to Claire's cheek, her arms falling away as she turned. She could hear the mare's soft footfalls, sense her nose inches behind as she walked over and ducked through the rails. She stopped in front of him, reflecting his posture, carefully meeting his eyes.

"I'm sorry," she said quietly.

"Yeah, well... you're dealing with a lot."

"I overreacted."

"You did." He held his hand out to her, and when she grasped it, started walking. "What do you say we take Jay and Chique into Woodbine tomorrow morning? Pacino left an empty stall, and we can bring Reba home. She doesn't need to be in there, and it will make up for taking Jay from Em. Now that the yearlings are on hiatus, she'll need something to fill her non-existent free time. You may think you two are not alike, but in that way, you are. Always occupied." He grinned.

"She might be worse than me." A wry curve tugged at her lips, then they fell into a twisted frown. "Everything's changing."

And she had no choice but to adapt.

CHAPTER TWELVE

NATE WAITED in line in the kitchen. The most recent incarnation of the old barn coffee maker had died without ceremony first thing that morning. Nate, being the most dispensable person between five and six AM, had volunteered to make the run.

"Would Timmie's really have been that much further?" Sue asked, frowning at the styrofoam cups in the tray, looking like she didn't trust the brew wasn't toxic. Her fears were justifiable.

"Should you really even be drinking coffee, Sue?" Nate said in response, nodding at the round abdomen she couldn't hide once her jacket was off.

She grumbled, snatching a cup and walking out of the crowded tack room.

Sue and Michel were going to Florida this winter, but her condition — somehow that word didn't seem right, but he was going with it — was another reminder how everything was changing. Track grooms didn't necessarily take mat leave, though at least Triple Stripe was an above-board kind of operation, so it would be an option. It meant next spring there might be a human baby on the shedrow. Liv was going to love that. *NOT,* with capital letters, italicized. But Sue and Michel were a big part of the barn family, so she would have to learn to deal. That was going to be fun to watch. He'd be the buffer; protect her from the worst of it. He had no illusions the presence of an infant would sway her on her own thoughts on procreation; the opposite was probably true.

"This is a big step down, Miller," Michel said, daring to drink his brew black. The guy had an iron stomach. One day his working-hours diet of untempered coffee and Jamaican patties off the food truck was going to eat a hole in his stomach, if it hadn't already. Maybe Sue made him eat better food the rest of the day.

"We should get one of those pod machines," Nicole suggested, loading her cup with cream and sugar. "Then everyone could have whatever they wanted."

"And we could contribute to the landfill?" Lest anyone forget, Emilie had once considered a career in environmental something-or-other before she'd made the jump to physiotherapy. Her hard stare and furrowed eyebrows made Nicole slink away, gaze averted.

"And I'd no doubt be the one expected to keep everyone's favourites in stock, so I second that with a hard no," Jo said.

"Well, Em, you could make a delivery from Triple Shot every morning. People would pay for that. You'd make a killing." Nate grinned.

Emilie's expression transitioned from barely suppressed indignation to thoughtfulness, the entrepreneurial cogs no doubt turning in her razor-sharp mind. "You might have something there, Nate."

"Because Em needs something else to do." Liv laughed. He noticed she'd done no more than cast a leery glance at the remaining two cups. She met his gaze. "I'll take the headache, thanks."

He shrugged and sipped his own. They'd been up extra-early to bring in Chique and Jay, so caffeine was caffeine. Someone would drink hers and the one he'd gotten out of habit for Roger, if the trainer didn't show.

"Why are you here, Em?" he asked.

Emilie waved a hand enigmatically through the air. "I'm everywhere."

"All right, time to get some horses out." Jo pushed between bodies to reach the white board outside the tack room, the morning's training schedule outlined in her neat block letters. It made Nate think of Roger again and killed whatever was left of the joviality inspired by the silly coffee discussion.

Next to the office, Chique bounced off the walls of her old stall, squealing and kicking the rubber-matted sides. It would be just like Chique to crack a sesamoid when she was only here for their very human desire to add another title, another trophy, to the collection. They'd shuffled Reba to an empty stall at the other end of the shed for the morning.

"Let's take Chique and Jay out," Nate said, and got the expected *you with the crazy suggestions again, Miller* look from Liv and Jo. For a few weeks, it would be like old times. Like they had a veteran D-line to hold the team together. Of course, one of those horses was Chique, so maturity and stability were relative concepts.

A little walkabout today would help the filly's mind when she was used to spending most of her day turned out. It just might settle their own minds as well, thoughts of Hélène a constant in the background.

Liv sighed. "I get Jay. You get Crazy."

"Naturally."

Chique was totally in his face as he entered her stall, the

strength of her upper lip wriggling against his waistline. She could smell the peppermints in his pockets. He slipped her one, like the Pez dispenser he was, and tied her to the back wall.

He curried her lightly, using a soft gummy comb to disrupt her coat. Once the decision had been made to bring her back, she'd been blanketed to discourage its growth. She was also under lights to influence her heat cycles artificially, and the mimicking of longer daylight hours tricked her system into thinking it was spring, so she was actually shedding the bit of winter coat she'd started. Another reminder this was just a detour from her future reality. A year from now...

A year from now, she'd be fat and two months away from producing the devil spawn she was sure to deliver. He couldn't wait. He couldn't have been more excited about that foal — one that had yet to even be conceived — than he would have been about his own human child. Which would never be.

"Where are we going?" he asked once they were outside the barn. The lights from the main track shone brightly compared to the glow from the shedrows and streetlight-like lamps throughout the backside.

"This was your idea," Liv said.

"The Field, then." It would be dark, but more conducive to the easy exercise he had in mind.

They took the long way, along the horse path that ran parallel to the E.P. Taylor turf course, the bank of which rose to their right. Chique had her old power-walk going, Nate in the familiar ready-for-anything posture. Liv had Jay on the knot, one hand casually holding the lines.

"I still can't get over how good he looks," Nate said. Then Chique slammed on the brakes and swung her quarters ninety degrees to face straight into the tunnel. Nate almost fell out of the tack laughing. "She wants to go to the main, I think."

"You're the one who suggested The Field," Liv said. "You explain it to her."

For half a second he thought about giving the filly her wish and going to the main track, but in the other half second he realized what a death wish that would be — a recipe to get run off with. So he turned her back the way he intended to go. Chique let out a huff and followed Jay.

The Field was deserted. When Chique was a two-year-old, he used to bring her here — his first mount of the morning — because the main and training tracks didn't open until six AM. It was a way to fit her in before his schedule got crazy, back in the day when he was the hot bug rider at Woodbine. The demand had never really let up, even when he'd become a journeyman... until he'd moved his tack to California's Santa Anita Park last winter. He'd been a nobody there. Now, since his accident... he might be something worse. He'd heard enough of the whispers to know those wagging tongues thought he might be a has-been. It was a fickle thing, this business.

Chique's current behaviour was reminiscent of that green-as-grass two-year-old, like she'd brought her juvenile self out to play for old times' sake. She was demonstrating an impressive giraffe impersonation, neck as close to the vertical as she could get it. Nate ducked his head to the side in case she popped. He didn't want to add a broken nose to his list of Why This Year Sucked. Jay jogged along placidly. It didn't settle the filly, but it shielded her from the rail-less infield, and perhaps pre-empt her dashing across it.

"Never grow up, baby girl." He laughed when she spooked at something — real or imaginary. At least there was a high chain link perimeter fence, so if she decided to go solo she couldn't reach the access road and potentially tour Rexdale Boulevard. She seemed to be eyeballing the high-rise condos over that way. Never a dull moment.

She leapt into a gallop to keep up with Jay's longer-striding jog. Nate let her, and Liv didn't grumble at him to bring her back. It was still too slow to keep her brain engaged — only speed work truly did that for the busy filly — so he kept his position defensive, his weight back. She wasn't pulling at least. She was just happy to be here.

Rounding the gradual arc of the narrow track until they were no longer facing suburbia, they now travelled parallel to the 427 highway. The rumble of traffic was of no more interest to the filly than the low-flying jet descending into Pearson Airport; they were not the goblins from which she needed to protect him. Finally, she dropped her head and downshifted into a lofty jog.

"It's a shame they're so closely related," Nate said. "You could breed her to Jay."

Liv pondered for a moment. "They would have a beautiful baby, except for the extra leg that would come out of its forehead."

"A unicorn. Chique should produce nothing less." He reached forward and scrubbed the filly's neck underneath her wild mane, which was desperately in need of a stylist. Liv would get to that before race day.

Race day! In just over two weeks, Chique would run. They were getting a bonus round. Overtime. A little fun to look forward to amid everything else.

Hard and fast, Chique propped, driving his knuckles so hard into her withers it sent a shooting pain up his left hand, all the way to the collarbone that still ached from the break that summer. Just as quick he was on his back, in the dirt. It felt like a recurring theme this year. That must've been a hell of a spin, because of the moves she'd thrown at him in the course of their partnership, he'd sat all of them but the very first.

What had he been looking forward to, exactly?

Oh, shit. He sat up abruptly, because all they needed was Chique loose for real. She'd been back, what, an hour? But Liv corralling her with Jay, her hand snapping out to snatch the filly. Sweet, kind, Jay. Nate wasn't sure that breeding Chique was the wisest thing in the world from a disposition perspective, but Jay deserved to sire babies.

"You okay?" Liv called. She was staring at him, looking as if she wasn't sure whether to be amused or show concern.

He started to push himself to his feet and felt the pain he'd momentarily forgotten in the panic of not knowing where Chique was.

"Shit," he said, this time out loud as he approached, trying to ignore the stinging in his hand. "I am not walking back, so just look the other way." He managed to throw his leg over the filly, easing into the saddle. "And you don't get to say a word about this."

Liv's laugh was immediate. "Oh, nice try, Miller. You're not getting out of buying the barn a case of beer. And no getting the cheap stuff. This is worth craft beer."

"You don't even like beer."

"So? I'm looking out for the crew."

"Nifty catch, by the way. You and Jay could join the outrider team." He reached for the lines — but the hand, the stupid hand. *Are you kidding me?* He arranged the reins into a cross and fisted his right fingers over it, praying Chique didn't have any more antics to throw his way.

"You okay?" Liv asked again.

"Not sure," he answered, gritting his teeth.

Her eyes narrowed. "What did you do?" Chique drifted away from Jay, and Liv leaned over and grabbed the line to reel the filly in. "Miller?"

He glared at the back of Chique's head. "I just jammed my hand. It's fine. I'll ice it and it'll be good as new."

"Well, rest it now. I've got you."

Great. Brilliant idea, coming to The Field. They'd have been better off going to the main. Or being sane and not taking them out till tomorrow.

Jo's eyebrows arched when she caught sight of them, Jay showing off his sainthood. Because how many four-year-old colts could pony a filly?

"Excitement in your travels?" she asked. "Did you part company out there?"

"No." He hopped off, careful not to jar his hand.

"The dirt all over your ass suggests otherwise."

"We were due a case of beer. Thanks, Miller." Michel, of course, hadn't missed any of the news. He grinned, then followed Liv to Jay's stall.

"Thank Chique," Nate grumbled.

"Does she need to be walked?" Jo laid a hand on the filly's neck, which looked pretty cool to Nate.

"We didn't do much," he said. "But I can take her a few turns if you let me get my boots off."

"Don't you have other horses to get on this morning?" Jo asked.

"Not sure that's happening now." He tried to flex his hand again, but the same shooting pain occurred. He'd better text his agent. Puffs of dry sand rose as he scuffed his feet along the shed like a sulking kindergarten student.

Liv was in the tack room, hanging Jay's bridle on the hook in the doorway. "Let me see."

He balked. Liv checking out his injuries usually only meant more pain. He eased his glove off and held it out — not to her, but to look at it himself. There was swelling across the back, but it was slight — so far. Liv peered at it, but thankfully didn't touch it.

"Pictures, yes?" Liv asked cautiously.

"See, if you'd become a vet, maybe you'd own an x-ray machine, and I wouldn't have to wait in the ER for three hours."

Liv rolled her eyes, then levelled them on Jo who had just appeared. "Got a few minutes?"

"Office?" Jo said. "Don't worry about Chique, Nate. Marc's got her."

Nate followed them, standing just inside the door. Neither woman claimed the chair behind the desk, the significance of its vacancy filling the space. Jo dropped on the couch, and Liv leaned against the wall of win photos, hands tucked in the small of her back.

"You heard about Hélène's surgery?" Liv said.

"Yes," Jo responded. "It's terrible."

The biopsy determined the tumour was cancerous and had infiltrated the nearby lymph nodes and tissue outside the abdomen. Diagnosis: Stage Three ovarian cancer. Abdominal debulking performed. Chemotherapy to follow. The news still made Nate's head spin.

"If you can handle things till I get to Florida, we'll talk again. I think we all need time to process," Liv said. The Triple Stripe string would leave next week, and in a little over a month, Nate and Liv — and hopefully Jay — would follow.

"After your wedding," Jo said. "At least we have something happy to end the year off with."

Liv met Nate's eyes with a soft smile. It erased the lines that had been much too common on her face recently and with it, some of his own trepidation.

"I guess that's it for now," she said, straightening as Jo stood and turning to Nate. "Time to go to the hospital. Will you let me drive you there?"

He finally broke into a grin. "I'd let you drive me anywhere."

He used a towel to hold the ice pack against the back of his hand, freezing away the swelling and pain — and the annoyance. At least this afternoon he had the Breeders' Cup races to distract him. But they didn't, not really, because he couldn't watch, couldn't see those scenes from Santa Anita without thinking, what if, after the Mile, Liv had said they were going? What if she hadn't retired the filly after the International? Chique didn't run on Lasix; she could recover in three weeks and be ready to compete at that level again. She was capable of anything... on the right day.

"How's it feeling?" Liv settled next to him on the couch in the Lachance's basement television room. He felt like he was becoming a regular, and still couldn't get over Claude and Anne's generosity regarding the house. One less thing to worry about, at least.

He tried to close his fingers, and winced.

"Maybe you should get it x-rayed again tomorrow," she said.

"It's not broken," he reminded curtly. They'd waited forever in the emergency room — despite it being deserted — when he figured he deserved VIP service after his injuries this year. The radiographs had been clean. The pain and inconvenience seemed trivial after what he'd been through this summer. A reminder to be grateful: this was trivial.

"Sometimes minor fractures aren't seen right away," Liv persisted.

"Well, if it's that small, it's not enough reason to stop riding. You wouldn't. You just want my mounts."

"While I'd be perfectly happy to ride Chique, and Jay, what I want is for you still to be riding when Chique's hellion is ready to run, not totally crippled with arthritis from undiagnosed fractures."

"The hellion that isn't even conceived yet? I'm supposed to preserve myself so that can be what kills me? And I had a diagnosis. It's not fractured. You're not legally qualified to offer a second opinion."

Emilie set a store-bought platter of veggies and dip on the coffee table in front of them. She rubbed her hands together. "Are you guys fighting? Is this a fight?"

"Nate's just feeling sorry for himself," Liv said.

"On so many levels, I do."

They looked at each other and laughed. It had become their joke whenever those words came up in innocent conversation. One day, soon enough, they'd say them in response to some gravely serious questions, which would be no joke. He was counting the days.

"I miss the drama. I miss the angst," Emilie said. "You two are already like an old married couple. Boring."

"Nobody misses the drama and the angst," Nate said. "But we're not boring."

"I'll tape it for you," Emilie said, bringing their attention back to the injured hand. "Before you know it you won't remember it's hurt."

"That's just great," Liv said with a scowl. "Instead of, you know, letting it heal?"

"Never let 'em see you're broken," Nate quipped. Because that's how it was. If you were hurt, and took time off, you lost more than mounts. You lost status. So you rode injured, unless you absolutely could not. Especially now, after those two months he'd been laid up... if they didn't take him out in an ambulance, he was riding.

"You have to at least wait for the swelling to go down," Liv insisted.

"With Em's miraculous taping job, it'll disappear in hours."

"It's a good thing you got that suspension, then." She gave him a fake sweet smile.

"Thanks for the reminder, honey."

She nailed him with a cushion.

The commercial break ended, panoramic camera shots taking them back to Santa Anita's pink hills. The view didn't have the same effect on him it might have a few years ago. He saw the shadows more than the California light, hard memories sticking stubbornly in the corners, hiding behind the prettiness. He didn't think he'd ever lose the immediate punch-to-the-gut feeling he got at the mere mention of the track. *Spill at Santa Anita this afternoon. One of the jockeys just died in hospital.* You could take a brush and stroke some fresh paint over the dark spots, but the shadows were still there, ghostly lines that showed themselves when the angle was just right.

It didn't prevent his disappointment. *We deserve to be there. When the hell are we going to have a horse in the Breeders' Cup?* He'd wanted it for Chique as much as for himself. The race they'd written for her at Woodbine was a glorified workout. She'd load in the gate, gallop along, kick clods of turf into the faces of her foes, and they'd collect sixty percent of the purse. Add start number three to her Canadian tally this season and beat out Ride The Wave for Horse of the Year — while collecting outstanding older filly and turf filly at the same time. But he'd always wonder what could have been.

CHAPTER THIRTEEN

WHAT, exactly, should she call the precipitation falling from the sky? It wasn't sleet — too cold. Wasn't icy rain — it melted too quickly. Not big enough to be hail. Not fluffy enough to be snow. Apparently, the temperate weather they'd been blessed with into November left town with the rest of the crew, rubbing it in for Liv and Nate that they were being left behind. Chique would love it, though. That fresh air? Filly weather. Just in time for race day.

The shedrow was barren, stripped of equipment and personalities. Liv tacked up Jay to the beat of Chique's incessant tapping next door, hoof on mat. *You'll be disappointed you don't get to gallop, but wait. Something better is coming.*

There were still traces of mud left on the chaps she hadn't worn since spring. March seemed so long ago now it might as well have been another decade. She zipped them on over her jeans for an extra layer of protection from the elements and cold, adjusted her neck gaiter, and tugged on a warmer pair of gloves. How many days left in the meet?

Fifteen. Nate texted her the new number first thing each morning.

The sun wouldn't be up for almost an hour, which seemed lazy in a place abuzz with activity. It might not be as busy as it had been a month ago, but as long as there was racing, there would be horses, though their numbers dwindled as closing day approached.

She wondered if anyone noticed when she took Jay around a second time; a stronger mile than the first. Nate got on him some mornings and insisted he was better than he'd ever been. In a couple of weeks, they'd find out if that was true. After cooling out the colt, leaving Chique now sulking at the back of her stall, she headed for Dean's barn to breeze Ride The Wave.

Dean still hadn't accepted she wouldn't be riding his colt in the Valedictory. He dismissed the fact she'd swapped her jockey credentials for that of trainer shortly after the news of Hélène's diagnosis. Despite her suggesting Cory as an alternative, Dean wasn't committing to another rider. Anything could happen, he insisted. And anything could. There were no guarantees Jay's name would be there on entry day, no matter how promising it looked.

When she returned to the Triple Stripe shed, Emilie was there. She met Liv in the stall and slipped on Jay's halter as Liv removed the tack. "I brought you cappuccino."

"Thank you." Liv smiled as she settled a cooler over Jay's back and secured it. "I'm going to miss it when we head south."

"I'm not feeling sorry for you," Emilie said, turning Jay toward the door. "I'll walk him. You can get your wild child out."

Chique lived up to her reputation, energy barely contained. One good thing about so many empty stalls — it left a clear path for power-walking. In hindsight, she should have put the tack on the filly and shedrowed her. She'd have more control on Chique's back than on the ground. Whether it was safer or not was a toss-up.

Despite an utter lack of worthwhile grazing left on the lawn, Liv let Chique pick at what hardy blades remained before putting the filly in her stall and tossing her a clump of Bermuda grass. She retreated to the office to stay warm while she waited for the vet, leaving Emilie puttering with Jay. Good luck messages flooded her phone, from those who weren't here: her parents who were back in Montreal; Jo, Nicole, Sue and Michel, in Florida; Roger and Hélène; Fay and Will. Nate showed up before the vet did, dropping onto the sofa next to her. Roger's chair remained empty, like an honorary place setting.

"This feels weird, doesn't it?" he said. "Like it's not a real race. Like we did this already."

Liv met his eyes. It was different this time. The tension before the International had been so unbearable she'd made herself ill over it, as much because of the friction between the two of them as the way she'd driven herself crazy, convincing herself the filly wasn't sound. That didn't mean Chique hadn't been checked from top to bottom before today, as promised. It would not do to come back for this celebration of the filly's career to have her pull up with an injury. And technically, Chique didn't have to win today to be eligible for the Sovereign awards, but a win was exactly what everyone expected. Even still, Liv didn't feel the same pressure she'd suffered last time.

Before she could translate thoughts into words for a response, Emilie cracked the door open, sticking her head in.

"You're both signing autographs on the frontside at the New Chapter table, right?" Emilie glanced from Nate to Liv. "I'll stay with Chique."

They'd settled on calling the race the New Chapter Stakes

to bring attention to the local Thoroughbred retirement organization, and Woodbine had built a day around it to showcase Thoroughbred aftercare. Liv had publicly announced a portion of any purse money Chique won would be donated to the cause. Normally Emilie would have been helping manage the table on the front side, but she'd insisted on being the one to take Chique over for the race — something Liv was especially grateful for, with everyone else gone. Emilie had done enough work beforehand to make up for her absence over there — printing up souvenir posters of Chique, enlisting Nate and some of the other riders. A token appearance was the least Liv could do.

"Sure. It'll help pass the time," she said. "When do you want me there?"

Fan favourites of Chique's calibre didn't come along every year. The melancholy she'd felt before the International crept back, because this time was it. No more encores. Maybe Jay's impact would be more enduring and next year they'd be signing a poster of him.

———

"Sorry, princess, Paz is basking in the Florida sun right now, and Liv didn't go for my suggestion that Jay could pony you."

The pony rider looked sideways at Nate like he was smoking something, clearly not deeming this assignment the honour it was. Chique eyeballed the unfamiliar pony with a similar expression.

"Don't take it personally," Nate said, and when the pony rider didn't so much as crack a smile, he focused on the large white flakes settling on Chique's ears and mane. It might be pretty on a Christmas card, but not in the post parade of the final race — reprise — of Chique's career. Could be worse, though. Could be rain, or that shit that had been coming from the sky earlier in the day.

It was a relief when he could finally break from the line to warm the filly up, leaving the humourless escort behind. Chique dropped her head and pinned her ears, galloping into the driving snow.

He didn't want it to end, this gift. The filly felt tremendous, and after Cam, also a joy. If he closed his eyes, maybe he could prolong it, or at least etch it on his brain to recall in detail once it was over. Except if he closed his eyes, Chique would likely throw out one of her nifty moves and leave him with a different kind of memory. *Trainer Olivia Lachance, please call the jock's room.* With Jay, Nate was pretty sure anyone could ride him. With Chique, it was a toss-up. Not that he'd been entirely successful dealing with the filly's games himself, but he liked to think she was slightly less likely to try them with him aboard.

Maybe Chique could be one of those mares who raced after she was bred. He hated the thought of her getting fat in a field. Like that was such a terrible life, Miller. He wondered how the odds compared: the chance of injury at the track versus in a field, or the risk of losing a mare from foaling complications. He'd bet, much to the horror of the anti-racing folk, that racing was the safest of the three. They just didn't keep stats on how horses tried to kill themselves on their own, or how scary reproduction could be when things didn't go right.

This race was custom made for Chique. A mile on the grass against fillies and mares, three years old and up. The competition wasn't the same class she'd faced in the Woodbine Mile or the Canadian International. As a result, she was the overwhelming favourite. Odds-on.

The previously kind weather had made such a request possible, because it was rare for the E.P. Taylor turf to remain in use this late in the season. Wildly fluctuating temperatures and plenty of rain typically made such a thought impossible, because this course was Woodbine's jewel, handled with appropriate reverence. This fall, the seasons had seemingly changed overnight: sunny and dry one day, cold and miserable the next.

Coming up behind the gate, it was like Chique knew she was on display for her groupies. She stood a moment after the starter's assistant met her, as if to make him wait a beat before walking straight in and standing like the professional she was supposed to be. Square beneath Nate, an ear flick as he laced his fingers through her mane to prepare for the break, then ears zeroing in on the lush lawn before them. He ignored the customary back-and-forth of the other riders until the bell pealed and the starter turned them loose.

Chique was out-footed. He'd been too casual, maybe, but he wasn't worried. He was glad she was relaxed, and willing to feed the delusions of the two over-eager three-year-olds who shot to the lead, thinking it meant something to rob Chique of that right. Being mid-pack in the middle of horses as they rolled into the turn made him feel as if he was on a different horse. And maybe he was; maybe Chique was gauging her competition and deeming them worthy of only so much effort. Or maybe that was him. He wouldn't be stuck in here. Things would open up in the stretch.

One big, long turn, and it felt like forever they were trapped in there. Hemmed in on all sides. He kept getting himself trapped like this. There were only six horses in the race, but he felt like Chique was being mobbed, buried in here as they barrelled down the incline. Chique was on the bit now, ready to break out, but there was no room. Something would open up, he told himself again. *Stay with me here, Chique. I'll get you out of this.* Because he'd gotten her into it.

The endless straight of green waited for them as they turned for home. *Lots of time.* But his heart was thumping.

These fillies and mares he'd dismissed as second-rate had come to play today. Served him right. Finally, one pacesetter gave way, losing ground on the outside. The bay filly on the rail pressed on, determined, but her rider let her drift out just enough to be in Chique's path, closing a hole as quickly as it had opened. Chique leaned on the grey beside her — but no one was going to give them any room. There's no way that bay could stick, though. No way. She was, though.

The bay led the way with an eighth to go: all out, driving. She opened up a length and a half, at last giving Chique room to escape. Nate pointed Chique at the opening. She was so small and handy she could slip through those spots. Finally clear, Chique swapped leads and released the fury she'd built, ears nailed to her skull. Cut the lead to a length, then three-quarters. The grey behind them pursued, nose glued to Chique's saddle towel.

Then the bay careened into Chique, sending her like a domino into the grey. It felt as if Chique's legs were going in every direction as Nate steadied her, but she insisted on resuming the chase, making up lost ground, threading herself into the space between the grey and the bay. Wedged between them, there was no room to engage his stick, so it was up to Chique. As if it wasn't always up to Chique. The three of them flashed past the wire, their momentum carrying them around the clubhouse turn.

He let her gallop out longer than he normally would, making himself savour this. When he finally pulled up, he turned her in, reaching forward to stroke the filly's neck, heat emanating from her skin through his gloves. She stared across the infield over her white shadow roll, ribcage like bellows beneath him. Scratch that: being a broodmare might be safer than playing bumper cars out here. When the red-coated outrider jogged up, he sighed — both for the relief Chique had won, and because it was time to let go.

"It must not have been as close as it felt," Nate said. *Glorified workout. Right.* They'd had to fight for every step of that win.

Liv was looking down, not at him, as they approached. Emilie took the shank from the outrider.

"Hold up a second, Em," Liv said.

Chique dragged Emilie for two steps before Emilie managed to stop her. Liv reached for the filly's right fore. When she straightened, she fell into step as Emilie walked Chique off again. She was frowning.

"Tore off her shoe and half her foot in that scuffle midstretch. The inquiry sign is already up."

At least this time, it wasn't him who'd caused the ruckus. Chique's win was quickly made official. They gathered for the win photo, just the four of them — Emilie, Liv, Nate and Chique, her nostrils flared.

Liv cooled Chique out herself, fast-tracking it. The whole "a few sips of water every so many turns" was an outdated protocol, even if the track clung to it like so many other routines. Chique submerged her muzzle in the bucket and Liv let the filly have a good drink of the warm water. She didn't have the nerve to let Chique guzzle the whole bucket. Old habits died hard. Chique's right fore was padded with sheet cotton and wrapped with vetrap. The rest of the filly recovered more quickly than that hoof would.

Emilie refilled the bucket after bathing Chique, and the filly sucked back another half before she was done. She'd always been a good drinker — an important thing for an athlete you couldn't force hydration on. The old proverb and all. Liv signaled one of the women in the office and led Chique to the designated stall, giving up the shank so the attendant could obtain the urine sample. She waited outside the door, listening to the repetitive whistle.

After witnessing the sealing of the sample and signing off, she spotted Nate with Emilie. Liv retrieved Chique, and he dropped his car keys into Em's hand. He walked with Liv and Chique to Barn Five, Em bringing the Porsche slowly behind them.

"I thought you had a mount in the last?" Liv asked.

"Booked off," he responded, not looking at her. "I wanted to get back and see how she was. She's short on that foot."

Now that the adrenaline from the race had worn off, Chique felt the injury. "Of course she is. You should see it. I'm calling the vet for x-rays as soon as she's back in her stall. Just to be safe."

Nate didn't mock her for being over-protective.

They released a collective breath when the radiographs showed no visible damage, though plenty didn't show up in those pictures. Sensitive tissue, bruised and torn. Somehow, none of them felt like celebrating after the vet left.

This is what she got for trying to be tough. Chique was tough. There was no question. But it was Liv's fault she'd had to prove it. She stopped, reminding herself. This was part of training. Chique would heal. *Be thankful for that.*

CHAPTER FOURTEEN

Nate Miller in her pool. Liv watched him from just inside the sliding doors. He'd wanted to switch up his fitness program, and she'd suggested this. Swimming was great. Cross-training. Low impact.

She'd never been into the whole men as eye candy thing — not even when Nate had been the eye candy the female farm staff were so excited she'd hired five years ago. It had always seemed superficial. What was below the surface was far more important. But now that she knew what was below the surface, she appreciated the exterior — as he drew himself out to the edge, not an ounce of fat hiding muscles ripped under pale skin that would soon soak up the sun's rays down south.

She turned away before he caught her, because while her mind wandered to certain things, she would honour his wish. They would wait, and she didn't want to make it more difficult than it already must be for him. Because it was harder for him. She didn't have the history to know what she was missing out on. She had to admit she was anxious about the unknown.

What if she was bad? Or when the moment came, she just... couldn't?

Emilie walked in with a tray from Triple Shot, cups jammed into pressed cardboard. Inadvertent chaperone, when Em would no doubt love to hear the two of them had stopped behaving like scared teenagers. Her sister saw no reason not to train her eyes on Nate in appreciation as he entered. That was what eye candy was for, wasn't it?

"Even though it took an excruciatingly long time," Emilie said so only Liv could hear, freeing one cup and holding it out, "I'm so relieved you finally figured *that* out."

Well... she hadn't figured *that* all out yet. There was still a lot to learn.

Nate looked suspiciously from one sister to the other as he approached, a sweatshirt now covering his upper body, towel around his neck. Liv resisted the temptation to run her fingers through his hair, damp and tousled. Again, not that Emilie would care, so why? Sometimes she was more self-conscious than others.

"What are you two up to?" he asked, eyebrows still quirked but now joined by a crooked smile.

Emilie handed him his cup. "Just admiring your athletic physique." She grinned.

He didn't have a quick comeback for that, looking dubious. As if he didn't know he was good-looking and fit. Right. His eyes flitted to Liv, and her core warmed, her own earlier thoughts returning unbidden.

"I'm going to change," he said, his eyebrows levelling but his lips still twisted. "Thanks for the coffee, Em."

When he returned, he had jeans on, the collar of a shirt jutting up under his sweatshirt. The gym bag he left by the front foyer was a reminder that one day this would be his home, too. It didn't yet feel familiar to have him around, but it did feel comfortable. He joined her on the couch, Emilie in the adjacent chair.

It had taken this long for them to find the time to sit down and talk about the farm. Chique had been home for two weeks, back to future broodmare status. Her parents were in Montreal finalizing the purchase of a home. In the last month, they'd spent more time there than here, staying with Claude's mother. There were only four racing dates left. Sunday, Jay would run in the Valedictory. A week from today, she and Nate would be on their way to Florida.

"So you think we can work this out?" Liv directed her question to Em. "Do you have ideas for the house?"

Emilie produced a sketch scribbled with notes. "Nothing major."

Liv glanced at the lines. A few simple adjustments — if renovations could ever be simple. Emilie had created a space that would be separate but still provide access to common areas, like the kitchen and living room. None of it seemed real yet. A month later, it still hadn't sunk in.

"How does that look to you?" Emilie asked. "You two are hardly around here, anyway. And I don't expect we'll be fighting over kitchen time."

Liv grinned at her. Emilie liked to bake, but while not as incompetent as Liv when it came to meals, she didn't put much effort into cooking.

"Are you okay with being here on your own over the winter, Em?" Nate asked.

It was the biggest question in Liv's head, aware she'd taken for granted the ability to come and go as she pleased. To spend winters in Florida, return for holidays. These changes created a stronger tie to the farm. But the farm was her place, now more than ever. Not just a place to return to.

"I'll be fine," Emilie said. "I was thinking of getting a dog, though," she added. "It's been too long. Is that okay?"

"Definitely." Liv agreed. *We'll have dogs.*

There hadn't been a dog on the farm since Geai's old black Labrador Napoleon had died, shortly after Geai's own death three years ago. It still broke her heart; just one more thing she hadn't been able to deal with then. It was longer still since there'd been a dog in this house. They'd lost Josée, Napoleon's litter mate, two years earlier. While they'd all loved her, her father had been Josée's person. Between his sorrow and their active lives, neither Liv nor Emilie had suggested introducing another canine. Now, though Emilie was always busy, her schedule was flexible.

"Not a puppy," Emilie said decisively. "That's as far as I've gotten."

"Now that we've taken care of the important stuff..." Nate's mouth crimped upward at one side. "I think the two of you should talk about this without me. This is your inheritance, really. That kind of thing needs to be discussed between siblings."

"It's okay, Nate," Emilie insisted.

"No, it's not," he said, standing. "I'm going to go, and once you have it figured out, I'll cook you both dinner and you can fill me in."

Leaning over with a light hand on Liv's shoulder, he kissed her, then gave Emilie a light poke on his way by.

"Where did you find him again?" Emilie said, still staring at the door after he'd left.

"He found us." Liv could only smile. Was that fate or providence? How many times had she shooed him away like a stray? But he'd stuck, ever loyal to this farm. To her.

She turned the cup in her hands. "I can't leave everything here to you, Em. It's too much for you to handle alone."

"I'll be fine," Emilie reiterated. "Austin is here, and the staff is solid right now — as much of a miracle as that is in the horse business these days. All I'll be doing is opening mail and pitching in now and then. And another thing — I can't take that money our grandfather left, Liv. I'm sure you can find a place to give it away if you're determined not to keep it."

Liv's eyes flashed toward her. She wondered how much Emilie knew. Liv had been willing to play along to protect her younger sister, and would be forever grateful Geai had stepped in when he had, and that her father had acted. Everything was worth it because Emilie had been spared. Maybe some of that tainted money could go to a charity for victims of abuse.

"All right," she conceded. "Maybe some for New Chapter. Or for around here, to start our own in-house thing."

Em's face lit up. "That would be amazing."

Liv was sure it had never been far from her sister's mind. "Can I leave that with you?"

Emilie glanced at the time. "I don't think we're done talking yet, but I have to go. And tell Nate he can pick a day for dinner. It better be soon, though. And I guess that will have to be our Christmas, if you're going to be in Calgary on the twenty-fifth."

"So he needs to be prepared to cook a turkey?" Liv grinned.

"I don't care if we eat grilled cheese. I'll just be happy to hang out with the two of you."

After Emilie left, Liv walked to Nate's apartment. She could hear music, and tapped lightly at the door before slipping in. He glanced over his shoulder from the piano as she kicked off her shoes, leaving her jacket over the back of the couch. She made her way over and slid to his right on the bench.

He retracted his hands from the keys and kissed her. He didn't need much of an excuse for that. "Missed you."

She laughed and shoved him lightly. "Stop that."

"I thought you two would be up to all hours planning the next phase of the Triple Stripe racing empire."

"It'll be a work in progress for a while. But Emilie says we'd better hurry up and pick a time for you to cook dinner for us."

He chuckled, his fingers resuming their position on the piano keys. "So? All good?"

"For now. Still feels strange."

"Do you know this?" He started playing chords, and it took about two seconds for her to recognize "Heart and Soul."

Anyone who'd ever sat at a piano knew it, so in response she jumped in with the simple one-finger melody, amazed, not for the first time, at the way their notes fit.

"We stayed for this. Let's make it worth it."

Liv nodded and threw Nate up on Just Jay. *"Bonne chance,* Miller. Safe trip."

A hired groom led them away as she watched, clutching her elbows to keep the heat in. The dark had closed in quickly. The sun set so early now, accentuating the chill and her need to get out of this province for warmer climes.

Closing day. Had she ever still been in Ontario for closing day? Silly question. Of course she had. Not that long ago; it just seemed as if a lifetime had passed since Chique and Jay had been weanlings, the next great hopes. They hadn't disappointed, but Liv was certain Jay had more to offer.

She was on her own to watch this one. Em and Faye were up to their elbows at the café, though Liv had thought Em would still get away for the race. Not so. She waited her turn to access the escalator, and even though it was cold, light flakes drifting down from the indigo sky, she made her way outside. It was one race;

she would survive, because races were best watched outdoors. The tall sliding doors opened automatically as she descended. There were only a few other people brave enough — or crazy enough — to be out here. It meant she had her choice of seats.

Someone shifted, looking over his shoulder, and her mouth fell open in recognition.

"Roger!"

She rushed over as he rose, her arms going around him, squeezing. Then she didn't know what to say. How many times could she ask, *How are you doing? How is Hélène?* But she did anyway.

He nodded slowly, his eyes tired, looking like he'd aged since she'd seen him last. "She's okay. Trying to think positive. You have to, you know?"

Hélène's chemotherapy had started, which to Liv was the definition of "what doesn't kill you makes you stronger." Poison your body and hope the good cells survive while the bad cells die. It made her shudder.

He continued. "Sylvie is visiting; that helps." The Cloutiers' daughter lived in Montreal.

"That must be nice." It sounded so lame, but she was still at a loss. "I'm sorry I won't get to see her before we leave."

The horses coming on the track provided an out from any further conversation, but didn't take the churn from Liv's stomach. The field jogged up to the front of the grandstand next to their pony escorts, lights towering above.

"The colt looks great."

"He's an easy horse to train," she said. "Here's hoping." And now she hoped even more, because it was like he needed to win for Roger — for Hélène.

Jay was more composed than the pony through the post parade, Nate silent and still on his back. Once the track announcer finished the introductions, he took the big chestnut off on his own to warm up.

"When are the two of you leaving?" Roger kept his eyes on the colt — he had his binoculars, posture with glass to brow mimicking Liv's.

"Tomorrow," she said, the words sounding insane as they left her mouth. But they were stopping — not the foolish trip following the transport she'd made other years. They'd stay overnight in Lexington, so they could rest properly. How grown-up that seemed, when she could still remember the trip three years ago when she'd insisted on doing it alone. "If we make it to Florida without killing each other, I think we'll go ahead with the wedding."

Roger chuckled, with echoes of his old laugh. "Definitely a good compatibility test."

The gate waited in the chute at the six-furlong marker. Jay would start from the outside, but in this three-turn race, post position didn't matter so much. Jay was by far the class of this field, too... but it was a horse race, so that didn't matter so much either. They'd been reminded of that with Chique.

When the gates crashed open, the horses came out without Jay. Liv groaned, but no, there he was. *Were you two meditating in there or something, Miller?*

"That was unexpected," Roger quipped.

It was fine. It would be fine. He had plenty of time to make up for that. Especially when the horse and rider who shot to the lead seemed to have forgotten this race was a mile and three-quarters, not six furlongs. They were flying. Jay trundled along at the back of the pack in a far more leisurely fashion.

He was even farther back when they passed under the wire for the first time. A mile to go, and the pacesetter was already fading, paying for those zippy early fractions. By the time they entered the backstretch, he was back with Jay, and Nate finally let his big colt pick up a few horses. But he sure wasn't in a hurry.

"Any time, Miller," she muttered as they rounded the final turn. Was he playing some kind of game? Did he think he was on Zenyatta or something?

The pace had slowed to a crawl now, and he was mid-pack, on the outside. He was gaining, but still looking as if he thought they'd go around again before it was time to get serious. Ride The Wave, Cory up, was rolling now. Liv bet he'd catch the new leader at the quarter pole.

"That's Aintthattheway and Ride The Wave leading the way into the homestretch. Just Jay has yet to make his move..."

Maybe they'd done too much long, slow distance, and not enough speed work. Maybe she didn't know how to train a horse for a mile-and-three-quarter race. Wait — she wasn't taking the blame for that alone. Nate was in on this, too.

Or maybe this was just Jay telling them he was done and wanted to be Em's event horse after all.

Now, though, signs of life. Three-sixteenths of a mile to go, and Nate roused Jay. Ready, aim... fire...

"And out of the clouds, it's Just Jay..."

She almost felt the *whoosh* as the big chestnut finally launched, his stride growing, hungry as it ate up the distance between him and the battling leaders. Nate pumped but hadn't seen the need to bring out his stick yet — *there are those hands, Miller* — and Liv and Roger clambered to their feet, elbow to elbow, binoculars cast aside. Screaming at the pair on the track, willing them to get there in time. Ride The Wave was alone in front now, but Jay swallowed him up and spit him out, the bright light at the wire spotlighting him as he roared under it, a length up.

She threw herself at Roger, letting Jay's bold effort erase everything else for just a moment, then watched Nate gallop the colt out — or watched Jay drag Nate all the way to the back-side — before Roger nudged her to initiate the descent to the winner's circle.

Jay wasn't done. Jay was back, possibly better than ever.

Jay was their Big Horse.

Nate's face lit up when he noticed Roger next to her, and he swung his arm out, then reached down to grasp the older man's hand. Liv merely smiled up at him, not sure her pulse had recovered yet from the heart-stopping stretch run.

Would that man ever not stop her heart? As long as it kept restarting, she'd be fine.

The track photographer waved them into position on the track, three — well, four, including Jay — familiar faces recorded in pixels. Years from now, would they look at that photo and try to remember the groom's name? Would it bring back how conflicted the moment felt? How trivial horse racing seemed when a friend was fighting much bigger battles? But it was horse racing that had brought them all together. Without it, they never would have met.

The brief memory captured, Nate hopped off, releasing the girth, his valet sliding the saddle off.

"I'll be right behind you," Liv called as the groom walked Jay past. She chased after Nate and Roger, hopping onto the boards that made a walkway across the snow-dusted turf, and caught up to them on the apron.

"You two did a good job with him," Roger said. "The horses are in excellent hands."

"You never know what we'll cook up to torment them. It'll be a relief for them when you come back," Nate said, putting on a grin that almost looked normal.

"You are coming back," Liv emphasized. "You have to. I'm not done riding yet. Can't let Nate get too comfortable winning races on all these nice horses."

"On that note," Nate said, "I'm off. Great to see you, Rog. Give Hélène a hug for me and tell her we're thinking about her." He met Liv's eyes. "See you back there."

"I'd better get home," Roger said after the briefest awkward moment when Nate left to weigh in. "You kids drive safe. Look after this horse, he'll take you places."

Liv hugged him again, clinging a little too long.

Then she was alone, and for a moment she just stood there, until the cold made it through the inadequate fabric of her coat. Time to return to the backside, because there'd be a groom and hotwalker to pay, and, once Jay was cooled out, a horse to do up — and last-minute things to pack for tomorrow's departure. It was dawning on her, though. She'd been naïve to think Roger's leave would be short term. He and Hélène were in for a long haul. And she'd have to figure out if this job — if for some unexpected reason Jo didn't want it — was who she was.

CHAPTER FIFTEEN

THERE WAS SINGING — something familiar, but distorted. Who was singing? And why? She was trying to sleep. She needed to sleep. It was her turn to drive next.

Consciousness pried its way in, and she cracked open an eye. The singing was real. Nate had an amazing voice, but it was strained as he belted out the lyrics while Spirit of the West's "Home For a Rest" punched from the truck's speakers.

"Pull over." She thought she'd yelled it over the music, but the quick glance he gave her let her know he hadn't understood. She pushed herself fully upright, and gestured with her hands to back up her voice, much stronger this time. "Pull over!" Now that she was awake, it occurred to her she should have just turned down the volume — which she did now.

He flipped on the right blinker, and obediently — looking decidedly relieved — eased the rig to the side of the road.

"Where are we?" she asked.

"Just the other side of Cincinnati." He closed his eyes and leaned into the headrest.

About an hour to go. She hopped out the passenger side and rounded the hood. The window on the driver's side was open — another sign he'd been struggling to stay alert. "Get out. I'll drive the rest of the way."

He pushed against the heavy door, sliding out and leaving her to take his spot.

"I'll wake you up when we get close to Lexington," she said, snapping the seatbelt on. "Seeing as you know where we're going."

He adjusted the pillow she'd left on that side, propping it against the window, then kicked off his shoes and tucked one foot under him, crossing his arms and closing his eyes again.

"This music all right?" he asked, lifting one lid.

He didn't wait for an answer, thumbing through his phone, the current song careening in the background with its pounding bass line — whatever it was — coming to an abrupt halt. Something that sounded suspiciously like a Gregorian chant replaced it.

"Don't put me to sleep while I'm driving. Maybe something halfway?"

He nodded in slow motion, looking as if he was trying a little too hard to focus on the screen. She should have picked her own music before starting to drive. Finally, he settled on The Killers. That worked. Except she could hear him humming, like he'd decided to help keep her awake.

"So... do you know what you're going to say to Jo? About training?" he asked.

"As far as I'm concerned, she should take over officially. She's been Roger's assistant forever; it's her right. She's got seniority."

"But you know if you want the job, it's yours. You're still the owner's daughter."

"I'm so tired of that being why I get things, though. It's never because I've earned anything."

"Maybe we should go somewhere else." There was something else on his face now; something wistful. "The two of us could just ride. Arkansas, or Fairgrounds. Be anonymous for a while."

"Nobody is really anonymous in this business, Miller."

"You're such a cynic."

"It's not as if we could do that now, anyway. I agreed I'd be around to help in Roger's absence." At least she wasn't having any trouble staying alert now. "And I think Luna's right. I don't think I can be a real trainer. Because Chique, and Feste, that wasn't real, was it? That was only about picking races from a stakes schedule. The only time I've ever really had to talk to the racing secretary was to tell him what I wanted for Chique's encore. Real trainers have to do stuff like that all the time."

"You talk just fine. It's all in your head."

"The thing is, I don't like it. Riding is more fun."

"Just as long as it's not because you're avoiding the responsibility."

"What?"

He dipped his head and half-shielded his jaw with one shoulder, like he was deflecting a blow. Okay, maybe the response had come out with more force than necessary. But really?

"You know..." he continued, anyway. Brave, brave man. "Like not finishing vet school?"

"You're on dangerous ground there, Miller." Her knuckles blanched as she wrapped them tighter around the steering wheel, firing him a dark look. She'd been responsible her whole life. It hadn't been ducking anything, leaving vet school to ride races. It had been following her true passion — you only live once, right? Riding races was not an old person's job; it was something best tackled in your youth. Even if it aged you prematurely. But... her jaw loosened, and she almost laughed. "I see what you did there. You only think I'm considering training because I feel obligated." To the farm, to the family, to her father.

"Did I say that?"

"You didn't have to."

"If you won't go to a therapist, you're going to have to put up with me pretending."

"My head was too messed up right after the funeral."

"That makes sense."

She laughed. Yes, it was absurd to think her head was too scattered to speak with a professional, because wasn't that the point of getting help?

"I found one, okay?" she admitted.

"You did? How come you didn't tell me?"

"Sorry. We were so busy, I didn't get to fit in more than the first appointment. And I figured I'd have plenty of time to bring you up to speed on the drive."

On one level, what he was saying about obligation was true. But on another... it was a legitimately tough call. Sure, riding was fun, but her love of this game reached beyond the thrill of extracting the talent and courage of a Thoroughbred in the minute or two those things were tested in the afternoons. The sport was about so much more than that. The hours — days, weeks, months, years — of preparation to get to that point. She loved it all. But she couldn't properly have it all at the same time.

"So what do I do?"

"Right now, you need to dial it down. You don't have to answer that tonight. Because at this rate, you won't sleep. And the less you sleep, the more I have to drive tomorrow."

"So now this is about you?" She grinned.

"Of course. But only as self-preservation."

He looked exhausted, and she felt guilty for her rant, for keeping him awake. He punched ahead a few tracks on the playlist to "All These Things That I've Done." Liv shook her head and chuckled. Nate never picked songs by chance. That choice was loaded with intent. At least it was great to sing along to. And while she was still usually too self-conscious to sing around Nate, because his voice was so incredibly brilliant, the words fell out anyway. Sometimes she felt just like that, like a soldier. Not a real one, but navigating her career choices was making her head some kind of war zone.

She pressed her lips together, glancing over at him, the gentle vibration dissolving in her throat. "That won't keep you awake?"

"Nope. I can't keep my eyes open any longer, Liv."

"I'm amazed you're still conscious."

"Trust me, I wouldn't be, if you weren't talking. Which is wildly ironic. See? You talk just fine, so you can stop telling yourself that. Just pretend the race officials you have to deal with are me, and I will laugh and pity their poor souls. You're perfectly capable of all of it."

She rolled her eyes and took the hint — at least about shutting up and driving. And didn't wake him until they reached the outer limits of Lexington.

She'd never lived here, but it still felt like a second home. Horse country, plain and simple. They left Jay behind in a posh stall generously banked with fresh straw at the layover farm. It hadn't been hard to find a spot to spend the night that wasn't a hotel. Well — Nate had found it, because he was closer to normal than she was. He'd known someone. Because he struck up conversations with people, unlike her. Maybe that was a skill worth learning.

This is what rational people did: stopped halfway to give

themselves and the horse a break from the constant motion, get some kind of sleep, then carry on safely for the second part of the journey. Even with two of them, he hadn't let her talk him into driving straight through.

He preempted any awkwardness in the room by promptly dumping his bag on a chair, then unzipping his hoodie and folding his jeans neatly on top of the bag. He turned back the covers on the bed and dropped onto it with a moan of relief.

Well, she wasn't sleeping on the floor. She at least brushed her teeth first before crawling in, facing him. His eyes remained closed, his breathing even until he pulled up the covers and met her gaze. The thud of her heart was so acute she had to catch her breath.

He wasn't going to last long, though, his lids heavy. After putting one pod in his ear, he took the other, setting it in hers so she heard the music transmitting through the wires. It was like he used music to program his brain. Did that work? He was probably so exhausted right now it didn't make a difference. She closed her eyes and made herself block out his nearness and soak in the notes — no lyrics; it was purely instrumental. It played just low enough to cancel out the strange sounds of an unfamiliar place.

In the past, she'd always dismissed the idea of seeing a therapist whenever the thought had worked its way into her overwrought brain. Therapy was fine for others. She applauded those who chose to pursue it, but she was smart and strong, and could handle it on her own. She'd muddled through with that belief for a long time. When he'd brought it up that afternoon in the Laurentians, she'd kept herself from expressing resistance. He was only trying to help when she wanted to believe he was enough. It wasn't fair to put that kind of responsibility on him, though.

Whether it was luck or fate, the psychologist she'd been

referred to was a good match, because if that first attempt had gone poorly, she never would have considered continuing. Working through her defences wasn't easy. Her logical left brain wanted to protect her right brain and keep those emotions where they belonged. She didn't want to release those repressed things. The process would probably take years.

How much of her behaviour was her personality, and how much was her past? Nature versus nurture. She wanted to science her way through it, and retraining herself to approach it all differently was a painful challenge. Like another of Nate's favourite songs. Learning to breathe. Learning to crawl.

Gradually the music slowed her mind, and her last thought was *how did I make it this far in life without the things I've learned because of him?* Who knew he'd become the life coach she'd once joked about?

It was a treat to go to the barn when the sun was up instead of arriving at work in darkness, not to mention wearing shorts and a t-shirt in December. They'd left the training centre in the middle of the night after putting Jay in the stall Jo had prepared, then driven the truck to the condo on the beach. He'd been exhausted again, but still opted to sleep in the spare room. With how good he'd gotten at restraining himself, he was starting to worry if he'd remember what to do when the time came he no longer had to.

Michel returned the keys to the Porsche with dropped shoulders.

"Thanks for driving it down for me, Mike."

"It was nice while it lasted." Michel sighed.

"You should probably look at minivans sometime soon, right?"

"Please tell me that will never be."

"I can't predict the future. But I can let you drive it again when Liv and I go to Calgary for Christmas, if that's any consolation."

"I'll take whatever I can get."

Nate laughed at him.

Payson hadn't changed, just the horses who occupied the stalls this time around — and their neighbour on the other side from them: a trainer from Chicago with six horses. He was six foot and built and could probably deadlift a guy Nate's size with his baby finger, so Nate figured he'd better stay on the guy's good side. Which he forgot at the exact moment he saw the pot-bellied pig shuffle around the corner to the Triple Stripe shed.

"What the hell is that?"

Jo laughed. "That's Hamlet. Elliot's emotional support pig."

"Is Elliot a horse, or...?"

"Elliot's the trainer. And I'm joking. Hamlet's the best friend of one of his geldings. Apparently he gets the credit for making the horse a stakes winner."

"I'm glad Chique isn't around to see this. It's bad enough there's wild boar out there without inviting a pig on the shed."

"Surprisingly, most of the horses don't mind. Except Paz," Jo said.

"Maybe he's offended. Or scared we might replace him."

"Lucky for him, I don't think the pony tack would fit a pig," she quipped. "Are you two ready for the big day?"

Ready? He'd been ready for weeks. Ready for the racing season to be done, ready to leave Ontario's fickle fall weather, ready for the sun. Ready for Liv and the future.

"Are you bringing anyone, Jo?" he asked.

"Nope. Nicole and I will go stag."

"Maybe Elliot would lend you his emotional support pig. I hear he's popular at parties."

"If I didn't know what a sweetheart Hamlet is, I might consider that an insult."

"Invite Elliot. If we're going to share a barn with him this winter, we might as well get to know him."

"Go ahead," Jo responded. "But it's not coming from me."

"What's left to do?" Liv asked, one eye on the pig as he searched for... what, exactly? What did pigs eat besides leftovers?

"We're pretty much all done," Jo said. "You two should go relax. When do people start to arrive? Do you have to go to the airport?"

"This afternoon, but they've insisted they'll rent cars in Fort Lauderdale and drive themselves," Liv said. "Faye and Emilie are still in charge of most of the arrangements, so thankfully there's not a lot for us to do."

"All the more reason for you to enjoy the calm before the storm," Jo said. "Go."

"We're coming in tomorrow morning, though," Liv insisted. "Tell Cory and Nicole they can have the day off. We don't need four people galloping."

"We'll be fine, Liv. And they've been getting days off, don't worry."

"No — I need this, okay?" she pleaded.

She would need it — to maintain her equilibrium and get through the social burden of the whole thing. Nate wasn't going to judge her for not gleefully looking forward to the wedding. The admission wasn't a newsflash.

"See you in the morning, Jo," he said, nudging Liv toward the Porsche. "C'mon. Beach."

Liv had been thrilled when he'd found out the condo was

available again. He'd handled the winter rental while she dealt with the farm and family drama. They picked up a few groceries on the way, but were on the beach in record time.

She walked to where the waves crept up the sand in a foamy surge, her bare feet leaving indentations. The ocean receded, then crashed, and withdrew again, her prints washed away with each new swell. Her shoulders were probably already pink from the sun, but they were both ready for the heat, craving it, and it would take a lot of willpower to keep from exposing themselves too long on this, the very first day. It was easy to forget how nasty a bad burn could be when you'd just come from snow falling in Ontario.

She pivoted, and he watched her return to him, his eyes bleached in the brightness. A knowing curve graced her lips, like she'd read his expression from behind her sunglasses.

That's a hungry look. No more starving yourself, Miller.

"Maybe a wedding present?" she said as she sat next to him, draping her arms loosely around her bent knees, the sand giving under her heels as she pushed into the graininess beyond her towel.

"This place? Sure, I'd like that," He leaned in, grinning, his hand curling around her bicep. Kissing her, he pulled her down with him, then yelped when she gripped his lower lip with her teeth. "Oh, you mean for me to give to you. Did you miss the part where I'm marrying you for your money?"

"Let's not talk about money," she said, smothering the grin from his face. "Let's not talk at all."

"But you're getting so good at it," he tried to mumble.

She wasn't bold enough to slide on top of him, not out here. The private beach wasn't all that private, so she kept herself to the side, draping her torso against him. He stopped himself from counting the hours.

"We should go inside. You're burning." He certainly was, and it was more than his skin.

"I thought we weren't talking." But she slowly rolled away and pushed herself back up.

The fridge was fancy, one of those monstrous stainless steel ones that made ice and filtered water. Nate pressed a glass against the lever, releasing irregular cubes in a clatter, then filled it with water and set it in front of her, repeating the process for himself. Liv sipped, watching him. Last winter when he'd come — for Chique, for her — he'd stood in this kitchen and made omelettes, and wondered whether they were done; not for the first, or last, time.

"What are you thinking about?" she asked.

"Omelettes," he said, and she laughed. "Want one?"

"I could eat."

When he pulled the frying pan from the cupboard, he figured it hadn't been used since he'd set it in that exact spot after cleaning it last winter.

"At least try to have fun these next few days," he said as he cracked the eggs.

"I'd rather just be here with you."

"Two more sleeps." He grinned. "Then you're stuck with me for the rest of your life."

Two more days, then it would begin. On the beach where, two and a half years ago, she'd told him they would never happen. The perfect spot to get married, wasn't it?

Blue sky. A breeze coming off the ocean that tossed into disarray the hair Faye had so carefully styled for her. A white silk off-the-rack shift. Her father walking her through the middle of the scattered chairs in what approximated an aisle.

Flowers clutched in her hands, because Faye and Emilie had insisted, *yes, you need a bouquet.* And Nate there, waiting for her. *No more waiting, Miller.*

Timeless, traditional vows, because writing their own would have made her cry, and she would not cry on this day. She wouldn't let him sing to her, not as part of the ceremony, because she wouldn't be able to hold it together. She wanted it to be perfect, and happy, and fun. She wanted to laugh at Faye and Em as they bawled. It would not be her. Because this was, in fact, the happiest moment of her life.

So they said the words with the sand between their toes. Barefoot. Grounded. And Em and Faye, and Connie and Anne, and most definitely Sue, and quite possibly Jo, cried the tears. But Liv couldn't stop smiling, Nate's face a reflection of her own. This was not a performance. It was a declaration, and she wouldn't think about how death could part them on any given day, doing what they did. Instead, she chose to believe there would be decades together; that they'd be that old couple who died within days, or maybe hours, of each other, when they were both old and frail.

When they kissed, they forgot anyone else was there until the whoops of the crew brought them back. Then she passed off the bouquet, grabbed his hand and dragged him toward the ocean in his dashing grey slacks and matching vest, a crooked grin on his face when he gave up resisting and ran with her into the waves, diving under them, because, hadn't they just taken the plunge?

"Now look what you've done," he murmured against her lips as the froth swirled around them. "You've gone and gotten all wet."

Her face was already flushed, heart pounding against his, so only her lack of a snappy comeback gave away her body's response to his words. With the taste of salt on their skin, she kissed him again. "Congratulations, Miller. Believe me now?"

"Think we can just stay out here? Then maybe they'll all just go away."

She laughed quietly. "You're starting to sound like me."

"That's not always a bad thing."

She would add this to her list of accomplishments, and maybe it was more important than the other stuff. Made it here. Did not even consider freaking out and running away. Promised to love, honour and cherish. For ever and ever. Amen.

They went inside to change, and he wrapped himself around her, the two of them dripping on the slate floor as their lips met, the lightest touch deepening, his hands on her lower back molding her into him and leaving her with no doubt where his mind was. His fingers drifted to her waist, and he shifted her, backing her slowly down the hallway, flat palms clenching to fists filled with the fabric of her dress. She wondered if this was it. The guests could wait. But stopping in front of the linen closet, he broke away, snatched out two towels, and pressed one to her.

"I've waited this long. I can wait a bit longer. Till we have the time to do it right."

One last look that left her with a tangle of exhilaration and apprehension, and he slipped into the bedroom and closed the door behind him. She laughed, and dropped her weight against the wall, silk clinging to her as she pushed her face into the towel and tried to catch her breath. Perhaps this was his plan, to build her confidence bit by bit so all the hesitation would be gone. Like taking time with a young horse, getting them so fit that when they first breezed, there was no question they would be fast enough to make the work sheet, they were so primed, so ready.

"Your turn," he said when he came out, looking more casual

— not to mention drier — in knee-length shorts and a clean shirt, his damp hair combed.

When they returned to the beach, Faye's head tilted, like she was trying to gauge whether anything had transpired during their absence. Liv met her eyes and rolled her own with a subtle shake of her head.

It was a "light refreshments" sort of party; then the music started. Nate had compiled all the songs that had ever meant anything to them, and others she'd never distinctly considered, but that connected in the context of this day. Not a single one was there by chance. Hand-selected. An endless playlist of their past, their present, and their future.

"Where's Faye?" Nate said, eyes leaving hers only for a split second. "I need a cheat sheet to know who I'm supposed to dance with when."

"You're not going anywhere, right now."

She didn't know if it was wrong that she danced more with him than anyone else, but she didn't care. Emilie was with Tim, Nate's younger brother, but as one song transitioned into the next, Em gave him a tight smile, leaving him and attacking a flute of champagne. Tim shrugged and drifted toward the food.

"That doesn't look to be going well," Liv said.

"Give 'em time. We didn't like each other when we first met."

"We didn't like each other three months ago."

"That's not accurate," he corrected. "We didn't like what was going on. We didn't hate each other or anything. Did we?"

"I didn't hate you, even when you thought I did."

"Sure had me fooled," he said, amused now instead of skeptical.

"Yet you persevered."

"And here we are." He kissed her lightly. "Oh well. A

matchmaker I am not, apparently. Either that, or my brother is an idiot."

She couldn't believe it, but this was fun. Two months ago, she'd been terrified. But they'd done it on their terms, and the only way it could have been more perfect would have been if they'd hopped on two horses at the end — Claire and Chique, ideally — and galloped away down the beach.

Instead, as the afternoon wore on and the tide crept in, the crew begged off, Sue and Michel mentioning there were horses to feed. Liv should have thrown the bouquet, but instead, she tossed it underhand at Faye like a softball pitch. Faye fumbled before catching it and raising one of her perfect eyebrows. Liv mirrored the expression with a head tilt of her own. Then Faye squeezed her.

"Time for the rest of us to disappear, and let you get on with it," Faye whispered in her ear, then kissed her on the cheek. "You'll be fine."

Jo gave her a rare hug. "Don't you two dare think about coming in tomorrow, or I will chase you off the shedrow with a pitchfork. You might not be going on a honeymoon, but you can take one day. Promise me."

"Oh, she promises." Nate said, catching Liv's eye as he grinned and grabbed her hand.

Faye and Will herded the family away, back to the hotel. And finally, they were alone. They sauntered up to the condo, Nate's fingers curled around hers. He poured two glasses from the bottle of champagne, chilling in the fridge, handing her one. Then he lifted the pendant — the one Geai had given her — from where it rested in the hollow between her collarbones; the bitter mixed with the sweet, a reminder of those who weren't here.

She sipped, bubbles exploding at the back of her throat like they had that moment after Chique's Queen's Plate victory.

The one where she'd first let herself fall. A palm on his cheek, she curled her glass to her chest and met his lips, falling all over again.

He started singing a sappy seventies song about having all the time in the world, and she laughed as he removed the flute from her grasp. Her trust in him trumped the fear. It was only the beginning of this good thing.

CHAPTER SIXTEEN

It was a relief when they all went home. They could go back to being who they were, or who they were going to be. When they showed up Saturday morning, the crew graciously refrained from joshing, for the most part — though complete restraint was unavoidable. Nate fielded their jibes effortlessly.

"Does this mean you can never fire me?" he'd asked Liv, emboldened by the audience.

"Of course not," she'd responded. "Can we go back to training racehorses now?"

"Yes, boss." He flashed that old grin.

A smile caught the edges of her lips. Not that the enforced day off hadn't been educational. Enjoyable. Amusing. Okay, delicious. A thesaurus of experience. For possibly the first time in her life, she hadn't missed the horses at all. She'd also slept better than she had in her entire life. She could guess what Faye would say. *So, do you get it now?* Yes, yes, she did — though she imagined she'd only just begun to understand.

Sunday morning, everything felt more or less like back to

normal. Jo hadn't marked the white board yet with the training schedule, though.

"You want to get Jay out first?" she asked, poised before it with a dry erase marker in her hand.

"Sure," Liv said. "Nate can get on him, and I'll get on Elemental."

"Have you decided where you're going to run Jay next?" Nate interjected.

Liv caught Jo's eye, both of them reminded of how different this winter would be for more sombre reasons. "Time for a proper talk. How about you come over tonight? I'll make Miller cook something."

"Nate can cook?" Jo looked surprised.

"I know, right? He can."

"Just tell me what time. I'll be there."

It felt good to head out to the track — Jay's first day training since they'd arrived in Florida. The routine out here was so ingrained, they didn't need conscious thought. Back up — jogging the wrong way along the outside rail. Turn in and stand on the backstretch. Set off the right way, galloping. Jay strode easily beside Elemental, content to stretch his legs over Payson's deep sand, and Elemental, though less fit, had no trouble staying with him at this pace.

Her mind drifted back to the Valedictory Stakes; the way Jay had toyed with the Ontario-based field. Gulfstream would be a different matter. She knew Jay was good, she just didn't know how good. They might have to consider travelling with the colt. They had the staff at Payson to do that, spoiled by a solid group and a reasonable human-to-horse ratio. Cory was helping gallop for the winter while doing some freelancing on the side, so with Nicole, they had plenty of riders.

They walked back to the barn, both horses relaxed on a loose rein, and Nate's phone buzzed. She didn't know how he didn't lose it, stuffed in his back pocket. She always left hers in the tack room.

"Kenny," he said, peering at the screen with a frown. He jammed it back in his pocket without answering. "Checking up on me."

He'd told her about his conversation with the agent — his voice and expression conveying suspicion. She'd only suggested Kenny call Nate and make the offer as a way of appeasing Kenny, not to torment Nate. But Kenny might be useful.

"What are you going to tell him?" she asked.

"I'm not interested in working my ass off this winter."

"I know. But if you're riding Jay — which I assume you want to do — he can probably find you a few mounts to keep you sharp."

"True. But I don't have the paperwork."

"Maybe look into it."

"I could let you ride and I'll just lie on the beach and get fat."

She tried to picture that, without success. Not the lying on the beach part — she imagined that just fine — but she didn't believe he would ever be that guy who let himself get soft.

Jo and Michel waited outside the barn with halters and shanks, and Jo came forward to meet Liv.

"Your phone's been ringing. What was the song, Michel?"

"'Perfect Girl.'" Michel said as he unbuckled Jay's throatlatch.

Liv paused, her hand resting on Elemental's bridle. "Emilie. I'd better check it before the next set."

The list of recent calls showed three attempts, and there was a text that simply said *call me*. Liv tried not to let her mind rush ahead to the worst. Life had seemed so incredible of late. It couldn't be ending already, could it?

"What's going on, Em?" she asked, her sister picking up after the first ring.

"Sorry to bother you. I know you're in the middle of training."

"That's okay. What's up?"

Emilie's exhale met her ear before she responded. "Men are swine. Austin, that... jerk..." She spat the word out, obviously self-censoring the adjective that came to mind. "He quit."

"What?" Nate appeared at Liv's elbow, a question on his face, and she relayed, "Austin quit."

"Are you serious?" Nate snapped. "What did he do?"

"I'm putting you on speaker, okay?" Liv said. "Nate's here."

"I heard," Emilie said wryly. "Austin... I may have messed up."

"What do you mean?" Liv said.

"I — had dinner with him last night. And when he dropped me off, he was going to kiss me and I... well, I bolted. And this morning, he was gone."

"He quit because you didn't let him kiss you after having dinner?" Liv asked.

"I'm going to kill him," Nate grumbled. "We're coming back so I can kill him."

Liv laughed. "No, you're not. On all counts."

"Plus, he's left. Like, the country. He's going to Florida, apparently."

"Oh, I hope he comes here." Nate all but rubbed his hands together. "I told him to watch his step."

"But—" Emilie protested.

"No buts, Em. He doesn't get to assume buying you dinner gets him anything," Nate said.

"You told him what?" Liv stared at Nate.

Nate shook his head and held up a hand. She glared at it, then at his face, her mouth slightly parted.

"I'll be okay," Emilie insisted. "I just thought you should know we have no manager again. I'll take care of everything. The timing just sucks. Faye's so busy, she needs my help. And I've still got hours to do for the physio clinic... but it'll all work out."

Liv glanced at Nate, who had the same concerned expression. "Em... are you sure?"

"Yes. Now the season's done, I can ask Dean to come if I need backup. I've helped him out with hay enough times. He owes me."

"Okay... but don't hesitate to call us, all right? We have more than enough people here." Liv's mind was already whirring, forming a contingency plan. If she and Nate flew back, it wasn't as if the crew couldn't function without them. They had been, for the past month, with only one less horse. "Do *Maman et Papa* know?"

"It just happened an hour ago, and they don't need to worry. Neither do you. If it gets to be too much, I'll let you know. I promise."

Liv disconnected and stared at Nate. "So this jerk has come on to Emilie before? I would have fired him myself if I'd known that. If I'd known sooner, maybe we could have found someone else."

"You told me not to give him a hard time. And you've had enough to deal with."

"No one needs to protect me, Miller. What's past is past. This is serious. No secrets, okay? Especially when it involves my farm." It was the first time she'd called it that. She kind of liked it. Except it wasn't quite accurate. "Our farm."

Sharing food and beverages with Jo wasn't unusual. Over the years there'd been many occasions: beers on the backstretch sitting on a cooler after shipping in to Gulfstream; stake parties at Woodbine; the holiday orphans' gathering Roger and Hélène always hosted on Christmas Day. This was far more formal. But Nate had it under control, setting Jo up with a glass of wine and sending them out to the patio facing the ocean.

"You are living the life, my friend," Jo said, both of them gazing over the deepening blue oneness of ocean and sky.

"Not sure what I did to deserve it," Liv responded, and sipped the wine, "but so I am."

"You deserve it as much as anyone else."

"We've got more important things to discuss." She needed to get right to it so they could move forward. "You've been Roger's assistant forever, Jo. The training job is yours. You've earned it a million times over." Jo's loyalty was admirable. Most in her position would have gone out on their own long ago. Liv was sure there were owners who would give her horses, yet she'd remained with Triple Stripe.

"Except I don't want that job, Liv."

It wasn't the answer she'd expected — or counted on. She didn't have a response prepared for that.

"Maybe I did once," Jo continued, her voice mild, "but I know now I'm better as the right hand."

More like an entire side. Jo had always been so much more than a mere hand.

"Are you sure?" Liv raced through arguments to convince the assistant otherwise, but came up empty. It didn't seem right to try and talk her into something she'd clearly decided wasn't for her.

"I'll just keep doing for you what I've always done for Rog," Jo said.

"But I don't want the job either."

Jo sat up, leaning forward with arms resting on her thighs, fingers wound around the stem of the wine glass. "You don't mean that. You've got the credibility and experience. You trained a Queen's Plate winner. And the alternative..."

She left it hanging, and Liv swallowed hard. The impossible time she'd had finding a farm manager who would stick didn't give her much hope for nailing down an appropriate trainer. Which meant moving the horses to a public outfit. Dispersing their dedicated staff. "Yeah. I know."

"We have a great crew, Liv. A totally rare one, these days. How many sheds do you know that have the same help year in, year out, with only minor additions and subtractions for hotwalkers and exercise riders? They're family. This news hit them as hard as it hit us, so we owe it to them to keep things as much the same as we can. And I'll be right there the whole time, so that you don't have to lose yourself in the job. Because you have to protect this." She waved an arm toward the sliding doors, and Nate inside. "I've given up a lot for this job. You can have it all. And I'll make sure of it."

Jo's insistence took Liv aback, and she was more than a little embarrassed she didn't know the assistant's entire history. Jo had always been there, quietly — or not so quietly, when necessary — running the shed, so Roger could focus on the other stuff. She was entirely capable of doing the job; she'd just found the place she preferred to be.

"So..." Liv ventured. "Maybe this will get back some of what you've given up, if I do this?"

"This job is the love of my life. Sometimes there's no room for anything else. Where would I fit it in? Between 8pm and 4am?"

"You won't get an argument from me." Liv wouldn't be the one to whimper on and ask, *don't you get lonely? Don't you want more?* Somehow, more had found her, against the odds, but she believed with her heart there was nothing wrong with being alone, defying what the world declared necessary to be happy. But she sensed a trace of regret in Jo's words. "Here's the deal then. You'll help me protect this..." Liv waved her hand in the same direction Jo had moments earlier, catching Nate's figure in the kitchen at the edge of her vision. "And before we go back to Ontario in January for Claire, you're going to take a week and go to some Caribbean island to recharge. Because I need to protect you from burnout. You might never admit it, but you're frighteningly close right now. Trust me. I've been there."

Jo's face fell, an admission of what she'd never say outright. "It's that obvious, is it?"

"Sorry, but yes, it is."

"All right. You have a deal." Jo held out her glass.

Liv met it halfway with her own. "Go have a fling with the bartender of whatever all-inclusive resort you land at. Just don't let him talk you into marrying him and bringing him home with you to Canada."

Jo snorted, her hand flying to her mouth. "Could you imagine? I'd put him to work, though. You never know when we might need another hotwalker."

Nate wandered out, like he'd been watching and perceived the serious part of their discussion was over. "You all ready for something to eat?"

Liv raised her eyebrows, lips curving upward on one side. "'You all,' Miller?"

"I'm trying to blend in with the locals."

"How many really are locals around here?" she wondered.

"Right?" Jo agreed. "Probably just as many snowbirds as native Floridians."

"This is what I get," Nate said. "Are you hungry, or what?"

They clambered to their feet, filing inside, taking their wine glasses with them. Best not to annoy the cook.

The table was set, plates waiting, the aromas filling the great room drawing them to their seats. Taking advantage of the readily available fresh seafood, Nate had prepared blackened grouper with a salad of tossed greens. Simple but mouthwateringly brilliant.

"This is incredible." Jo said, not hiding her appreciation after the first mouthfuls. She glanced at Liv. "Does he clean, too?"

"Fortunately, she's pretty tidy." Nate quipped and topped up their glasses before settling back into his chair. "So now that you've sorted out whose name is going in the program, what about Jay? What's next?"

And really, that's all this discussion was for. Because though Liv might have been voted leader in an official capacity, moving forward, they would execute plans together.

"I know what I want to do," Liv admitted.

"So, spill," he said.

"The Pegasus."

His expression didn't change. Had he heard her? She'd thought he'd be happy about her ambitious choice; it was a three million dollar race. Did he think it was over Jay's head? Then he rose and came to her chair, leaned over, and, angling his head, kissed her. She thought he was going to knock her out of her chair.

"Maybe I should leave..."

Jo's voice made Liv push Nate's shoulder back with a light laugh, catching his eyes. "You approve, I take it?"

He straightened, returning to his seat as if he'd just gone for a walk on the beach. He smiled and sipped his wine. "Hell yes. I love this new you even more than the old one."

"This new me?"

"It's a very bold decision," he said. "I'm impressed. Go big or go home, baby. Next year's not even here yet and it's already better than this one."

Liv launched into her rationalization. "It's just another race now — no more putting up a million dollars if you want to play, because that never would have happened."

"I think Cal Preston is planning to send Paradise for it," Jo inserted.

Nate's face clouded, grim, as he responded. "Let's hope this time we get a chance to give him a run for his money." It was Paradise who had presided in the race that had seen Jay and Nate go down in that horrific spill at Santa Anita.

"Who says it's his money?" Liv said.

"Touché." He raised his wine, his comment echoed by the clink of glasses. He pushed up from the table. "Time for dessert."

Liv smiled at Jo. "That must be in your honour. Dessert's not usually on the menu."

"Don't get too excited," Nate said as he set plates of Key Lime pie before each of them. "I bought it."

"But you bought the right kind, with real crust," Jo said. "So you get points for that."

"Cappuccino?" he asked.

"Seriously?" Jo said.

"Faye and Will gave us an espresso machine as a wedding gift," Liv explained.

"Nice." Jo nodded "Yes, please."

"It's only fair," Liv said. "They spoiled us in Ontario and got us used to it. Heaven forbid we go a whole winter without posh coffee. Want help?"

Nate shook his head. "I'm good."

Indeed, you are.

"You know," Jo started once Nate was steaming milk, "I

haven't always been sure about you two, but I think he's a keeper."

Liv laughed. "I haven't always been so sure of the two of us either, but you are dead right."

While she'd long called Jo a friend, their relationship had always been as co-workers, colleagues. Faye was the friend who made her acknowledge she was female and not just one of the guys. Jo was becoming something else. Someone who fully understood the conflict of this game. The willingness to sacrifice relationships for the life. The dichotomy of it: love for the sport versus love for the animal. Those two things had a hard time coexisting, and it was harder yet for most women, wasn't it? A woman couldn't let it show, or she wouldn't be taken seriously, as Luna had so succinctly pointed out. Yet, that compassion set women apart from their male counterparts. Gave them a special edge. It should be a strength, not a weakness.

Nate reappeared with three cups on a tray Liv hadn't even known they'd owned. Thank goodness one of them was domestic. He distributed the beverages and pulled his chair up to his slice of pie.

"What weight will Jay carry in the Pegasus?" he asked, pausing before putting a forkful in his mouth.

"Just eat, Miller. It's over a month away," Liv replied.

They were all quiet for a few minutes, dessert commanding their attention. Jo was right. This was the life.

"How are Michel and Sue doing?" Liv asked, directing the question at Jo.

"Sue's fine. It helps that she's a swing groom this winter, so she doesn't have a full four horses, though she likely would have done a regular groom's job if I hadn't told her that was how things would work."

"Michel needs to step up, big-time," Nate said. "They can't raise a baby in the dorm."

"Do they live in the dorm?" Liv looked at him in horror.

"That might be a small exaggeration," Nate admitted. "But right now, they're in the trailer park down the road from Payson. And at home they rent some dark basement apartment. The guy needs a house. And Jay's going to buy it for him." The groom's stake from winning the Pegasus would certainly contribute to the down payment.

Once both plates and cups were empty, Nate cleared the dishes, then topped up Jo and Liv's glasses — but not his own. "I'm going to bed. All three of us can't be dragging our asses in the morning. 'Night Jo."

"I guess that means we have Nate's permission to get drunk." Jo reached for her glass and held it aloft.

"Cheers," Liv said with a nod, though the thought didn't appeal to her. "You can sleep over if that's the plan. There is a spare room."

"Thanks for the offer, but I'm not sure I want to be a stone's throw from the newlyweds."

"I guess that means you've better stop drinking then, or I'm going to have to get Miller to drive you home." Liv gave her a stern look, which transformed into curiosity. "Where will you go on your forced vacation?"

"I've always wanted to go to Barbados. I want to see them swim the racehorses. Bucket list item, you know?"

"That would be cool."

"We'll see how long I last."

"See?" Liv said. "Don't judge me for vetoing a honeymoon."

"I'm not. I'm just the enforcer of your work-life balance."

"I'm not sure you have any credibility in that department. Be grateful I'm not like Faye, or I'd be trying to set you up. Dean, maybe."

She thought Jo would laugh, but Jo returned an amused

smile. "We went on a couple of dates once, actually. He's a nice guy, and of course we had lots to talk about, but there just weren't any sparks, you know? And if I'm going to have a relationship now, there'd better be sparks."

That tidbit was worth another slug of wine. "You dated Dean Taylor? How did none of us know about this?"

"Tell Nate and I'm quitting. You can say goodbye to that work-life balance."

Liv choked back a laugh and almost sputtered out the sip she'd just taken. "Sworn to secrecy."

"You're leaving for Calgary on the twenty-third?"

Liv nodded. "Back late on the twenty-sixth."

"Not really a lot of time."

"I know. I feel bad about that, but at least it's something. It's going to be hard for Nate's family." It would be the Millers' first holiday since the accident that had claimed the lives of Nate's brother and sister-in-law.

"You're serious about the Pegasus?" Jo asked.

"Why not?"

She would do it.

She would do it for her warped family, and that tainted family name — which she would keep. For Geai, who had always believed in her.

She'd do it for Roger and Hélène and the crew.

She'd do it for Feste, because she felt as if she had something to redeem there.

She owed it to everyone to be confident. The whole Triple Stripe family. Jay was their big horse, and if Roger said he'd take them places, they'd give him places to go.

CHAPTER SEVENTEEN

It had been right to spend Christmas in Calgary. Not exactly easy, but right. From the pervading absence of Phil and Cindy to more trivial things like his mother's insistence on playing bad Christmas music. Normally, he appreciated his mother's taste in music, but not during the holidays.

His father had been gruffly civil — *we don't see you for five years, then we see you four times in one* — and even greeted Liv with a stiff hug. Connie had battled through grief so obviously just below the surface, bravely holding it together when Nate would have been perfectly fine with her falling apart. He'd played the piano and sung carols with her, and embarrassed Tim about Emilie. Liv had been touched Connie had made a traditional tourtière for Christmas Eve. The hardest part might have been seeing Phil and Cindy's twin toddlers, because he saw so much of both of their parents in them.

They'd returned to Florida in time for Jo to go on her vacation, and had an easy week at the barn — typical for the days between Christmas and New Year's — though he couldn't help but gallop Jay with more intent, if not more intensity, since the decision about the Pegasus. Nate didn't entertain the prospect of total embarrassment, showing up for a race in which some might think they had no place running. Liv was not one to enter a horse just for the prestige; they needed a reason. They had a reason. A reason named Just Jay.

With Jay, the skeptics couldn't say the horse was running off Roger's training. They couldn't give Liv flak about that. Jay was all theirs, from the minute they'd commandeered him from Emilie. That said, Em had played a significant role, even if it was inadvertent — because the base she'd put on the big chestnut with her trot and gallop sets was responsible for the rock solid foundation moving him forward. Forward into greatness.

Naw, he wasn't high on this horse at all.

Jo would be back tomorrow from her escape — New Year's Day. Then January second, holidays were over for everyone. It was time to start pointing the runners to races.

There was a minor blip in the continuity of their Pegasus prep. He and Liv were going back to the farm in Ontario to be there for Claire. Claire had always read the book, and he was trusting her to foal within reasonable proximity of her due date — even if due dates with mares were more a suggestion than a hard marker, like they seemed to be with humans. Claire would not be that one whose offspring cooked a full year. Because if that's the way things went, they'd have to leave her, and Liv badly wanted to be there for the arrival of that baby.

He'd been content to take it easy this winter, but now they had a goal, he was grabbing it with both hands. Maybe it was like they said — a change was as good as a rest. Or maybe Kenny was right, and now that the wedding was behind him, everything was clearer, fatigue forgotten. There was no point in engaging the agent before they went back to King City, but he'd call the guy about starting up something when they returned, if the offer was still up for grabs. The break had been nice, but now Nate was antsy. The opportunity to ride in a three million dollar race might've had something to do with that. Nothing like a good horse to reignite the fire.

He took the big chestnut an easy two miles while Liv galloped once around with Elemental, which meant he walked back from the track alone. How many times had he travelled this path? How many of those times with Chique? He missed the cheeky little bitch, who he could always count on to keep him on his toes. None of this strolling on the knot, gazing at the surroundings.

Another horse jigged up beside him, head in the air and lines snug against a sweaty neck. Chique hadn't been nervous like that, only impatient. Nate glanced at the rider.

"Hey, you okay?" he asked instead of the usual nonchalant greeting he offered to those coming and going.

The girl on the horse's back grimaced more than smiled, a short, dark ponytail poking out from under her red kerchief and black helmet cover. She was very straight-backed, gripping her crossed lines with a white-knuckled fist while she tucked her left hand into her midsection against her safety vest. Her face was pale enough, the slight flush when she glanced at him barely registered.

"What happened?" he tried again when she didn't answer.

"I don't know. He dropped me on the turf course. Someone was right there and caught him, and I thought I was okay, so they tossed me back up. But —"

She held out the hand, already red and swollen. Something like his had been after Chique had pulled a quick one on him back at Woodbine in November.

"That looks angry. You're on a colt?" Nate nodded at the horse's head.

The girl's eyebrows knitted briefly — like what did it matter — before she gave a quick shake of her head. "Gelding."

"Better still," Nate said, and nudged Jay over. "Do you mind if I help you out and pony you home?"

Again she looked more embarrassed than agreeable, but answered, "No. Thanks. All I need is for him to duck out from under me again."

"Where are we going?" He wrapped his fingers around the closest rein. Jay, Pegasus Invitational hopeful, part-time pony. Liv would only kill him if he let their big horse get hurt.

"Elliot Kay's barn."

"Oh yeah? We're on the other side. Sorry I haven't noticed you."

"I just started."

She didn't say much — kind of inverse of Cory, who was blonde and chatty. He felt as if he was annoying her. It made him remember the good old days when that's the vibe he'd gotten from Liv.

Michel was waiting with the halter, and Liv wandered off the shed when she saw him approaching.

"What did you find out there, Miller? A stray?" Michel asked.

Nate gave a quiet head shake because the kid was obviously horrified enough her little mishap was going to get out. Not that she could avoid it with that hand.

"Hey Liv, can you lead them over to Elliot? She hurt her hand, and the horse was being a twit."

Liv grabbed a shank and snapped it to the gelding's bit. "Nate did that a few months ago," she said, jutting her chin toward him. "It ended up not being broken. A couple of days on the ground and he was back at it."

"I can manage now," the girl said, dismounting. "But thanks."

"Borrow the shank," Liv said, handing it to her after the girl had awkwardly run up the stirrup irons.

"Thank you." She walked away with the gelding in tow, her eyes scanning the ground dejectedly.

"That was weird," Liv said, looking at Nate.

He suppressed his grin. The exercise rider's manner was quite familiar, he'd thought. "She got dropped on the turf course. Someone caught her horse and threw her back up, and it wasn't till she was on she realized her hand wasn't right. I thought it might be easier if I played escort."

"I'm not questioning your decision," Liv said, the corners of her lips lifting. "I'll go check with Elliot that she's okay before we get the next set out."

He saw the kid walking the gelding around the shed when he was ready to get on his next horse. Clearly, the injury didn't need immediate medical attention, but she wouldn't be galloping any more horses this morning. Liv came up to him, leaning in.

"Elliot asked if we could help get his horses out when we're done."

"Sure," Nate said. "It's not like we're busy."

Elliot's horses weren't as well-schooled as the Triple Stripe bunch, that was soon obvious. No surprise the kid got dropped. There was some remedial work happening with the first one Nate got on. The good news was Elliot only had five right now, and with the gelding the girl had been on done, they took care of the remaining four in short order.

"You guys are lifesavers," Elliot said at the end of the morning. "I owe you."

"You'd better take the kid to get pictures of that hand," Nate said.

"I have five horses to do up first."

Nate hadn't interacted with Elliot enough to have formed

an opinion before now, but at the moment, he was coming off as a jerk. "Maybe one of us can take her." He looked at Liv.

They nominated Sue, who didn't appreciate it when Nate suggested she needed to get used to taking kids for x-rays — any more than the girl appreciated being referred to as a kid, if the look on her face was any indication. He didn't feel sorry enough for Elliot to offer to help do up, so he headed off to do the tack instead. Once Sue had departed with the girl, Elliot suddenly seemed to have time to come over and talk.

"Thanks for helping me out. I feel bad the kid got hurt."

"Does the kid have a name?" For whatever reason, Nate had never asked. Maybe because she hadn't been inviting questions.

"Marie. I just hired her, and had no right to put her on that gelding, but I was stuck." Elliot shrugged. "Hard to find help when you only have five horses. I can train them and groom them, but I'm not getting on them."

Nate ran his eyes from the guys's size eleven feet to the black-crested top of his six-foot frame. He was probably two hundred pounds, easy. "I guess not. You might have yourself a hotwalker now, though, if the kid's hand is broken. Can the pig ride?" He hadn't seen the pig yet today. Off somewhere doing his job.

Elliot chuckled. "Probably better than some of the help around here." He leaned on the cinderblock wall opposite the tack room. "You riding at Gulfstream? Maybe you can ride for me."

Nate peered through the bridles. "How do you know you'd want me to?"

"Wasn't that long ago you won an Eclipse award. And you've won some big races, even if they were just in Canada."

"Just, yeah. Nice to know I haven't quite faded into obscurity. I don't know how much I'll be doing down here. I'll let you know."

Nicole produced the birthday cake, which she'd kept hidden in Elliot's fridge, because New Year's Eve was also Liv's birthday. Liv did her best to play nice. She hadn't changed that much — she didn't like a fuss being made over such events. In honour of that, they agreed to refrain from singing "Happy Birthday." He could do it later just to irritate her.

"This needs to be the last day for cake," he said as Liv sliced it and handed him a wedge on a paper plate. Sue returned at that moment with Marie, the cast on Marie's left arm all anyone needed to know. "You definitely need cake," Nate said, and handed her his piece, then wondered if she could manage to eat it. With her fingers, for sure.

"Here, Miller. You don't need a full slice." Liv held out a forkful, and he couldn't resist closing his mouth over it, meeting her eyes. She grinned.

They took turns driving the Porsche. It seemed only fair they should share. He loved the way she looked behind the wheel, especially when she was taking them to the condo and he could let his favourite version of Poe's "Hey Pretty" run through his mind — the Drive-By 2001 Mix, with its spoken word layered over the tune and chorus. Sometimes, if she thought he was sleeping when it came along, he'd catch her singing it, and it took everything he had to keep up the ruse and not try to talk her into playing out the story.

"You making friends with Elliot this morning?"

He cracked an eye open, fantasy rudely interrupted. "He asked me to ride for him."

"Maybe we'll have his horses going good by then."

He laughed. "Right? What a rogue bunch."

"You'd better get on that paperwork, Miller."

"See, I should have taken your name so you couldn't call me that anymore."

"I would anyway. Old habits and all that."

They'd fallen into a routine most afternoons. A run on the beach, followed by a dip in the ocean, letting the sun dry them off after. He fell asleep for real under the warm rays, enough days into UV exposure not to burn. Did he really want to give this up to be driving down to Gulfstream? But when he got on Jay every morning, he remembered why he'd have to do it. Why it would be worth it.

He tried to make dinner a little special for her birthday without going overboard. No gifts because she'd made him promise, claiming all she wanted was a nice evening. As they sat down, he wondered if she was remembering that awkward meal they'd shared with Roger and Hélène three years ago. When he lifted his glass and paused, meeting her eyes, he thought yes.

This time there was a wry curve to her lips as their glasses touched, her voice soft and low as she said, *"Santé."* After she sipped and set down her glass the sultry smile dissipated. "I wonder how Roger and Hélène are holding up."

Hélène had always been a private person. There were no social media updates on what she was experiencing or thinking or feeling, so it felt as if they were doing a lot of wondering. They heard more from Emilie, who was friends with Roger and Hélène's daughter Sylvie, than from Roger and Hélène themselves. It felt wrong to be so far removed from the reality of it.

Later, they sat on the beach in the dark as midnight drew near, and as he laced his fingers through hers he remembered every last New Year's Eve since the one that had started his hatred of a night that was supposed to be a celebration. *New Year's Eve is just for drunks and people in love,* he'd told her three years ago while they'd polished off a bottle of wine between them, each engrossed in their own self-pity. She'd been surprisingly bold that night, facing off with questions. Agreeing — with a little prodding — to dance with him to the song that had become his sad tradition. He hadn't planned on kissing her. And last winter, as they'd kept vigil while Chique battled deadly laminitis, their kiss as one year passed into the next hadn't felt any more hopeful. This year, though. This year.

He turned to her, eyes adjusted enough to the low light to make out the softness of her features. He didn't have to reach for her; she met him halfway, fingers weaving into the hair at the back of his neck before she pushed into him, or he dragged her down... it didn't really matter.

"You're a quick study."

"Hmmm," she breathed. "Good teacher, maybe. Should we even bother staying up till midnight?"

He let that question hang, because that would mean getting up, and would it be so wrong to stay right here? But he rolled her to her side, drawing back enough to break off the kiss so he could see her face, though there was a powerful impulse pulling him back.

"Yes. We're seeing this year out, because it needs to go already."

She scrambled to her feet so quickly he was left feeling robbed, and for a terrifying moment, like he'd said something wrong. But as he clambered after her, he noticed her smile.

"I've got just the thing," she said, skipping into the condo.

He followed as far as the door. The calendar she'd hung in the kitchen last January remained on the wall, and she pulled out the thumbtack holding it there, then rifled through a drawer. Matches. He grinned.

Just enough beyond the building to be safe, she handed him the matches and held out the calendar. He struck the head against the rough side of the box, watching it flash yellow-orange, then set flame to paper. The edges of the glossy stock curled and blackened as it slowly blazed.

There were fireworks — some up the beach, some down — the cracks and pops and sizzles reaching them like a dubbing delay after the bursts of colourful sparks and flares. The calendar was ash at their feet. He'd clean it up tomorrow, because now there needed to be a proper kiss before going inside.

This was how it was supposed to be. Time for new traditions. Six years of miserable New Years Eves, but tonight all that changed.

CHAPTER EIGHTEEN

HIS FEET DANGLED around Chique's elbows, the — mare now, no longer a filly — swinging her head to the side every so often to show him a bright eye peeking through her long forelock. *This is different,* that look said. But she seemed to like it. And if she decided she didn't, well, the snow was over her knees in some places, so at least he'd have a soft landing. Reba trudged through the powdery white stuff in front of them, leading the way through the woods. Emilie glanced back and grinned from under the peak of her helmet, a scarf wrapped around her neck and tucked securely into her red jacket.

When was the last time he'd ridden bareback? Maybe when he was ten, or even before that, at Will's grandfather's farm in Canmore. As soon as riding had become a job, as much as it was a job he'd always loved and considered himself lucky to be paid well for, that layer of tack between him and the horse had always been there.

"Maybe I'll move to South America where they gallop horses bareback. What do you think, Em?"

She shifted again on Reba, hitching a hip so she could rest

one hand on the cantle of her saddle — because she'd decided she should keep hers in case she needed to rescue Nate, or Chique. "No one's stopping you from doing it here. What a feeling that must be, eh?"

It would be, to breeze a horse with nothing between you. It would require even more core strength and finesse than was already necessary.

They emerged by the clearing near the stallion barn. Geai's cottage — because he would always think of it as Geai's cottage, not the farm manager's cottage — stood in front of it, the path to the door he'd walked up so many times covered in an undisturbed layer of white. He nudged Chique into a jog, and she trotted up next to Reba with a contented snort. She definitely wasn't taking offence to this. *Huh.* Maybe she was just glad to be doing something.

"How's the farm manager hunt coming, anyway?" he asked.

"Chip's friend from out west is flying in this week to see the place and all going well, she'll take the job. We've been speaking on the phone since Christmas, and I'm trying not to get my hopes up, but I really like her. In the meantime, Dean's been a big help. He's spelled me a few nights watching Claire. His first mare isn't due till the middle of February. And he's close if I need a hand for something. Even Will comes sometimes."

The farm's latest addition, a compact black Labrador named Holly, bounded out of the trees, rejoining them from wherever she'd been. Tracking rabbits, no doubt. Holly had joined the farm Christmas Eve, Emilie declaring she'd been a foster fail even before she'd officially agreed to take on the Lab. Chique shied into Reba like she'd just realized the Labrador was there, when Nate was pretty sure her horse radar had known the dog's exact location all along, as well as if she'd had a phone and Holly a GPS collar.

Nate stilled his seat and pulled back on the neck strap — he wasn't completely insane, so he'd thrown that much on the filly-now-mare. Chique halted and swung her hindquarters so she faced the dog. Holly wagged her thick tail with her big Labrador grin, and Nate let the lines slip through his fingers so Chique could dip her head, stretching out bravely to touch the dog's black nose.

"Next year's Christmas card!" Emilie called gleefully from the spot ahead of them where she'd stopped Reba, reins in one hand, phone deftly held in the other.

The farm's two resident stallions lifted their heads in their individual paddocks as Chique and Reba approached. This could be interesting. His landing wouldn't be so kind if Chique decided to be silly on the snow-cleared laneway, so he ducked her to the far side of Reba to use the younger filly as a shield. *Yes, I trust a three-year-old more than you, Cheeky.* Just Lucky jogged to the fence, a lift to both his head and his tail, a poof of powder rising each time a hoof dove through the snow. He followed them along the fenceline as they passed. Starway returned to his hay. The older stallion must've checked the calendar. Breeding season was still over a month away. Even Just Lucky's reaction was civilized.

"So I take it you didn't hit it off with my brother." Nate looked sideways at Emilie.

Emilie's shoulders lifted and fell with a long-suffering shrug. "You all thought we'd have this instant bond, like it was predestined. That's a lot of pressure. And I expected him to be like you, just without all the baggage." She smiled with mock sweetness. "But he's nothing like you, except for the resemblance."

"Yeah, he's not. He's more like your sister."

She tilted her head. "How so? Other than being quiet."

"He still likes his own company better than anyone else's.

And he takes his hockey seriously. He has to. I get that. He hasn't figured out a girlfriend wouldn't have to get in the way."

"Maybe he needs to find one who plays hockey too." Her eyes fell back to Reba's ears.

That looked like regret. So had Em found something to like in Tim, despite how things had gone at the wedding? "It's a different life from this, so I don't think that's a prerequisite," he said, because he knew she was trying to compare it to his relationship with Liv; that common ground of a passion for horses and this sport, the thing that'd helped her see their potential. "Not that I'm trying to talk you into it, but what he probably needs is someone who's independent and self-assured enough to deal with that life."

"He friended me on Facebook. We message back and forth sometimes. It's a modern romance." The laugh she probably meant to sound light came out a little flat. "It's not a romance at all. That's okay. I'm sorry to disappoint everyone who decided we were meant to be. How did anyone think it could really happen? I'm not going to move to wherever he is with whatever team on the off chance we might become a thing. I'm not that desperate. So I'll go on being everyone's friend or little sister again. Whatever. Everyone thought it would be Liv who would be the reclusive spinster. Maybe we switched fates."

This wasn't a place for a pat answer, so he said nothing at all. She sounded like she was more upset about it than she wanted to admit. Which would be interesting if it didn't make him hurt for her a little. Emilie deserved the magical romance they all hoped she'd find, even if she didn't need it. She was amazing all by herself.

What would Claire have done if she'd slipped on a bridle, thrown a leg over that broad back, hugged her expanded ribcage once astride? The poor mare was far too uncomfortable for Liv to actually consider it, but she'd always been so close to Claire; shared so much. They'd grown up together, even if it had taken reaching her late twenties for Liv to think she might be getting there herself. Claire would always be the wiser of the two of them; the mature one. That just meant she had to live forever. That went without saying. *If only.*

Claire's head popped up, ears zeroing in on something behind Liv. Liv turned, leaning back against the fence. There they were, looking like a festive greeting card, coming down the snow-covered lane with Holly romping alongside them, a piece of coal with legs. All the Labrador needed was a red ribbon around her neck, and the scene would be complete. Even with the holidays done this time around, there was something about that sight. She'd missed Christmas on the farm.

"Good ride?" she asked. Nate was still on Chique, though whether he'd been up there for the duration of their winter hack was up for grabs. Claire nuzzled the pom-pom on her toque over the fence from behind.

"Nate's going to ride in Argentina. He's done with saddles," Emilie quipped.

"I see Claire didn't foal while we were gone," Nate said wryly.

"Smartass." She walked up to meet them and thought about dragging him off Chique's back into a snowbank, but she, at least, was going to treat Chique like the valuable addition to their broodmare band she was supposed to be — instead of Nate's pony.

"That was fun," he said as his feet hit the ground. He only cringed a bit. They were probably cold, if not frozen, even if the rest of him was warm. He lifted the reins and neckstrap over Chique's neck.

"See you two later," Emilie said, walking Reba toward the training barn.

Liv followed Nate and Chique, standing outside the stall as he pulled off the bridle. Chique rubbed her head on his shoulder, and Liv didn't bother chastising him for it. Let him have his moment. It's not like this was a daily occurrence.

"I'll stick around after I turn her back out if you want," he offered, sliding the door shut. "If there's stuff at the house you want to get done."

"All right. I can take the bridle to the tack room on my way out." She left him snapping a shank to Chique's halter.

It wasn't cold by Ontario-in-January standards, only compared to what they'd become used to in Florida. She kept her chin tucked to her chest under the collar of a down-filled coat that hadn't seen action since last Christmas, and marched to the house.

It seemed eerie, devoid of her parents' presence. Emilie took up so little of it, the evidence of her there, but minimal. There were more signs that a dog lived there than a human. A stainless steel water bowl on the kitchen floor. A couple of toys and a chew bone on the living room carpet. Her mother would have a fit. Liv thought it helped the place look homey.

Progress on the renovations was slow, but might pick up now the holidays were over. It wasn't as if they were in a hurry — hopefully, by the time they returned from Florida in April, it would be ready. Right now, Nate's apartment was a cosy and logical place to stay, with Claire living right underneath.

This trip to King City was like a pause button on their track life — modulating the anticipation of running Just Jay in the three million dollar Pegasus Invitational. With so much back and forth and here and there in the last few weeks, she didn't know what to call home. Would this house be it, come April? Or was home wherever Nate was? Wherever they were. *Wherever I lay my hat...*

She wandered upstairs to her room. Her old room, now. The box rested where she'd left it — and, she admitted with chagrin, forgotten about it. The box of Geai's things.

There hadn't been time — at least the right time — to nestle herself in a corner and open it before travelling south. She carried it downstairs to the living room, clearing the coffee table and setting it there, then poured herself a glass of wine in the kitchen before returning. She tucked a leg under herself and rested on the sofa in front of it, imagining a glow emanating from inside.

A simple cardboard box, not even taped shut; just the four folds pushed and pulled to close it, a technique it always took her brain a minute to remember how to do. Lift one edge. Pull up the opposite. Opening it was easy, though. And not so easy.

Resting on the very top of the contents was a framed eight by ten photo. She'd seen it — Geai and Francie's wedding photo — because Geai had prominently displayed it when he'd occupied the cottage. Liv hadn't volunteered for the job of clearing the place out. Her mother had likely done it with her father's help. She'd been too weak, too broken, and only now did she let herself remember why.

Next was a stack of win photos. Why had she never seen these? She knew he'd ridden, his career brief because weight had quickly become an issue. He'd never had Nate's lithe build, so as soon as he'd matured, the muscle that had come with it had put an end to those aspirations.

They were black and white, and Geai looked so young in them, she barely recognized him. Most were from Blue Bonnets in Montreal, which had once hosted Thoroughbred racing. Some of those photos included who she had to think was Francie. Another froze her, a chill travelling up her arm to her heart. Next to Francie, his arm around her slight shoulders... Liv checked the information at the bottom. Daniel Lachance, owner. Geai had ridden for her grandfather?

She didn't try to process it now, setting it aside and reaching for a ziplock bag full of snapshots. First, a small one in black and white. A woman cradling a baby. Francie, she now recognized with ease. She and Geai had no children of their own. Liv flipped it over. *Tante France avec Claude.* Her father.

Posed baby photos. When she only knew the subject as an adult, they always looked to her like grown-up faces pasted on pudgy little bodies. Her father's smile hadn't changed, except for losing that naïve charm. Of course, his face was thinner now, and he had more lines. He'd kept the hair, though. It was just salt-and-pepper these days.

More images. Her father, growing up, with her uncle Julien... then her mother appeared, often on a horse. In one she wore tall boots and breeches, riding a big jumper. In another, she was on a racehorse. Her father wasn't in that photo. Had that been before? When she'd been dating a jockey? The one who had lost his life on the track?

All of it a lifetime before Liv.

Her parents' wedding photo... then... there she was. She'd better hide these, because if Nate ever got his hands on them, they'd show up at inopportune times.

An eight by ten of her on a pony. A real pony, maybe twelve hands, though her feet barely made it a quarter of the way around her steed's stout barrel. She was bareback, but held the reins like she remembered how she'd been taught, which was something at that age. Four, maybe? She didn't remember the pony at all. Geai posed, holding the gelding on one side. The grin on her face. She'd always had a quick smile for Geai; for ponies. Everyone else had to work for them.

About that time, Emilie appeared. A photo of the two sisters with their grandfather. Liv already looked uncomfortable in his presence. Emilie appeared oblivious. Had it started earlier than she remembered? Had she blocked more of it out? *So young.* But her grandfather owned the ponies. Sacrifices were made for ponies when you were a horse-crazy girl.

Next, extended family photos with several people she couldn't name; possibly three or four generations represented. Geai and Francie always there, though not unlike her, never smiling.

Francie had died shortly after their move to Ontario, the cancer that had taken her swift and ruthless. Geai had gone on with his duties stoically, though he travelled no further than the grocery store. Never returned to Quebec. Now she knew there was more to that story.

A fractured family. A patriarch with an unspeakable secret. Geai, she now realized, was her great-uncle by marriage. He and Francie had always felt part of the family. She'd just never known that they were family. Why had no one ever said?

Something made her look up, like she expected Geai to be there, ready to answer all her questions. But it was Nate — though she had a strange sensation of Geai standing behind him.

"A picture paints a thousand words?" he asked quietly, eyes falling to the photos now strewn about her.

At first she couldn't speak, and he remained where he was, like he wasn't sure she seemed ready to share whatever she might have discovered. But she untucked her foot and shuffled over to make room by way of invitation.

"Yeah," she said as his weight compressed the cushions next to her. And what a story.

She pieced it together — using pictures more than words — until they sat in silence amid the history before them. Nate reached for her empty wine glass, retreating to the kitchen and returning with a refill and a glass for himself.

"Does it change anything?" he asked.

"No... not exactly. It brings him closer again, when it felt like he was slipping away. And it places him where he always belonged, anyway. I just wasn't aware."

"Em's keeping an eye on Claire," he said, preempting Liv's query, but he brought up the camera view on his phone, the expectant mare all but filling the frame as she munched hay in her stall. "Hungry?"

She nodded, realizing she was, and that she hadn't thought about Claire until Nate appeared.

He made them something to eat, leaving enough for Emilie, and they finished the bottle. It made Liv sleepy — not the best state with a night of watching ahead. But they had each other; would spell each other. They weren't missing this baby, if this baby decided to come while they were at the farm.

Nate sent Em a text that there was food for her, then went ahead to the apartment without Liv — promising to check on Claire, despite Emilie's *all is quiet* response and the camera view of a contented mare in the stall. Liv returned to the living room to pack up the box. She hadn't even made it to the letters and notebooks. The photos were probably enough for the first pass. But she couldn't help reaching for a small cluster of notepaper, bound with an elastic. She slipped one from the envelope, noted the date, and almost put it back. A letter in Geai's handwriting, to his sister, sent early spring of the year he'd died.

They remind me so much of Francie and me in our early days. She is so talented, but stubborn. So reluctant to accept help. And he is determined, but someone has stolen his confidence.

How will they ever see what I see? How will they ever figure it out without me to help them?

Liv gulped a breath and squeezed her eyes shut. He had known, then. And he hadn't told them. Because he didn't want to be a distraction. It was just as Nate had suspected.

If only he'd prepared a manual. Then again, maybe he had, and it was somewhere in this box. All the things she'd refused to deal with in the wake of his passing; new fodder for the sessions her therapist had agreed could continue via video while she was down south. Maybe now she was brave enough to tackle it all.

CHAPTER NINETEEN

HE SWAPPED AWARENESS WITH EMILIE — that's what it was, this foal watch thing. One person at all times dedicated themselves to keeping the mare top of mind. This foal's arrival would not go unwitnessed. Nate would put money on Claire waiting for Liv, anyway. He liked to think they were that in tune, even if the concept was a bit bad-horse-novel.

It wasn't long before Liv joined him. He'd picked out the stalls and topped up waters, making sure Chique and Claire both had hay. Liv grabbed the broom and swept the aisle silently, then disappeared into the office.

He found her as he had so many times before, sitting at the desk under the iconic painting, the story behind it woven through the canvas fibres under the brushstrokes. Somehow the newest details hadn't been a surprise, like they'd always intuitively known without being told. Not that familial connections mattered. Geai was who he was without the genealogy. The surrogate grandfather, making up in no small way for the one who had failed her. Nate only wished he'd had the chance to meet Francie Doucet too. He dropped into the old overstuffed chair.

Liv glanced up. "I just confirmed the booking for the van taking Chique to Kentucky."

For the first time, Chique would go off without either of them. The farm in Lexington always took amazing care of the Triple Stripe mares, but it didn't make it easier. It had been so nice to have Claire stay home, bred to their own stallion, Just Lucky, but there wasn't a suitable match for Chique in Ontario.

"Who are you breeding Claire to this year?"

"Let's see what she produces," Liv said.

Which meant she hadn't booked the mare to a Kentucky stallion, though Claire was certainly worthy of it. But why go to Kentucky if her foal by Just Lucky turned out to be spectacular? And next year, how about Just Jay? After he'd won the Breeders' Cup Classic, of course. The thought made Nate a bit restless; a bit torn. Eager to be back at Payson prepping the big horse for the Pegasus, but needing to be here.

"I'm going to see if I can sleep," he said, rising. "Wake me up at two, and I'll take over." He yawned, stretching.

"Stop that," Liv chided, her hand going to her mouth as she hid a yawn of her own.

Upstairs, he sat at the piano — something he definitely missed about this place. How the hell would they get it out of here to take to the house? That might be easier than getting it in had been. He was glad he hadn't been part of that.

His fingers communed with the keys like old friends until the notes started running together as tiredness took over. When he crawled under the covers, his mind drifted to a year ago. He and Jay, prepping for a significant race. Holding onto the prospect of success because it was all he had, with Liv a continent away and the wavelengths transmitting between them interrupted. And it had gone how it had gone — disastrously.

Now there was a peace to their plan. Together, they were unstoppable. Chique was only the beginning.

Her body was a tensegrity structure, angles shifting and softening. Claire's once-tucked abdomen was misshapen; edges instead of roundness, like the unborn foal was on its back now — one corner the hip, one corner the withers. The mare's topline appeared nearly flat as her pelvis adjusted, ready for that twist and dive into the birth canal, transforming fetus to foal.

Claire would not be a sneaky one, like Sotisse had been with Chique five years ago. Claire had read the book. Liv merely checked the boxes.

"Just give her a phone and ask her to call when she's ready to go," Nate had joked earlier.

With flashlight in hand, she peeked first under Claire's tail, then at her udder, the bag more swollen, teats full, a tiny crystal at each tip. She did the check several times a day, looking for the subtlest of changes. The breaking down of the muscles in Claire's croup, the alterations in colour and consistency of the excretions — evidence of the forthcoming milk, building colostrum that would provide the foal with life-sustaining antibodies.

Soon, but not yet. It was a sense, a gut feeling that told Liv so. Not that her intuition couldn't be wrong. So she wouldn't trust it; she would watch. Obsessively. She checked water buckets before turning off the aisle lights and trudging up to the apartment.

The bedroom door was closed, Nate likely well into sleep behind it. Liv wandered to the small kitchen, contemplating making a coffee to keep herself alert. Too early for that. It was only ten, so she'd save it for when she'd need it more. It was just one of a stack of how-to-stay-awake-when-your-body-wanted-to-sleep ploys. She opted for a green tea instead, thinking how Connie Miller would scowl at her for heating the water in the microwave instead of brewing a proper pot. *Mom.* She hadn't quite been able to bring herself to call Connie that yet, but it was only a matter of time.

Foal watch was isolating; not a job for the lonely. She'd done her share of stints on the night shift when the Lachance family had first moved to the farm and kept broodmares at home, giving Geai a break from the upside-down routine. And while she'd never thought of herself as lonely before Nate, she wondered now if she'd just been in denial about the whole thing; if it had been a defense mechanism all along.

No. She'd been solitary, for sure, but being alone didn't have to mean lonely. It didn't bother her to be on her own, and sometimes she still wondered how Nate had assimilated himself into her life. The only problem she could see with it now was the thought of life without him, a dull ache rising in her chest, thinking how debilitating it had been to lose Geai. But now she would believe it was better to go with it; a reminder it was all the more reason to cherish every moment.

The stillness in the middle of the night always seemed peculiar; that realization she remained conscious when everyone she knew was in their beds. Sleeping when it was dark was a privilege she took for granted until foaling season came around again, and it had been years now since she'd been part of it. She felt for those who had no choice — shift workers, nurses, foaling attendants. It messed up the body's circadian rhythms. This was elective for her, though how could she not watch Claire? Emilie was grateful for a few nights of sleeping rather than the fitful slumber of grabbed daylight hours that never seemed to satisfy the basic need. Thankfully, the next mare wasn't due for several weeks and hopefully they'd have a new manager to share the night shift by then. Emilie would not last, trying to keep up with everything. She needed to complete her hours at the physio clinic if she wanted to graduate this spring. She'd cut them back drastically for Claire.

Once it hit one AM, she started on her list of creative ways to stay awake. Just another hour, and Nate would take over. Television bored her. Reading put her to sleep. Cleaning was good, but how many times could she clean the apartment? It wasn't large, and both of them were tidy. She could go downstairs and groom the two mares, but Chique wasn't one to endure fussing, and Claire was uncomfortable at this stage of her pregnancy, so that didn't always go over so well. The closer she got to foaling, the more Liv needed to leave her alone. Besides, Claire was doing a good job blowing her furry winter coat on her own with her changing hormones. *She wants to look good for the photos once her baby's born,* Nate had explained, ever anthropomorphic.

On camera, Claire nibbled hay. After a couple of nights, Liv knew her habits. When she ate. When she dozed. When she listened. When she lay flat out and made Liv strain at the screen to be sure Claire hadn't foaled without the warning signs she was convinced the mare would show.

One-thirty. She staved off her craving for coffee now, because it would only keep her awake when she could finally let herself sleep. She put on headphones instead, connected to the keyboard, and tried to remember the scales she'd learned as a child. The piano was still in the apartment, but Nate had borrowed the electronic instrument from Will so he could play while she slept when it was his turn to watch.

"You going to take it up again?" His voice made it through to her, because she'd kept the volume low enough to hear him when he emerged.

She turned, mildly self-conscious because her fingers were so clumsy on the keys compared to his. "Maybe."

"You could do with a hobby."

"Why does everyone keep saying that?"

He laughed and pulled her to her feet. "Go sleep, while the bed's still warm."

It would have been warmer with him there, but she crawled between the sheets gratefully, like it was the most amazing luxury in the world. She breathed in the traces of him left on the sheets as her head sunk to the pillow. Was there something in the scent of someone you loved that contributed to feeling content; safe? How did scent connect to the brain? She'd have to look it up... but now... sleep drew her in.

When her eyes opened again, it was light, and the indulgence of it struck her; it was so rare she woke after the sun was up. Surfacing to Nate rinsing out a dish in the kitchen was like tuning into a show partway through the broadcast.

"All quiet?" she asked after he pressed a kiss to her lips and a glass of juice in her hand.

He nodded. "I fed them and turned them out. I'm going to run to Triple Shot and grab cappuccinos, okay?"

"Sounds brilliant. Say hi to Faye for me."

She bundled up and trod downstairs to check Claire — not that she didn't trust Nate; it was just a compulsion at this point. Liv squeezed through the fence rails and Claire swung her head sideways slowly, then huffed out a sigh — tired of carrying around the extra weight; tired of Liv hovering over her. The tiniest translucent bead clung to each teat. *Closer.*

She started stalls, stripping off layers of clothing once she was moving, her body heating up. Every few minutes, she glanced outside. Each time, Chique and Claire were quietly nibbling their hay. Claire couldn't hold out much longer. She was huge, her body so relaxed Liv was sure she could probably reach in and pull that baby out right now. But the age-old wisdom remained true: *the foal determines the day, the mare decides the hour.* At least now her stall would be ready with a nice, fresh bed of straw.

Liv was setting evening feeds and checking the outdoor camera on her phone — Nate had proven himself handy, installing that one in addition to the one inside — when he returned with the cappuccinos. And, of course, Triple Shot's specialty: butter tarts.

"Still warm, even," Liv purred, reaching into the paper bag to remove the golden pastry, not hesitating to bite into the sweet filling. The cappuccino was probably too hot to drink yet, anyway. As always, the tart was perfect. Buttery caramel with a flaky crust. A melt in your mouth breakfast.

"I'm going to get on some horses," Nate said, crumpling up the paper bag and tucking it into the feed sack which served as trash. "You should come. You know she's too civilized to foal outside."

"I'll check her again and decide."

He laughed, heading for the door. "Yeah. You're not coming."

She smiled at his departing form and took her cappuccino upstairs, glancing again at the camera view on her phone — even though she'd done so seconds ago. Nate was right, she should have gone. Something to distract herself and pass the time. But she couldn't bring herself to be even that far away.

She'd brought Geai's box from the house and set aside the photos, lifting out the bundle of letters. Below them were note-books, and she dug deep. Journals? Geai wasn't the type. No surprise to discover they were Francie's. She couldn't help herself; she started reading when she found where Geai entered the picture.

Some of it she knew: Francie had wanted to be a jockey too,

but in the late sixties it was a fight for women to get licensed, let alone ride, so the dream never became reality. Some of it she didn't: they had eloped, because her family wasn't in favour of the relationship.

She was still curled up on the couch when Nate walked in, the last half inch of her cappuccino cold in the paper cup — a crime to waste even a drop, but she'd been absorbed. He tugged off his boots with the jack and hung his coat by the door, running a hand through his hair after jamming his toque in the jacket's pocket. Liv set down the notebook and rose, stretching.

"How'd it go?" she asked.

"It wasn't as bad as the last time I galloped in that indoor arena in January." He grinned, his Florida tan not hiding the pinkness left from the cold.

"That was... the year Chique was born. I remember that winter. It's when we learned the words *'polar vortex.'*" She shuddered just thinking about it.

"So what do people do around here when there's no beach in sight?"

He kissed her, lips lingering just long enough to tantalize, but palm to his chest, she pushed him gently away, toward the bedroom. "Go have a nap." Claire needed all her attention right now.

And when they brought the two mares in at feed time, opaque globules of classic wax tipped each teat. Liv was as sure as she could be. *Tonight.*

———

A voice, a touch, nudged her awake. She blinked, an arm across her brow as she rolled onto her back, Nate silhouetted against the door-shaped illumination.

"Show time," he said.

His voice was quiet, but she flung back the covers, as alert as if he'd thrown cold water on her. She grappled for her jeans and tugged them on, grabbing her sweatshirt and pulling her hair into a messy ponytail before she followed him into the bright living room. Finding her phone on top of the piano, she fired a message to Emilie. Em had said she wanted to be there, if it worked out.

Claire had a good steam going, the vapour rising from her creating a broodmare-shaped mirage. Nate had wrapped her tail, the long hairs contained under a navy bandage. But she was just standing. Liv looked at Nate. A mare could heat up and cool off again. "Are you sure?"

"She sent me a text, all right?"

Liv laughed and shook her head. She wasn't the only one who ran on instinct around here. He'd been watching her for the last two hours; she'd go with his gut. And sure enough, Claire dropped her head and made a slow circle of the stall. On the second circuit, Liv saw the glistening white bubble under the black tail held aloft.

The wait was excruciating — she wanted to dart in and pierce the membrane; make sure that baby was properly aligned in the birth canal. Nate felt it — his hand rested on her arm in a suggestion, not restraint, so instead she held off until the bubble broke from the pressure of the fluid inside it. She didn't have to ask Nate to hold Claire; he did so automatically, though she'd bet Claire would have stood on her own.

Liv nodded after finding the foal's position as it should be and stepped back again. Nate removed Claire's feed tub and water bucket before rejoining her. More waiting, watching, while Claire toured the stall again. The funny alien foal feet were visible now, precariously vulnerable. Claire crumpled to the straw in a sensible spot. Definitely read the book, this one. Nate and Liv positioned themselves behind her, ready.

The mare pushed with a grunt, the foal's legs, exposed mid-shin, both white. Nate cleared the sac so they could each take a one, and when Claire strained, they applied traction... but it felt like the foal wasn't budging.

"It's huge," Nate gasped when their effort yielded an unsatisfactory result. "Only fair the Amazon mare would have a monster of a foal."

"Here," Liv said. "We'll swap. You take this leg." That crossed the foal's legs, effectively making the shoulders narrower.

"Hold up," Nate said. He gave a smooth pull on his leg and grinned. "See that? The knee was jammed. It's a beast. We should be good to go now."

The nose appearing with the next contraction was pink. "It's going to be as flashy as its momma," Liv predicted.

Claire heaved, and they heaved — clearing the shoulders — and the slippery body came free in a whoosh. The foal was already working to right itself before Liv had the placenta pulled back, a shrill nicker escaping. Claire rumbled in response.

"Just rest, mare," Liv murmured.

"You're a rock star, Claire. Every mare should be like you." Nate gently drew the foal far enough out that the hind legs were free, but the umbilical cord remained intact. "Tell Chique how it's done, okay?"

"What is it?" Emilie asked, peeking through the bars. She'd been watching silently, leaving them unaware of her arrival.

"What's the pool say?" Nate quipped.

"There's a pool?" Liv tilted her head. She was never in the know about this stuff.

"Of course there's a pool." Emilie moved to the door, sliding it open. She held up the phone. "Okay, who's doing the honours?"

Nate looked at Liv, shuffling out of the way with a dramatic sweep of his arms. "Has to be you."

Emilie hit record. "And here we are for the gender reveal!"

Liv didn't correct her — Emilie studied enough science to know it was sex, not gender. Vets could predict a foal's sex at specific windows during a mare's gestation, but Liv hadn't wanted to know. Hadn't needed to, from a business perspective, because Claire hadn't been going to the breeding stock sale any more than they would sell this foal at auction. This one wasn't going anywhere. Liv maneuvered herself near the baby's hind end and grasped the top of the stumpy tail to peer underneath.

"We have a filly," she said, glancing up at Emilie — and the camera — as Nate leaned in, an arm going around her shoulders as he pulled her to him and planted a kiss on her cheek. Of course, Em caught that too, and the smile that illuminated her face.

She hadn't cared, not really, but she loved fillies, and now she had a dark bay replica of her big mare... and only eighteen months to wait for her first lessons to begin.

———

"Isn't she gorgeous? Just like her mother. So perfect."

Nate laughed as Liv gushed. *Can't stand to be within ten feet of a human baby, goes ga-ga over a new foal. Sounds about right.* The baby was pretty damn perfect. A really nice first foal.

"I've just lost rank," he said wryly.

Liv grinned at him. "You know not to take it personally."

"You want to put them out?"

She nodded. "Grab Claire?"

She cradled the foal — one arm around her chest, her other hand holding the tail like a rudder. Claire rumbled anxiously, and Nate let her stay close without actually running over Liv as Liv maneuvered her baby into the aisle. With head held high and Liv guiding her, the filly boldly made her way to the small turn-out paddock next to the barn with mincy little steps.

At first, the pair just stood. Every few seconds, Claire dipped her head to touch the filly with her nose, as if to assure herself the baby was really there, and hers. Then the filly began exploring her new world. Cautiously at first, before lifting into a jaunty little canter, lighter than air, like the law of gravity did not yet apply to her.

The filly's rollicking steps grew more confident, propelling her through soft powder that came up to her knees. Claire jogged behind her, the hovering mother hen, murmuring in a throaty voice. When the foal stopped, Claire's neck bowed, reaching forward to touch muzzle to muzzle. Another possessive whicker escaped from the mare, the filly answering with a lyrical whinny.

It never got old. This was the definition of hope, the embodiment of a dream that started the moment the decision was made to breed a mare — part practical, part passion. When they came out like this one, you had the first part right.

"You haven't named her," he said.

"That might take forever. It has to be as perfect as she is."

"Of course it does." He chuckled. Liv was still really just another horse girl at heart.

"You'll probably get fed up with me and call her something horrible." Liv's gaze swept sideways to him.

"First off, I could never call Claire's baby something horrible. But I will threaten to, if it hurries you up. Baby needs a name. Just a barn name, for now."

Registered names could take more time — you could claim a name without penalty up to two years from the foaling date, officially. Geai had nicknamed Chique. Liv had named Claire. *Who will you be, baby girl?*

"Léa," Liv said suddenly, definitively.

"Wow. That was quick." He grinned. "As in Princess?"

"Absolutely. Without the i, though."

"Warrior princess." He nodded. "I like it."

Liv mucked the stall quickly while Nate retrieved a bale of straw for her and cleaned the water bucket and feed tub. Chique grumbled at him in the next stall, unimpressed at being left out of the excursion.

"What do you think, Cheeky?" He let her nuzzle his palm before finding a peppermint in the pocket of his jacket, along with a handful of hay chaff. Some things you could count on being in a barn jacket. "That should be you next year."

Chique got to go out after Claire and Léa came in. While Liv fussed over the new mother and her baby inside, Nate stayed and watched his original claim to fame, wondering if life was going to bless him with a fresh, new one.

With her winter coat, Chique looked black, a strong contrast with the bright white of her surroundings. The mare circled the small paddock with nose trailing the snow as if tracking the unfamiliar scent; that small, strange thing that had replaced her as Claire's companion. Nate had no idea if she sensed anything more than a disturbance in the routine and the ranks. She stopped and pawed, the snow rising in puffs, then flopped down and rolled, flipping easily from side to side. When she launched to her feet, she erupted into a gymnastic routine, bucking and farting her way around like she was a bareback bronc in the Calgary Stampede. He was glad she saved such displays of athleticism for times when he wasn't on her and limited herself to simple one-eighties under saddle, even if a couple of those had been quick enough to unseat him.

Chique propped and spun on the opposite side of the

paddock, then stood stock still, discharging one of her goblin-clearing snorts. Then she jogged over to him, stretching over the top rail like she expected a reward for her performance. He scrubbed her fuzzy neck, pressing his lips to the soft warmth between her nostrils, melting the dusting of snow there.

"I see you've moved on already."

He turned to face Liv as she reached the spot beside him. "She did love me years before the thought ever entered your head."

"Sorry, but true." Chique, an equal-opportunity pepper-mint seeker, pushed her muzzle into Liv's face. Liv kissed it too, but also came up empty on the peppermint demands. "This has been nice."

"Here's the bad news," he said. "We have to go back to Florida."

"Reality calls. Or maybe this is reality, and that's fantasy. Running in a three million dollar race named for a mythological horse?"

"It all seems like one big daydream." He pulled her in, laughing as Chique snuffled at their toques. "I'm glad it's not."

Emilie drove them to the airport. "I will send you photos daily, I promise. With the fancy DSLR you gave me for Christmas."

"That was the whole idea, Em," Liv said.

"And Chip's going to call you tomorrow," Nate said. "He can help you out at least till the end of February, when they open up Woodbine for training again. That will let his friend get settled in as manager. She's going to be busy right off the bat, getting here just before breeding season starts."

"Thanks, Nate," Emilie said.

"Take care of yourself, Em," Liv said, hugging her sister outside the terminal.

Emilie squeezed back. "Tell Jay I'm proud of him, and I'll be cheering."

"You should come for the race." Nate filled the space left when Liv stepped back, crushing Emilie to his chest.

"We'll see," Emilie said.

"You sound like Liv." Nate released her with a crooked grin.

Emilie laughed. "We are related. Have a safe flight, you two. See you when I see you."

CHAPTER TWENTY

SHE COULDN'T HELP but remember, parked here at the five-eighths pole. Except she didn't really remember. She remembered the before — turning in with Nate and Paz beside her, galloping around as they escorted the big filly to temper Claire's enthusiasm — sharp, sharp from the intense training routine. The quickening on the backside — both the pony horse who had been a racehorse himself once upon a time, reliving the thrill, and Claire, her stride switching like a circuit from efficient gallop to that smooth-as-glass stride just shy of racing speed. Then they soared — around the turn, into the stretch, Liv's only job to stay out of the way because Claire needed no encouragement to fly. But the memory faded to black somewhere inside the sixteenth pole, even though it hadn't been till the wire the loose horse had taken them out.

The movie in her head jumped to the next scene. Struggling for consciousness in a nondescript white space. The vague hum of voices. The registering of pain making her beg to be unconscious again. An indeterminate time later resurfacing, this time aware of the intravenous needle in her left hand — no doubt there before — and pain still pinning her to a mattress. Drawing all the clues together to identify a hospital room — and Nate, slumped and rumpled in a chair at her bedside.

"Keep your head up out there, Miller," she said, sounding a little grim as he pulled down his goggles and adjusted the lines.

He grinned and nodded. "Got it, coach."

There was no repeating of history today. No one got in Jay's way, and this work might hush some of the doubters and convince them their Canadian-bred horse deserved to run for three million dollars as much as the other invitees. Everything seemed to be going right. She started making plans for race day.

They'd work the barn the day before — all except for Jay, of course — which would make for an easy morning. Maybe Elliot could feed for them, so the crew could come watch. They'd done enough favours for him, galloping and breezing his horses. It could be like Christmas in January, except with a day at the races instead of a big dinner and awful movies.

Emilie was keeping her promise with regular updates on both Claire's baby girl and farm happenings. She reported when Chique was on her way to Kentucky, and the farm in Lexington called Liv when the mare arrived. Chip was helping at the farm and his friend was ready to start as manager in early February. A woman, this time. Perhaps they'd have more luck with this one. Things back home were under control.

Liv flipped through the latest photos and video of little Léa and Claire. She checked Instagram every morning because Emilie often posted them on the farm account, so there was no sense in her sending them directly to Liv, too. Emilie was getting good with the camera. And at a week and a half old, Léa had lost her newborn gauntness, adding layers of plump muscle under her foal fluff. Her long pins tethered her more securely to the ground, but she still cavorted with grace. She'd been gorgeous the minute she'd come out, but she was more gorgeous now. It was just as well Liv was two thousand miles away. At the farm, she'd get nothing done. She'd always be with that filly.

It wasn't even noon by the time the van pulled into the sandy drive at Payson, but most barns were quiet, done for the day. Elliot and Jo sat on overturned buckets drinking beer on his side of the shed, the pig snuffling along in front of the stalls. Elliot always had beer in the fridge.

Can't Catch Me's whinny rang out, more challenge than welcome, as Liv led Jay off the van. Cam would run the week after the Pegasus in the Holy Bull Stakes, a Kentucky Derby prep. Why not? But it was early days yet on the road to Churchill Downs, and she wasn't making any predictions on Cam earning a spot in the gate in Louisville. The Queen's Plate was still the actual goal.

Jo tied up Jay's haynet as Liv snapped the webbing in place. "How'd it go?"

"Great," Liv answered with an assurance that had never been customary for her, but there was no point hedging when it came to Jay's work this morning. Nate was unloading the equipment from the van, and Elliot had gone to help.

"You two want a beer?" Elliot asked after Nate parked and unhitched the trailer.

Nate shook his head. "Time to get out of here. Beach day."

"Beach Day? Seems a little cold for that."

"You come from Chicago, and you think this is cold?"

"For lying on the beach, yeah." The ocean didn't seem to be Elliot's thing. "So, are you going to ride that colt of mine at Gulfstream this weekend? Jo said she'd put in a good word for me."

"I did not." Jo laughed.

"Call my agent," Nate said. He looked at Liv. "Ready to go?"

"See you both in the morning," Liv said as they climbed

into the Porsche. Once she'd started the engine, she glanced back toward the shed, a furrow in her brow. "Was Jo flirting with Elliot?"

"Kinda looked that way, didn't it?" Nate grinned, likely as much at her obvious expression of concern as the observation.

"That cannot happen. I will not let it," Liv insisted.

"A Jo and Elliot thing? Why not?"

"Because what if she does something crazy and falls in love with the guy? Goes back to Chicago with him? I hear Arlington is really nice. She cannot leave us. She's supposed to be my Number One. That was the deal."

Nate laughed. "Good to know you haven't changed completely. You're getting way ahead of yourself."

"Easy for you to say."

"Just relax. If it comes to that, she'll just have to talk him into coming to Woodbine. Arlington's in trouble anyway, from what I hear."

Liv had heard the same thing. "Maybe we'd better put the Arlington Million on Jay's dance card, so we get to see it before it's gone. Think he'd like the turf?"

"Jay? Jay likes everything."

Oh, the places they would go.

Nate had seen the overnight entries, so he wasn't surprised when he walked in the jock's room at Gulfstream Park the morning of the Pegasus International.

"How'd you get the mount on that horse, Acosta?" Because Acosta was riding favoured Paradise, who would be the toughest to beat. Funny how his desire to punch the guy came right back, with no Liv around to stop him. But he resisted all on his own.

Acosta's dark eyebrows rose before recognition set in and he broke into a wide grin. "Ah, Pretty Boy, so nice to see you again."

"Likewise," he said, when he felt the opposite.

"Don't get too comfortable with my agent. I might want him back."

"I hope things work out for you on the west coast, then." It was Nate's turn to grin before conceding, "He's only doing it as a favour, don't worry."

"For your girlfriend? The lovely princess?" Acosta's eyebrows arched again, a smirk twisting his lips.

"My wife."

"Congratulations."

Nate didn't know if the comment was genuine and didn't really care. "Thanks."

He wished he was back at Woodbine, where he would have been busier instead of stuck here for most of the afternoon. He rode a couple of other races, both longshots. Warmups for the feature; the reason he was here at all.

The Pegasus World Cup.

Jay would not be offended by the gargantuan Pegasus and the fire-breathing dragon-beast in the parking lot. No, Jay would dance with the monstrosity, breathe fire himself, as bright and red as his own coat.

"Earth to Miller."

He turned to smile at Nicole as they walked onto the track for the post parade. "Just remembering that time Chique blew the turn here because she caught sight of that mythical monster in the parking lot."

"I watched that race." Nicole grinned back, her arm loose at her side as she held the long, thin piece of leather looped through Jay's bit. "You really think that's why she did it?"

"I'm just happy she didn't jump the outside rail to get a

closer look." Jay's head, in front of him, nodded in time with his stride while Paz, neck arched, jigged next to him. *Who's the pony here, old man?*

Paradise was the odds-on choice, and the fact Ricky Acosta was on him just made Nate want to win all the more. It wasn't a vengeance thing — neither Paradise nor Acosta was in any way responsible for that accident a year ago. Acosta hadn't even ridden at Santa Anita last winter. But Nate would always harbour resentment for the guy, after everything that had happened on BlueGrass Day at Keeneland two years ago: the aggressive riding that had bounced Chique around in one race, and taken Wampum down in the next.

This wasn't about the money, either. It was about proving they belonged on the world stage with the best. That a good horse could come out of a modest stable and compete in the upper echelon. And a three million dollar race attracted the top runners, especially now that the entry requirements had changed.

"Good luck, Nate. Go Canada!" Nicole said as she passed him off to the starter's assistant.

He nodded down at the Canadian flag on his boot. That, too.

The race was for four-year-olds and up, and they all behaved like the seasoned athletes they were. No trouble-makers in here. It made for a quick break, the starter sending them away with the bell ringing in their ears, the roar of the excited crowd greeting them with a wave of sound. Paradise shot away, but Nate didn't rush Jay, though he couldn't afford to let him fall as far back as he had in the Valedictory, with these horses. But he was happy here, out of trouble, where they could see everyone in front of them. It was almost as if they were both unconsciously hovering at the back of the pack, so they had a clear view of impending disaster. More likely it was conscious for Jay, a horse always reading the surrounding environment. Not that they could play it safe, but there was no point taking unnecessary risks.

Wow. He'd better stop thinking and start riding, or else retire and spend his days on the couch.

Paradise started his move on the final turn, stealthily sliding through horses; first outside, then cutting inside to creep up the rail. Each efficient stride wore down Get Ready For It's lead. Acosta rode confidently but not actively, still waiting to unleash the final assault, so much more left in his horse. And now second choice Arrow of Air came hard on the outside, swallowing up the distance so those three were splayed like a troika.

Time to go, big horse.

The thought was all the motivation Jay needed, the big chestnut leaping forward as he changed leads in the straight and began the chase. Get Ready For It faltered in the tight quarters between Paradise and Arrow of Air, the pressure too much. Nate adjusted Jay's path so they were clear, but they had some serious running to do if they wanted a say in the result, because they were at least four wide now.

Arrow of Air abruptly closed the gap left by Get Ready For It, then Get Ready For It was a jumble of flying legs, diving as he scrambled, tossing his rider over his neck. His head flew up as he tried to get his limbs under him — and maybe avoid the jock, suspended precariously off the side. Time seemed to stand still for a split second before gravity won, sending the rider toppling to the track.

Nate's reflexes kicked in, and he looped Jay wider still to avoid the fallen rider. Jay stumbled with the overcorrection — enough to give Nate a heart-stopping jolt without throwing him around too much. He caught a glimpse of the jock rolling slowly to his knees and hoped that was a good sign and not adrenaline fueling a fight response. No time to worry about that right now, because in the drama they'd lost precious ground.

Get Ready For It ran riderless, lines flapping. They had to get past him, fast. He might look like he was playing along for now, running with the herd to maintain his position in third all on his own, but a loose horse was a loose horse — and Jay needed to be out of the way before the outrider could make any attempt to catch him.

Jay's ear flicked, assessing, and he tried to drop closer to Get Ready For it... because that would be a good idea? Nate switched his stick and hit him left-handed, sending his energy forward to convince his chestnut that horse was not the one to be concerned with. *It's a straight line from here to the wire, buddy* — even if they were in the middle of the track now. It was kind of like dancing alone out here. He didn't expect Get Ready For It to dig in, come on again, line up Jay. But the horse did.

Are you kidding me?

Well, there was no rule against keeping a riderless horse at bay with your whip, was there? He intentionally made the way he waved his stick alongside Jay a little sloppy — more about warding off Get Ready For It's desire to keep Jay company than propelling his own horse. Jay pinned his ears to help the effort, driving now, while Paradise and Arrow of Air were doing battle where battles should take place, close to the rail.

There was an upside to this — it was like having an invisibility cloak out here. Because those two were so locked onto each other, Jay barely registered as competition. He was far enough away for them not to feel him. *The element of surprise.* Arrow of Air was losing the fight, Paradise on top by a half now... then a length. But Jay was in beast mode, driven by Get Ready For It's brief challenge and Nate's insistence there was a job to do here, a big one. He couldn't think about how close they were, because it was impossible to tell; all he could do was ride the hair off Jay's sun-drenched copper hide, and let the photo figure it out.

Their momentum hurtled them past Paradise after the wire, Jay leaving him far behind, galloping out. Nate finally slowed him on the backstretch, turning him in to stand facing the infield for a breath before wheeling him around to return to the grandstand.

They were leading Paradise to the winner's circle when he and Jay got there. *Damn it all.* One more jump and they would have had him.

Michel, next to Liv, snapped the shank to Jay's bit and planted a kiss between his flaring nostrils. The groom looked as proud as if Jay had won that race; justifiably so. Nate only wished he had. The big horse had run his guts out, avoiding disaster along the way. *One. More. Jump.*

"Holy hell, Miller!" Liv's comment came out in a gasp, like she'd been holding her breath from the quarter pole until this moment.

"Just another day with Paradise." Nate grinned.

"So close. So amazing," Michel said, rubbing Jay's forehead, still in awe.

Liv stepped in to squeeze a sponge of cold water between the horse's ears, and Nate reached for it, dragging it down Jay's neck before he tossed his whip to his valet and hopped off.

"Where'd that horse finish?" Nate asked. Unofficially, of course. Get Ready For It was being held by an outrider while the groom and valet took the tack off. He looked very proud of himself.

"Fourth," Liv said.

But they didn't give cheques to horses who parted company with their riders before the wire. Too bad.

"And preliminary word on Marty is he's fine," she added, bringing him up to date on the fallen rider.

That was the best news of all.

"See you at the test barn," she said as he walked away to weigh in.

Marty was indeed fine, at least the rider's version of it.

"Yeah, I can't feel my foot exactly, but it's not broken, I swear," he said as Nate watched the replay with him. Hopefully, there was some of that magical kinesiology tape Emilie had around.

"You should've nominated that horse for Dubai."

It was Acosta speaking. Nate twisted away from the monitor, just his shoulders, and eyed the guy. It didn't matter that it wasn't Nate's job to nominate horses for stakes. Any comment that acknowledged a Triple Stripe horse was worthy of such consideration — the world's richest horse race, the Dubai World Cup — was huge, coming from an arch rival. It showed respect he didn't expect from someone like Ricky Acosta.

Nate liked to dream big, but he'd never dreamed that big. They hadn't even been to a Breeders' Cup yet. "He ran a big race," was all he said in response.

He showered and changed quickly, shouldering on his jacket as he slipped out the door, bag slung over his shoulder. Liv was at the test barn, supervising Michel giving the big chestnut a bath, while the hotwalker, Marc, held him.

"How is he?" Nate asked.

"Mostly just mad." Liv smiled.

Nate laughed. Jay wasn't like Chique, who told you exactly how she was feeling. Jay had always been more polite. But the chestnut was simmering. "Me too."

"Acosta still have all his teeth?"

"Me too." He grinned to prove it. "And he made an interesting comment."

"Oh?"

"He said we should have nominated Jay for Dubai."

"How would he know if we hadn't?"

"Have we?"

That was quite a look, a little smug, a little sultry. He liked it and looked forward to taking it home.

"Bold," he said quietly, into her ear. "I've apparently underestimated you yet again."

"Never do that, Miller."

A refrain of low rumbles welcomed Jay back to Payson as Michel settled the chestnut into his stall. The groom checked his bandages and felt his neck to be sure the horse was still cool, then strung up the haynet and prepared his feed. Jo had left the tub hanging on the stall door. Michel poured in hot water, mixed it up, and let it soak a few minutes before snapping it in place in the corner. The racket as Jay dove into his dinner was a good sign the race hadn't taken too much out of him.

"We can stick around, Michel," Liv said. He and Sue, now seven months pregnant, would be tired after such a long day. "Thanks."

Michel nodded, taking one last look at his charge before he left. "See you in the morning."

Liv and Nate checked water — habit around horses when killing time, though the nightwatch person must've topped them up not long ago. The evening was dark and still, no sound but that of horses rustling as they munched forage and Jay working on his tub. All of it was so far removed from the bustle and crowds at Gulfstream. And no matter how nice their condo on the beach was, Liv would always love this best. Nate didn't seem in a hurry to leave either.

"Did you tell Michel about Dubai?" she asked. She'd driven her car back with Sue as her passenger, following Nate, Michel, and Marc in the van.

He shook his head, humour playing on his lips. "That's the trainer's job."

"It's not a sure thing. I think they have to invite us, officially."

"Also the trainer's job, to know stuff like that, isn't it?"

"Probably. So we'll just have to hope they do."

"You're uncharacteristically nonchalant tonight."

"Are you complaining?"

"No. I like it. Whatever you've done with your life to bring it about... it's working for you."

She matched his grin, sidling closer to him. "You're not suggesting you have anything to do with that, are you?"

"I could hardly take credit."

"Right."

Liv wandered down the shed one last time, contenting herself that everyone was happy. Nate was coming out of Jay's stall when made it back to the chestnut's stal.

"Still fine?" she asked.

"Yep. Ready to go home?"

There was that word again. Home. Their home away from home. "I'll just lock the tack room."

She closed the door and clicked the padlock shut, but stopped before turning off the barn aisle lights, glimpsing a car. Jo's car. Jo had offered to be the one who stayed back at Payson to feed so the rest of the crew could go for the big race, but...

Nate waited behind her. "What's up?"

"Is Elliot still living in his tack room?"

"As far as I know. Why?" Nate responded, coming closer. Then he laughed, quietly. "Ah. He has a guest, by the looks of it."

"It's not funny."

He put an arm around her shoulders and steered her away. "I agree. You'd think they'd go to Jo's. That'd be classier."

Liv swatted him and hissed, "If she's going to fall for a guy and abandon us, it shouldn't be for someone who lives in a tack room."

"Okay, Mom. But I'd put money on it just being sex. People do that, you know." His arm dropped from her shoulders to her waist, pulling her back to his side.

She pushed him away, but it was half-hearted, and he caught her again.

"Don't forget, you're the one who insisted she have a life," he said.

"It appears I've created a monster."

"Oh, please."

When they reached the Porsche, she tugged the lapels of his jacket, catching his lips as he pressed her against the passenger door.

"Home, Miller."

"I think you should drive."

She slid her hands down to his pockets to find the keys. He was humming; she felt the vibration of it. She shook her head, grinning as she recognized the tune. "Hey Pretty," of course. *Wanna take a ride with me?*

"Let's go."

CHAPTER TWENTY-ONE

TICK... tick... tick...

The long, slender hand seemed unusually loud as it marked each second. Who had decided to call it a hand when it didn't look like a hand at all? Liv flipped through the pages of the biography resting under her fingertips, convincing herself she was reading, when she wasn't registering a single word. For the fifth time since the poorly named indicator had completed a circuit of the clock face, she checked email on her phone. Nothing. She shoved it across the counter and dropped her head to her folded arms, willing herself not to watch the time. Squeezed her eyes closed. Maybe she would fall asleep, and when she woke up, it would be there.

Even when the door clicked open, followed by shuffling and the soft pad of bare feet, she resolutely kept her head pinned to her crossed arms. One of them was going numb.

"Bad news?" Nate asked.

Plastic shopping bags rustled, a slight poof of air tickling the tiny hairs on her skin. She pushed her head up, grimacing at the arm that remained attached to the granite like it was made of lead. Totally numb. She had to physically drag it into her lap with her other one.

Nate laughed at her. "Hello, gorgeous."

She squinted back, brushing the hair out of her eyes with the hand that still had feeling and waited for her head to clear. Nate reached across the counter, closing fingers around the front of her t-shirt, and leaned in, the play of his lips on hers helping chase away the fuzziness. Then her eyes flew open, and she looked at the clock. It still went *tick... tick... tick.*

"Were you actually sleeping like that? The bed too far, or something?"

"Pass me my phone." She tried to lift her left arm. "Ouch."

"You okay?" He raised an eyebrow at her, his expression a combination of concern and amusement.

"My arm was asleep. It's just waking up." The rest of her was alert now, sensation returning to the uncooperative appendage in painful sparks. "Phone. Please."

He set it in front of her and started putting away the groceries.

Twenty minutes, she'd been asleep. Her sluggish limb finally responded to her wishes. She unlocked the phone, the email app still open, and waited to see if any new mail downloaded.

And there it was, announced with a bold *ping!* She took a breath so deep and dramatic it attracted Nate's attention again. Her finger hovered over the sender's name for two hard thumps of her heart before she tapped the screen. *Dubai Racing Club.* She quickly scanned the letter — *blah blah blah* — to get to the important part. Read it twice, then sighed, flopping her head on her arms again.

"You going to tell me what all the angst is about?"

She sat up, smiling, then spun the phone to face him, watching him do exactly as she'd done.

"How can you just sit there?" he burst out, racing around the counter and sweeping her to her feet.

He kissed her so hard it left her gasping with laughter. Then he twirled her around. "We are going, right?"

"Well, I have to talk it over with Jo..."

"A formality."

"Is it? It's insane."

"Of course it is. But you've got me on this crazy ride with you. And you thought enough of him to nominate him all by yourself. For the Dubai World Cup. So proud."

She rolled her eyes. Ever the smartass.

Handicappers around the globe would begin making their predictions and setting odds, but Liv didn't care where Jay fit into their analysis. There were still several steps between this one and Just Jay standing in the starting gate at Meydan. They couldn't skip any of them, but with the invitation began the most ambitious ride of her life, and she wasn't even the one on the horse.

The name was like a drum beating in time with the cadence of Jay's stride. *Dubai, Dubai, Dubai.* Nate had to focus on it or his head started to spin. Would Liv go through with it? Really? This was the woman who'd refused to take Chique to California for the Breeders' Cup. Would she really fly a horse halfway around the world? All he could do was wait and see. *Welcome to horse racing, Miller.*

Jay felt bigger, like he'd grown in stature and power at the mere news of the invitation. His hooves skimmed Payson's sandy surface, defying its deepness. Instead of tiring, he got stronger with every stride. *Dubai, Dubai, Dubai.*

Liv joined him shortly after he pulled up and turned in on

the backstretch, standing Can't Catch Me parallel but a good six feet away. It was a safety precaution, because the three-year-old colt thought he was even more *all that* after a good second in the Holy Bull Stakes. It was like he knew his performance was a stepping stone to Kentucky on the first Saturday in May. Jay blatantly ignored him. The older chestnut's head turned casually to gaze down the backstretch, as if he was admiring the way the rising sun painted the track a bright raw sienna. Or else wishing he could go around again.

Liv didn't speak, merely glancing at Nate before opening her left line to direct Cam toward the off-gap. Cam flung his head in an arc, the martingale rings making a thunk of leather against leather; a clink of snap against ring. Liv kept her stick angled out, her elbow cocked; a reminder to behave in case the bratty colt made a move for Jay. Nate grinned, holding the older horse on the knot. Just like the old days, only swapped — back when Liv had been on the angelic Claire while he dealt with Chique's non-stop antics.

Chique, who would be bred soon. He wondered what the cheeky mare would think of that.

Michel waited beside two buckets in the stretch of coarse grass between barns, his arms crossed, halter and shank looped over his shoulder. He remained silent as he stepped forward, unbuckling the noseband and throatlatch and unclipping the martingale snap.

"He's training like a million bucks," Nate said as his boots hit the ground. "Or should I say, twelve million?" That was the total money on the line for the big race in Dubai.

Michel still didn't respond. Nate unbuckled the girth and dragged the tack off Jay's damp back, cradling it in his arms. Still not a word. He eyeballed the groom as he slid the bridle and martingale off in one smooth handful. When he returned from depositing the tack on the rail, Michel had already started

Jay's bath, holding the shank in one hand as he doused Jay's head. Jay likely would have stood there on his own had Michel just let go, ground-tied like a cow pony.

Nate grabbed the shank and sang, "If I Had A Million Dollars." Even that didn't get a smile out of the groom. "I miss smartass Michel. Grown-up Michel is boring."

Michel glowered as he drew the sponge down Jay's full tail. "Just because getting married didn't make you any more mature doesn't mean the rest of us want to be like that."

Nate laughed. "Seriously, what's up your butt this morning? You rub what might be the nicest horse in the whole damn world."

"I don't get to go with him on the big fancy trip, though, do I?" He carried the bucket around to start the other side. "Sue's due date is literally the same day as the race."

"Oh. That sucks." Nat had been so psyched about the prospect of the trip he'd forgotten how close the arrival of Sue's baby was. "Sorry, buddy. But what you're doing is bigger than the Dubai World Cup, continuing the human race and all. And if it's any consolation, you can drive the Porsche while I'm gone."

"We have to go back to Canada for the birth," Michel said glumly.

"Oh. Are there incentives for Canadian-bred humans?" Apparently he couldn't stop with the smart-assed comments.

Michel scowled. "Like universal health care?"

"Right." Nate rubbed a glob of dirt out of the corner of Jay's eye. "You drove the Porsche down here; it'd be handy if you took it back for me. And if Sue goes into labour along the way, you'll be ready to make a dash for the border."

He really wasn't surprised Michel didn't appreciate his humour. The question that flitted into his mind, unwelcome, remained unasked. *Would you trade?* A family, for the freedom to go across the world with a horse for the planet's richest race? His eyes fell on Liv, holding Cam for Jo. There was really no question. It would be ridiculous to give up this flexibility. And at this exact moment, he would not.

"We need to hit the road," Nate said, passing Jay to Marc to walk once Michel finished his bath. "The rest of you can take it from here. You get to play Dad, Mike." He laughed and was lucky Michel didn't flick the dredges in the rinse bucket at him.

One of Elliot's horses was running this afternoon. The gelding was already at Gulfstream — Elliot had sent him the day before, because it was that nervous gelding Marie had come off of when she'd broken her hand. Jo was running the horse for him, which left Michel in charge of the shed as next-in-command. Nate didn't think the rest of the crew would give him any trouble.

It felt good to bring home a winner that wasn't a Triple Stripe horse, even if it was for Elliot, on a horse he'd spent a decent amount of time on at Payson. Kenny had begrudgingly agreed to Nate's demands — he would ride, but he wasn't running around like a crazy person, like Liv had done past winters. Even with Kenny O'Connell managing his book, he was only so popular down here anyway, so they settled on a middle ground.

Elliot insisted on taking them out for dinner after the races. Liv, who'd come along, was sure to think that was cute. A double-date with Elliot and Jo. Nate showered and met them outside the jock's room. Kenny was there, chatting with Liv. Next to him was a slim, dark-haired woman in heels that gave her two inches on Liv, who never wore anything but flats.

Nate didn't recognize her at first glance, and grinned as the realization swept over him. "Luna Russo."

Elbow to elbow with Kenny O'Connell, no less. What a small, small world, though it wasn't unusual to see someone from Woodbine here. Luna might be galloping for somebody, or just visiting. She wore a colourful tank top and black capris that skimmed a figure that was fit, if not riding weight. Her style was a definite contrast to Liv's sleeveless sheath — the dress matched the steely blue of her eyes. She was trying to keep from grinding her teeth, he was sure. If the tightness of her jawline was any indication, she wasn't having success.

"You know each other?" Nate asked Kenny, slipping his hand into Liv's and squeezing it. He tried not to flinch when she crunched his fingers in return.

"Not really," Kenny said with his Irish lilt and broad smile. "We figured out we have friends in common and were just getting acquainted."

Friends. Yeah. Nate was certain that's what Liv was thinking.

"Ready to go?" Elliot asked, oblivious, an arm comfortably around Jo's shoulders. He jutted his chin at Kenny and Luna, adding, "Come along. My horse won and got claimed. I'm buying."

Clearly, Elliot wasn't upset about losing the horse. Nate wouldn't miss galloping him, that was for sure. Liv was bristling when she climbed into the Porsche.

"You up for this?" Nate asked as he turned the key in the ignition.

She pushed both hands in the air, palms up, and shrugged. "Why not."

They both turned down wine at the restaurant — Nate because of the prospect of the hour and a half trip to the condo, though if Liv wasn't drinking, he had no doubt she'd be happy to take him home. She wasn't letting her guard down tonight, staying mostly silent as the rest of them talked. Not even the topic of their lofty aspirations with Just Jay dragged her out from behind her barrier. That was fine.

"I'm proud of you two kids," Kenny said. "I'm just sorry I can't take credit for any of it."

Liv cracked a smile at that. "Won't keep you from trying though, will it?"

"You are going, right?" Kenny asked.

Liv played coy and didn't confirm or deny. Nate felt like echoing the agent. *We are, right?*

They said their goodbyes when the others started contemplating coffee and dessert. Jo had the next day off and Nate wasn't about to ask what her plans were, because it seemed self-explanatory at the moment.

Luna said, "Good luck in Dubai." Apparently, she thought the decision was a no-brainer.

"Thanks, Luna." Liv's smile was reserved. "Thanks for dinner, Elliot."

"Any time. You're both cheap dates."

"That wasn't so bad, was it?" Nate asked as they walked to the Porsche.

"Good move, leaving before we had to find out if anything would transpire between Kenny and Luna. The thought of that isn't worth any part of my imagination."

He opened the passenger door for her, but caught her waist before she folded herself in. "You're so right. There are much, much better ways to use that." For now, he just kissed her and left her to ponder them.

Her lips twisted upward briefly before she pressed them back together. "Do you think taking a horse to Dubai makes me worthy of Luna's respect?"

"Do you still think you should care?"

"You're right. I shouldn't." Once he was behind the wheel, she added, "You won't talk me out of being worried about Jo and Elliot, though."

"You can have that one, for now."

"Very benevolent of you."

"Want to talk about it?"

Liv kicked off her shoes and tucked a bare foot under her thigh. She snapped the seatbelt in place. "No. Yes. Damn it. Jo and Elliot look so cosy. I know it's selfish to want her to stay with us. I do want her to be happy."

"You realize you're being ridiculous, right? You're talking like it's a done deal."

"And what about Sue and Michel? When the kid comes? What if Michel has to get a real job?"

"He's not going anywhere. Even if he can't go to Dubai with the horse, he's not giving up Jay. How many grooms get to rub a horse like that? We just have to win the race so everyone stays."

Going to Dubai wasn't supposed to be about money. It was about honour, teamwork, and adventure. But what was the point in going if you didn't think you deserved a piece of the prize?

The only thing that would stop Liv from taking Just Jay to Dubai was Jay himself. As long as the horse stayed healthy and sharp, they were going. What's crazier than going to Dubai? Not going to Dubai. And Jo was fully on board.

"This is going to be your honeymoon," Jo said.

"Closest thing we might get to it, that's for sure," Nate agreed with his trademark grin.

"An all expenses paid trip to Dubai with one horse? That certainly qualifies as a vacation," Liv said. Not that this winter in Florida had seemed much like work at all, especially compared to her first one, bouncing from place to place, working the horses Kenny lined up for her as she tried to build her career as an apprentice. The three of them here made it work, and work well. Imagine that — a racetrack life without the constant threat of burnout.

And now, this, though she felt guilty. "Are you sure you're going to be okay?" she asked Jo. "It seems a little unfair, two of us leaving."

"We've had more than enough help all winter. Now it'll just be like a normal barn. And one less horse."

"Until Sue and Michel go home," Nate interjected.

"So maybe we should send a few horses back early." Jo shrugged. "But Nicole is good. She'll do extra. Cory too. We're still going back to Woodbine sooner than we usually would, so she'll have time to prep for the season. And you guys will be back by then. It'll all work out."

"Look at you, all mellow and shit." Nate nudged her with a fist to her bicep.

"Roger would be proud of us, working together so well," Jo said as she smiled back.

"Was he worried we wouldn't?" Liv asked. Jo spoke with him more than she did.

"I think he's just been worried, period."

For good reason. Hélène wasn't even halfway through her chemotherapy, with all of them hoping — some of them praying — it was successful, against the odds. Long-term survival rates were less than encouraging. The numbers were horribly disconcerting, like thirty-five percent, with the likelihood of the disease returning high. It refreshed the goal here, with the three of them; all they could do was ensure Roger didn't have to worry about this one thing they could control.

"It still changes everything though, doesn't it?" Liv said.

"What do you mean?" Jo asked.

"Well... do you think he'll come back?"

She and Jo exchanged a look. The question had been on

her mind for a while now. Things had been going smoothly this winter. Roger and Hélène had already been through so much — and it was far from over. What if he retired? What if she didn't get to go back to riding? It was fine, right now — a horse like Just Jay made up for just about anything — but what about Claire's new foal, Léa? Sure, it was a way in the future, but...

Nate watched her, his gaze a reminder. *Two years away, Liv. Take a breath. Stay here, in this moment.* She couldn't deny there were times she wished their positions were reversed; that she was going to ride in Dubai, and he was the trainer. He could train just as well as she could. Better, probably, because he was more adept with humans.

But right now, the job was hers. And there were worse positions than being responsible for getting a horse ready for the Dubai World Cup. Sure, there was pressure. Stress. But also opportunity. Pride. Had there ever even been a Canadian horse in the race? Just going was a huge honour. Anything else was a bonus.

"So," Nate brought her back to that task. "How are we getting him there? And I don't mean by plane."

The time span between the Pegasus and the Dubai race wasn't ideal, but factor in a fourteen-hour flight across eight time zones, and Jay would need to acclimatize. Liv had to make a choice: find a race — any race — at the end of February, or just train into it. It would be easier on home turf. She could do something like she'd done with Chique going into the Plate, when she'd had nearly three months between races. But it was easier still to race a horse fit. Nothing quite compared to those conditions. She could work Jay against Cam — the three-year-old was the only one in the barn who might come close to having the kind of talent Jay had — but Cam was now training toward the Fountain of Youth Stakes, and all his energy, as abundant as it seemed, needed to be channeled into that effort. They'd work with what they had with Jay: an honest, malleable horse, and a jock with a clock in his head.

Liv crossed her arms, zeroing in on said jock. "What would you do?"

Nate smiled. "Leave it with me."

An email notification lit up her phone, and she swiped the screen, hoping it was news from the breeding farm in Lexington. Chique's date with Megalodon was that morning. When Liv opened the message, it was so long she was surprised they hadn't phoned.

"Uh-oh," she said, but couldn't help chuckling as she read.

"What?" Nate asked, looking perplexed by her reaction.

"Well... it should surprise no one that covering Chique wasn't exactly straightforward. She wasn't bad, per se, but she wouldn't stand for the stallion." *You want me to let him do what?* "Apparently Megalodon is a shy breeder. So she hopped away a few steps each time he tried mounting her. Poor guy. That won't help his confidence." She could imagine the mare, restrained to keep the stallion safe from being kicked, but somehow still finding a way to evade the intended act.

"That's my cheeky little bitch, playing hard to get." Nate laughed. "Did they get her bred, or do I have to go have a talk with her?"

"They got her. Now in two weeks we'll see if she caught."

Three horses tacked up and waiting as the sun breached the horizon. Time to do this.

"Are you ready? We're gonna work like the big barns do." Nate grinned. All he was missing was a whiteboard, but Jo wouldn't have been happy if he'd messed up the one with the training schedule on it. The plan wasn't really that complicated, anyway. He explained it to Liv and Cory.

"Go ahead and put their bridles on," Jo said, lifting one off the door of Elemental's stall and nodding at Sue and Michel.

"You should get on the pony, Jo," Nate said, though he'd never seen her on Paz.

Jo shook her head. "I'm one of those people who's better off on the ground. Nicole can go out with you."

"Did you ever ride?" Cory asked.

"A bit, as a kid. That's when I figured it out," Jo said with a wry smile.

It was hard to believe there were people into horses who didn't ride, but loved them enough to still make a career of them. Of course, if he ever lost his ability to be on their backs, he'd be one of them. In the meantime, it was still his favourite place. Michel legged him up on Jay.

"You coming out to watch?" he asked the groom.

"Hell yeah," Michel said, walking a turn with them. "We all are."

Once the troops were outside, Liv and Elemental fell into step next to Nate on Jay. In front of them, Nicole, astride Paz, chatted with Cory, who was on an older horse named Excursion. He'd been a Plate hopeful Nate's first year working at Woodbine and had levelled off into a useful runner who consistently picked up cheques in allowance company — though the coveted "black type" gained by top-three finishers in stakes races had eluded him. Now he'd reached a crossroads in his career that many older horses faced. He either needed to be dropped to the claiming ranks to remain competitive, or find a new career.

"Want to trade?" Liv asked, her eyes running over Jay rather than Nate. Analyzing. Appraising. Filing away a *before* picture in her brain.

Nate raised an eyebrow. "Horses? No way."

"Jobs?"

He laughed. "No way there either, trainer. I'm just the choreographer."

He was way more excited about this than he should be. It was probably the end goal, not the opportunity to exercise some creativity in the training process. The drumbeat started up in the back of his mind. *Dubai, Dubai, Dubai.*

A mist hung over the sandy track, the cool night warming into day. Jo gave the clockers a heads up as the four riders filed their charges through the on-gap. Cory allowed Liv to go ahead, giving Elemental a head start as they backed up. Liv pulled down her goggles like she was activating the persona — race rider — setting aside her trainer alter ego.

As they jogged the wrong way along the outside rail, Cory settled Excursion next to Jay. Liv was heading off to gallop the right way around the oval, counter-clockwise, when they stopped to turn in.

"I'll hang out back here in case someone needs rescuing," Nicole said. Nate guessed she was scouting out the best vantage point from which to watch it all unfold.

Jay could sense it. He was tougher to keep next to Excursion than he would be on a gallop day; neck bowed, his neat mane leaping like a sailfish's dorsal fin. Today might have been the day to have Nicole and Paz break them off, but it was too late for that.

Liv was far enough ahead with Elemental Nate had lost track of her in the traffic of gallopers. They'd tried to gauge where exactly she needed to be when, but ultimately they'd just have to see if it all played out like it did in his head. On the clubhouse turn, Nate and Cory let their horses speed up a couple of ticks, then on the backstretch, dropped to the rail.

Stride for stride they travelled, Nate dictating the pace.

Excursion had no problem with this part. He might not be as fast as he used to be, but he loved to run. Breezing was still fun. But when the crunch came, Excursion was no match for Jay. Even under Nate's hold, Jay was inching ahead as he swapped leads leaving the backstretch. Cory chirped at Excursion to keep him from falling behind and managed to stay next to Jay until midway around the turn. Jay caught sight of Elemental before Nate did, Liv sending the four-year-old at the quarter pole ahead of them.

Once Jay locked in on the new challenge, Excursion disappeared from Nate's peripheral vision as Jay set to work catching Elemental. Jay's ears swept forward as he took up the chase, Nate's hands and voice feeding his drive. The drumbeat of hoofbeats — and that name inside Nate's head — came faster and faster as they closed in on their target.

Liv poised like a statue on her colt's back. She didn't look behind, but Nate knew she knew he was there, feeling Jay's energy. Before Jay reached Elemental, she picked him up with a sharp series of clucks and a sweep of her arms. Elemental pinned his ears, Jay's head now at his hip. He dug in, not about to let Jay blow by. Eli was making Jay work, which was the entire idea.

A couple of jumps, and Jay was next to Elemental. Liv kept after the colt so he stuck with Jay — and Jay responded all on his own, stretching his stride with each thrust of his neck. He pushed his nose in front, then hit the wire half a head up as they streaked past.

Nate freed a hand from the lines to slap Jay on the neck. He glanced at Liv, her smile enough of a reaction for him to know she was happy with that.

"That was good," he called over.

"I'm sure it was better from where you were sitting." She grinned back.

Coming into the backstretch again, they pulled up where Nicole and Paz waited, bathed in sunlight against the backdrop of the tall green hedge. The scene robbed Nate of some of his exuberance because, how many times had it been Roger on that pony? This race, this trip, the culmination of this whole winter... if only it all could have ensured Hélène's future wellness too, like collecting some kind of health points in a video game that they could pass along to her.

When they finished for the morning, Jo pulled out her phone. She'd been up in the clocker's stand to video the work, and Nate and Liv leaned in on either side to review it with her.

"Damn, he looks incredible," Nate said.

"Send it to Rog," Liv suggested.

Not that she felt she needed his approval; she was keeping him in the loop, letting him know he wasn't forgotten... and hoping things worked out that he'd come back and assume the helm. She didn't need to travel to Dubai to prove herself, in Nate's eyes. She didn't need to prove herself at all. He wouldn't fault her for always aiming higher, as long as she understood neither success nor failure defined her self-worth.

Roger's response came a few moments later. *Told you that horse would take you places.*

The drumming started again in Nate's head. *Dubai, Dubai, Dubai.*

Can't Catch Me looked as if he was getting ready to take a chunk out of Paz, his head tilted so Nate could just see the glint in his eye, the quiver of his lips. No one was higher on Cam than Cam himself. Nicole took a snugger hold to prevent the audacious colt from following through.

"Better stay with me." Nate swiped his eyes sideways at

Nicole as horses started to break from the post parade for the warmups.

"Today's a good day to come to your senses, Nate." Nicole grinned, then sobered. "What are we going to do with him when you and Liv go to Dubai?"

This week, leading up to the Fountain of Youth Stakes, Liv had finally decided she was done galloping Cam. *You get on him,* she'd hissed with shaking arms. It had become Nate's job to keep the brute from running off every morning as he prepped for the race that would determine if they continued on the Kentucky Derby trail.

"Flip a coin?" he suggested.

"I can't hold him. He's way too tough for me. Do you think Cory can? We might have to pony him, or you'd better start scouting out freelancers."

"We're going to have to figure that out." It could be a legitimate problem if they didn't find someone to get on the colt when they were away. Could they talk Chip into coming down? "Maybe swim him in the ocean?"

Nicole choked on a laugh. "I'd like to see that."

By the time they got to the gate, Cam seemed just annoyed. This could be even more interesting than usual. The colt loaded remarkably well — considering the Gulfstream gate crew didn't know him — but once he was in, he was never really still. Nate was actually happier he was on Cam's back instead of hanging onto the frame, holding the colt's head. At least until the doors opened. Cam shot out with a fierceness that was mildly terrifying. Nate asked him to take back, and the colt totally blew him off and kept going.

Fighting wasn't going to get either of them anywhere, but hotfooting it into the clubhouse turn was a death sentence. This was not how this colt ran. He was not a speed horse, but he was determined to go with the speed today. The race was already feeling like a write-off.

On the backstretch, the speed levelled off, and so did Cam. Nate tried to convince him to come off the pace a little — *save it for the stretch, buddy* — but Cam didn't want to give up any ground, keeping a nostril at the pacesetter's cheek. Guess they were going to see how much depth he had. They were playing with the big kids today, sussing out his worthiness to compete among them.

Two horses surged on the outside as they rounded the turn for home. The frontrunner had dropped even with Cam and Nate thought for a beat Cam was fading with him until he swapped leads and decided to take on the new rivals down the lane.

They had the rail now, the shortest trip home, but the challengers loomed large. Cam held his own to the eighth pole. It was harder to get to the sixteenth pole; the elasticity leaving his tendons and ligaments as he tired. The big colt wanted to stick, but he was paying for his premature effort earlier in the race. Nate carried him with a hand ride through the wire, the colt's nose trailing the runner-up's floating tail. They were beaten maybe a length and a half.

"Well, that took some oomph out of him," Nate said as Michel met them in front of the grandstand, Cam blowing as he sucked in the humid air. His chestnut coat was dark

Liv was at the groom's side, running her eyes over the colt as Nate dismounted; joining him to walk to the scales as Michel led Cam away.

"We'll see how he cools out," she said. "He ran great, considering he totally sabotaged himself. He's got a lot to learn if he wants to be worthy of the Kentucky Derby."

Just like Liv wouldn't take Jay to Dubai only because it would be a cool trip, she wouldn't take Cam to Louisville for a chance to run in the Derby, even if he managed to collect enough points to earn a spot in the gate. He had to belong there; have a shot at the money.

As it turned out, the decision was made for them. When the poultice came off the next morning, there was mild filling on the inside of his left fore, just below his knee. He wasn't lame, but he flinched when Liv palpated the check ligament.

"See what happens when you don't listen?" she said, standing up and running a hand down Cam's neck. The colt not trying to bite Michel, who held him, was proof the race had tired Cam out. "We'll get an ultrasound to see just what he's done to himself. Sorry Miller, no Derby this year. Dubai will have to do."

CHAPTER TWENTY-TWO

THE PLANE TAXIED from the runway to the terminal, reaching a slow and steady halt. It didn't pull up to a gate, instead staying a distance from the building. She caught glimpses of workers in fluorescent vests scurrying about, chocking wheels, positioning a staircase, and carrying out whatever other important duties they had before the flight attendants freed the passengers from their prison. If she hadn't been so tired, she'd be completely stir-crazy. What a long flight.

Then immediately she was alert, the impact of it all hitting her as a voice in her head announced in a stilted GPS-lady manner: *you have arrived.* Because on the world stage, wasn't this it? An all-expenses paid trip to Fantasy Island.

She disembarked in a daze, the smell of airplane fuel filling her nostrils as they walked across the tarmac. Nothing but darkness seemed to exist beyond the grey concrete shapes of the airport and the white bodies of the sleek jets. Inside, after collecting baggage and clearing customs, a shuttle whisked them away, heading, she assumed, to the hotel. She wanted to go check on Jay, the whole reason they were here, but it was late. They'd train extra-early here, so what were a few more hours, especially if it meant sleep? In an actual bed? There was no chance of anything making sense until that happened, so she gave up on the idea of finding out how to get to the stables. If Jay's accommodations were on par with theirs, she didn't have to worry. She was asleep within seconds of her head hitting the pillow.

When the alarm droned, the only thing familiar was Nate, turning away with a groan to hit snooze before rolling back and nestling against her again.

"He's just walking," he mumbled into her neck. "We don't have to go yet."

"We do," Liv said, dragging herself away to sit on the edge of the bed. "I'm having a shower. You can sleep a while longer."

She willed the hot water to revive her, thinking Nate had a point about Jay only walking today. They didn't need to be there this early. But responsibility and separation anxiety won out. After dressing, she explored the room and found just the thing to help kick-start the day — a coffee maker.

"Get up, Miller," she said, the machine gurgling. "We'll have more hours in the day than we know what to do with. You can sleep later."

She didn't even bother trying to calculate the time difference. The best plan was to just go with it; push through and accept the new reality. Outside the climate-controlled cool of the hotel, warmth settled on her skin, though it wasn't as humid as Florida. Another shuttle took them to the quarantine barn, and seeing Jay grounded her a bit. Shavings stuck to his bright chestnut coat, mane and tail bejewelled with them.

"Clearly you approve of your bed," she said, laughing quietly. She turned to Nate. "Walk or muck?"

He opted to muck, just as she'd hoped he would. She needed locomotion right now. After brushing Jay, picking every persistent wood chip from his silky long tail, she wound the shank around the noseband of his halter and began touring the barn. Jet lag seemed to apply less to horses than humans, Jay taking in the surroundings with a sweeping gaze.

One horse. What did they do with the rest of their day? They'd be back here more than once with all that time to kill.

"Breakfast?" Liv suggested.

"Then maybe we can check out some of the city," Nate said. "It's either that, or sleep."

She wasn't a good tourist, but maybe that was because she'd never really been one before, save for that walk down the main street of Banff last May — unless beach time in Florida counted. While she checked in with Jo at Payson and Emilie at the farm, Nate scouted possible things to do that weren't already on their agenda.

They decided on an informal tour along Dubai Creek in an abra instead of a fancier cruise. The waterway was lined with traditional dhows laden with cargo destined for locales like Iran and India, juxtaposed against the modern skyline. She wanted to get away from the shiny, glass-faced buildings and find the old and historic. Half the time it left her wondering what was real and what was man-made.

The taxi ride back to the hotel was exactly like the one they'd taken to the abra station — jarring and hair-raising. Pedestrians definitely did not have right of way in Dubai.

"Remind me not to walk anywhere around here." She'd stick to the gym for exercise and was ready for a break when they were safely in their room. Time to visit Jay, then find a bite to eat and call it an early night — but she'd check her email once more first.

She was expecting an update from the farm in Kentucky because today was Chique's twenty-five-day check. The mare had been pronounced in foal at fourteen days, and today would be ultrasounded again. All being well, they'd see a heartbeat; the very essence of a racehorse.

But the news waiting in her inbox wasn't what she wanted to read.

"Twins? How do you miss twins? You're Kentucky. Kentucky doesn't make mistakes like that," she muttered at the screen of her phone, totally aware her comments were unfair.

"What?" Nate quirked an eyebrow at her from where he'd propped himself on the bed.

"Of course Chique conceived twins," she said, shifting on the chair to meet Nate's eyes.

And, of course, they'd been so perfectly lined up that they missed the second embryo when they confirmed the pregnancy earlier. At this stage, it was too late to pinch one off, the most successful way to reduce twins.

They could take their chances, pray that nature would take its course and one growing mass of cells would naturally out-compete the other, shrinking until it absorbed, but there was considerable risk in that. The risk of abortion late-term. Risk of a complicated foaling if the mare carried twins to term. Risk of both foals dying because they were improperly developed.

Liv didn't like risk, when there was a way to avoid it. *Control freak.* She was what she was.

Even losing one weaker foal would be tragic. Once they were out, took their initial breath, they grabbed the first piece of your heart. And if they didn't survive... there went another slice.

She figured out the time difference and called the breeding manager at the Kentucky farm. He outlined options. Then she drew in a deep breath and blew it out slowly. "Okay. Let me think about it for a couple of hours. Thanks."

"So?" Nate hadn't moved, but he'd watched her throughout the entire call.

"Ugh. How did they miss it?"

"Those vets check dozens of mares a day during breeding season. It can't be a surprise that sometimes stuff gets by them. Especially something like that."

"Especially with Chique."

He laughed. "I guess we don't have to worry about her fertility. She's an overachiever, apparently."

"Let's hope this is a one-off." But Thoroughbreds statistically had a higher rate of twinning than other breeds, and mares often made it a pattern.

"You could leave her be and see what happens."

"Please don't tell me you're living in that fantasy world where she has two healthy foals, and three years later, they face off in the Kentucky Derby?"

"And of course the small one wins." He grinned. "No, I'll save the fantasies for other things, if that's all right with you."

"It would be such a shame to abort them, but that's really the safest way to go." She sighed. It was simple and fast. An injection of hormones; the mare cramped for a few moments, and it was over. Then they started again.

"She'll only be a month or so behind, if they short-cycle her." More manipulation through hormones, to bring her back into heat sooner than would happen without them. "That's not too bad."

"There is another possibility, a reduction method they can do up to thirty days... so it would have to happen pretty much immediately."

"Yeah?"

"It has to be done at the clinic. Lower success rate with a unilateral pregnancy like hers than if it was bilateral. The usual risk." That being, the mare could end up losing both embryos.

"So, a straightforward decision, isn't it? We're in Dubai with a World Cup horse. We can handle risk."

Her science-geek side won out over the concept of the simplest option probably being the best. She wished she could be there to observe, but Dubai had gotten in the way. *Dubai.* This was officially the most bizarre and frightfully exciting time of her life. She called the manager back.

And now what do we do?

It was the breeding business. *What do we always do?* Wait. It was just difficult, flooded with the sentimentality she tried so hard to avoid in this game... waiting for something to die. But by doing so, they gave something else a chance to live.

Jay galloped in the darkness under the lights at Meydan before the sun showed up and wilted them, though it wasn't as hot as he'd expected. Today they faced the same issue as yesterday: after the weeks leading up to their trip across the Atlantic to the Middle East passed at light speed, now time crawled. One horse was not enough to keep them occupied. They stayed at the track for a while, watching horses train as it became bright, and took advantage of a breakfast event set up on the apron. A haze hung in the air, like someone dropped a warm sepia filter over the scene.

"What are we going to do today?" Liv asked.

"We should go to that indoor ski hill. The one in the mall. This might be as close as we get to that parallel universe you keep talking about where we get to go skiing."

"Skiing in a mall? On artificial snow? No, Miller."

Nate could tell she was feeling as displaced as he was. He checked the weather to see if that helped with the decision-making, and the current conditions literally read *dust*. So that's what was happening with the sky. He didn't know where the desert was, exactly, but right now it was everywhere; particulate matter in the air. An oasis city rising from the sand; greenery growing in defiance of aridity; fountains flaunting richness. It was a region of extremes, with no middle ground.

He showed the screen to Liv. "Is that beach weather, or no?"

She laughed. "Dust? Maybe it acts as a filter, so it's safer? UV radiation and all. But I'm betting that's a sandstorm blowing in, so, no. We might want to get back to the hotel."

They caught the next shuttle.

"I hope it passes or I guess they won't be taking us to the desert camp thing," Nate said once they were in the room again. He peered through the drapes. The wind rushed outside the window, visibility becoming so poor it was getting hard to see the tall buildings just across the street. It was bizarre.

"I hope it passes so we can keep training our horse."

"Shit." He turned to face her. "That didn't even occur to me."

"Maybe it is best I'm the trainer."

He laughed, but he was on the way to her laptop, googling, *How long do sandstorms last?* Would they cancel a race of this magnitude if air quality was poor? What a stinker that would be, to come all this way only to not run at all.

"We're still four days out, Miller. Surely it'll clear by then. I expect we'll find out more at the draw tomorrow. Like, if it's a big deal, they'll say something."

"I will be mad if we don't get to go to that thing in the desert. I want to ride a camel," he said.

"Considering a career change?"

"I think I'm too big. And too old."

"Or too human?" Liv quipped with a slight tilt of her head.

"Do they really use robots?"

"They do."

"I can't see it being the same rush as a racehorse. But how long before they have robot jockeys for them?"

"That's not going to get you out of riding Chique's little terror, Miller."

He chuckled and turned back to the computer screen. "It would be wrong to miss out on the desert, either way. We owe it to ourselves to explore every experience this trip offers, don't you think?"

Liv sat on the bed, appearing unconvinced, and checked her phone. "You're probably right."

He wasn't getting anywhere with his search, so he slapped the laptop shut and came to sit next to her. "What's up?"

She was reading something intently. "They did the procedure on Chique today."

"Here's hoping they picked the right one."

"And that he survives."

"He?"

"Oh, yes. She's going to have a colt who makes her seem like a dream."

"Aw, she is a dream."

"How short your memory is."

"Selective, not short," he said, a hand drifting to her neck and pulling the elastic from her hair. He caught the corner of her smile with his mouth, and she tossed the phone aside.

What else were they going to do in a sandstorm?

The air quality improved enough by the next morning Liv's concerns about training disappeared. She'd claimed one day on their big chestnut's back to say she'd done it — she'd galloped at Meydan. She was happy with the post position draw, and the event in the desert turned out to be entertaining.

Riding a camel was an awkward contrast to her jaunt around the Dubai oval on Jay. She'd stick to horses. There had been fireworks and falcons. A simple henna tattoo wrapped around her wrist under the bracelet of Feste's hair, a memento of this trip that would soon fade. She hoped the memory of the race would last much longer. They were down to mere hours to post time.

Jay was flat out, his head resting on the deep bank of shavings, a fan gently ruffling his mane. Now and then he'd twitch and let Liv know he was actually alive.

"I need to take his temperature." She couldn't help fretting at this point.

Emilie laughed. "Don't need to take yours, because you're running true to form. He's fine. He's chill. He's a pro."

"Did Nate set you up with a script?"

Em laughed again. "I'm not new."

"I'm so glad the new manager is working out so you can be here," Liv gushed uncharacteristically and squeezed her tight.

"I'll seriously spend more time in the air than I will on the ground."

"Let's hope it's worthwhile."

"It's already worthwhile."

Texts filled Liv's lock screen, and she'd already fielded calls from Jo and Faye and her parents. The only one she hadn't heard from was Roger... then the phone came to life with his ringtone, which she'd changed to one of Nate's Switchfoot songs: "Hope is the Anthem."

Liv couldn't speak for the lump in her throat, seeing Roger and Hélène's faces on the small surface. Fortunately, they didn't push for any more of a reaction. Hélène just said "Bonne chance," and Roger said, "Whatever happens, we're proud of you all."

She disconnected and recomposed herself, swiping away

the tears. Jay chose that moment to right himself, resting on his sternum before his head curled around to his belly.

"Uh-oh," Liv muttered.

Then he climbed to his feet and shook, releasing a funny vibration that sounded a lot like a laugh. *You're right, buddy; joke's on me. You were just being cute.* He stretched his neck up, tucking his chin in before pressing against the screen in hopes of a peppermint. Cool customer.

The fireworks got a rise out of him. Not a big one, but enough to make him wide-eyed, his ears perked, a flare to his nostrils. It was a unique call to the post, that was for sure. Liv was sorry she was missing it; the big pregame show the frontside would see. She'd heard it was spectacular. But she wasn't leaving Jay now, with the hours breaking down into minutes. She wondered if Chique would have had as untroubled a reaction. Not likely.

It wouldn't be long until they tied Jay to the wall, removed his bedazzling of shavings, applied rundowns — the white self-adhesive bandages smoothly molded to his hinds — and dressed him in their newest racing bridle of rich Australian nut brown. The blue-lined browband and noseband complimented Jay's intense colour and set off his gorgeous head.

Emilie placed the quarter marker stencil along his powerful gluteals, back-brushing. Neither of them had ever learned — or bothered might be more accurate — to do the checkerboard pattern by hand. Liv might be a purist about a lot of things, but in this case, the stencil did an admirable job, and saved a boat-load of time.

The brass on his halter gleamed, carefully polished, Emilie slipping it over his nose on top of the bridle and buckling it behind his erect ears. Jay was tuned in now, fully aware that he was running tonight. They weren't just tourists over here. Emilie laced the chain around the halter and brought it under his jaw to the back ring closest to her; Liv snapped a paddock shank to the off side, and without needing to exchange words, off they went.

Walking over for the Dubai World Cup. Had it even sunk in?

The lights were so bright they were blinding, and it took a few moments for her eyes to adjust. People crowded the rail, locals in National dress making up the throng showing the same fervour for racing they saw at home. Maybe more. Wasn't this where the three Arabian stallions credited with the Thoroughbred's foundation had originated? They were the horses to which today's racehorse owed its speed and stamina; its beauty and strength. The Middle East was their cradle of civilization; the breed and those desert-bred founding fathers celebrated tonight.

Jay marched into the paddock like he belonged and Liv believed with her whole heart he did. The blood that ran through the veins of his rivals here — harkening back to the Barb, the Arabian, the Turk — flowed just as fluidly through him.

"I kinda feel like I did in middle school when I was the smallest kid in class," Nate said when he joined her, matching her crossed-arms stance. Liv didn't care that their elbows touched; that the hand he had tucked under the one closest to her discreetly found her fingers and squeezed.

"But I bet you were that scrapper kid who ran circles around those bigger kids," Emilie said, a grin spreading over her face.

"Got that right." He nodded with assurance.

"There's nothing tiny about Jay," Liv said. "Look at him. He's a monster. The good kind. Have fun." She pressed a kiss to Nate's lips and at the riders up call and legged him aboard.

Her words were a spin on her usual *bonne chance*, because

being here was unreal enough they could do nothing less than enjoy the experience. Win, lose, finish up the track — this trip was, plain and simple, wild and crazy fun.

This was it. He felt as if he should do something symbolic before he entered the gate, like some riders genuflected, but he wasn't Catholic. He pressed his fingers to his lips, then to the flag on his boot, casting a glance to the black sky beyond the dazzling lights.

Let's do this, big horse.

The last set of doors slammed shut, and Jay's ears swept forward, crosshairs through which Nate narrowed his focus. Just another horse race, on the other side of the world. Just another race to win, when some days he felt he'd forgotten how. Two thousand metres — about a mile and a quarter — of sandy loam, and whatever desert magic the duststorm had blown in. The gates crashed open, and they were off.

Jay popped out neatly only to be hammered on either side, Nate wrestling in the big horse's trajectory with a string of curses; a hard *stop* when everything said *go*. It was the only way to avoid disaster thanks to that squeeze by their less than friendly neighbours. Jay's stride stabilized, coming long and easy, assuring Nate he was fine, and now they had tons of room. Because they were alone at the back. Way, way behind. Not an unfamiliar place for the big Canadian chestnut; just not where Nate had planned to be on this day, in this momentous race.

He urged Jay to make up ground, but Jay would not be rushed. They passed the wire for the first time and headed into the clubhouse turn, Jay picking up a couple of horses with natural speed instead of effort.

Jay stayed tucked behind the tight pack, three paths out

from the rail, and they cruised around the bend and into the straight, maintaining position along the backstretch. They had to be ten lengths behind; five from Paradise, who stalked the trailblazing pacesetter relentlessly. It was going to take some kind of move to turn the tables on the American today. Nate asked for a little more and Jay said, *sure, I'm good with that,* offering a subtle increase in energy.

The final turn took its toll, the field stringing out as runners tired behind the honest fractions. With his new momentum, Jay swept around them, Nate's eyes locked on Acosta's black helmet cover.

One thing about being back here, he wouldn't be subjected to any of Acosta's games on the turn. Paradise was in the clear at the head of the homestretch, Jay sailing by the three horses in the flight behind the new leader and closing the gap. He eclipsed the fading pacesetter, only Paradise left to vanquish.

There was no element of surprise this time, like they'd had in the Pegasus. Acosta glanced back, seeing Jay coming. *Let that be your tragic flaw, that moment of hesitation.* Nate threw more coal on his freight train and bore down on Paradise in paradise, Acosta riding hard now, whip flailing.

Jay caught his rival at the eighth pole, but Paradise wasn't giving in; he wasn't folding under the pressure. He was fighting back. Nate expected nothing less. This was going to be an all-out stretch duel — chestnut heads pulsing in unison, copper bodies fused, differentiated only by the colours the riders wore. With each thrust of his arms and strike of his stick, Nate called on every microgram of Jay's reserves. That's what this race would come down to.

There was no telling at the wire which nod presided — the answer was so slow in coming Nate thought it had to be a dead heat, the first in the race's history. The suspense was killing him. Emilie led them in circles in front of the grandstand as they awaited the verdict, Jay sucking in breaths and expelling them, his neck dark with sweat under Nate's hand.

The crowd roared and all his anticipation didn't prevent him from being so totally stunned, he nearly fell off Jay.

Their big horse had done it.

Liv reached for his hand, and he grabbed it, kissing her knuckles because even with Liv on her toes, her lips were too far away. Then Emilie passed her the shank, and she led them to the winner's circle.

They made a quick trip to the beach before Emilie left, the landmark Burj Al Arab towering like a sailing ship in the Persian Gulf. The colour of the water was so perfect it looked synthetic. It was beautiful, but it didn't have the same calming effect as what she'd come to think of as their own stretch of the Atlantic.

Liv had yet to absorb what had happened. Seven million dollars — the winner's share of the World Cup's purse. The money didn't matter; it was such an exorbitant sum she couldn't even fathom it. Even when you took out Nate's ten percent and gave bonuses to everyone who worked for Triple Stripe — because they were a team — it was still a lot of money.

"What do people do with that kind of money?" Emilie asked, as awestruck as Liv.

"Papa's the money guy," she answered. "We ask him."

"We could build a bigger arena for the aftercare horses." Emilie lit up, toes in the surf.

"I'll give you my vote." Liv grinned.

Nate's nod of agreement was absent-minded; rote. He looked like they all felt. "It buys us the power to do things the way we want from now on," he said.

"You sound like a lottery commercial." Liv eyed him.

"It's true though. Think of the possibilities. We worked hard for that money."

It probably didn't appear that way from the outside. Horse racing was easy money, wasn't it? An easy way to lose money, that was for sure. But she prompted him. "All right, Miller, so what's your grand plan?" Funny that it obviously wasn't to retire and go live by the ocean, or construct a dream cottage in the Muskokas.

"We could build a training centre. Have a true European-style gallop," he said, meeting her gaze.

"A covered track," she added to the list.

"For the poor people who stay behind in the winter, because we're still going to Florida." His lips twisted into a smile.

"And you won't have to ride horses you don't want to ride," she said.

"Except the Triple Stripe ones, like Chique's evil twin baby," he reminded.

Liv laughed. "Chique's not having twins. And come on, you're going to love whatever comes out of that mare, scales and all."

"You'd better plan to buy some mares to breed to Jay," he continued. "Actually, you'd better plan to breed Claire to Jay."

"I'll have to look at the pedigrees, of course..." The possibility was magical, though. For this year, they'd already bred the flashy mare back, confirmed in foal to Just Lucky. "But he's been so much fun, I'm not ready to let go of him yet."

She'd already had interest, Jay an overnight sensation. Those calls were coming from Kentucky. Big players, now that his resumé was fashionable. Once they got their talons into him, she'd relinquish control, even if she maintained a majority interest for Triple Stripe. That's just how it worked.

He'd only run three times since his comeback. So many horses retired early and were sent to the breeding shed. Did Jay have to be one of them?

"So, keep him in training." Nate said. "And the first cheque you write from that big fat purse he just won goes to the insurance company."

It was a risk, of course. But this could never only be about the money for Liv. "He'll come back to Woodbine with us, regardless." Base camp, for future adventures.

"Seven million dollars sounds like a lot in the beginning," Emilie said wryly. "But somehow I think we could spend it pretty quick."

What was it they said? Horses, the most expensive addiction in the world.

Their dizzying trip was wrapping up. One thing Liv knew for sure: this was not home. It was an honour to visit, but she didn't want to stay.

CHAPTER TWENTY-THREE

PAYSON PARK SEEMED quiet and ordinary after the glamour of Dubai, but she needed ordinary right now. Here she could disappear into the cinder blocks and blue trim. It wasn't like Woodbine, where everyone knew everything about everyone else and there would be a flood of congratulations. People calling on the way out to the track. Visitors frequenting the barn. Media showing up to do stories for the Toronto papers and Canadian magazines. Which would happen anyway when they returned to Ontario.

Not that no one here knew the latest Dubai World Cup winner was among them, but the training centre lacked the same sense of community afforded by their home base in Canada. There wasn't the same intermingling here. They were transients. The barn across the way could have the next Derby winner standing in stall twelve, and they wouldn't hear about it until after the fact. *You remember that horse?*

The crew, however, welcomed them, demanding a celebration. It was only days now until they would journey north, but even Liv agreed they deserved a party and she gave Nate the go-ahead, because she sure wasn't planning it. That was his department.

On the shed, things were mostly the same, though Sue and Michel had gone home early. Because their baby — a few days overdue now — needed to be foaled in Canada under the umbrella of Ontario's health insurance.

Everyone else was here. At the end of the morning, they gathered on overturned buckets as Elliot passed around beers. Cory and Marie had bonded, probably because it was a perfect fit: Marie smiled and nodded at Cory's endless chatter and didn't need to talk. It was nice to see Cory have a break for the winter, to just be a horse girl again — galloping in the mornings, sitting on a bale of straw sketching after she'd finished the tack, then locking in her tan at the beach in the afternoon. At Woodbine she'd be back to being the track's top bug, with four months left of her apprenticeship to take advantage of.

Emilie had returned directly to King City. The farm had survived her absence, the new manager passing that test. Liv was starting to think her sister was feeling a little proprietary about the place. But Em was finishing up her Masters, getting ready to take the exams that would qualify her as a real live physiotherapist. Still, it wouldn't surprise Liv one bit if she abandoned that career for the farm, which was revealing itself as her true passion. You can try to deny it, but in the end, is it worth fighting?

Liv accepted a can of Budweiser though she debated even opening it, because she'd waste more than she'd drink. Setting herself on an unoccupied bucket next to Jo, she rolled the cool can between her palms and enjoyed the comfort of this place. She could breathe again.

The pig trundled over, and she peered down at him with

caution. What was an appropriate way to greet a pig? Scratch it behind the ears? Food would certainly be welcomed, but he was the official Hoover around here, ready to mooch everyone's leftovers, and she adamantly refused to reinforce that behaviour any more than she would have with a dog. In vet school, pigs had been commodities, not pets. Hamlet was friendly enough, but not so much that she wanted a porcine pet herself. The thought of Emilie's new Labrador brought a smile. They had a dog to go home to. And Claire and Léa. And in a few more weeks, Chique would join them. Much of the family would be together again.

Jo sipped her beer and gave Liv a sideways glance. "Don't think I didn't see what you did."

Liv tilted her head, still using her can as a prop instead of refreshment. "What are you talking about?"

"Running off to Dubai so I ended up training these horses after all."

Liv grinned. "Oh, come on. You told me to go. Called it my honeymoon."

"True enough. How was that, anyway?"

Liv elbowed her, Jo laughing as she rocked sideways on her tippy seat. "I think we just got over the jet lag in time to come back." She cracked the beer open and swallowed a mouthful because it was cold and her throat was dry. Then she pressed her lips together, levelling her eyes on Jo.

"What?" Jo's gaze narrowed, her brow furrowed.

"You are coming back to Ontario with us, right?"

Jo's laugh was immediate. "Of course. Why would I not?"

Liv inclined her head toward Elliot and spoke quietly, even though he seemed engrossed in telling Nate a story. "I thought someone might steal you from us."

Jo smiled in response, not without affection. "That was just

fun. The fling you said I should have. But no spark, you know?"
She winked at Liv. "Besides, someone's going to have to manage
the home squad if you end up globetrotting with Jay. What's
next?"

"Royal Ascot?" Liv tossed out. The mere thought gave her a
thrill. It almost made her want to start a Pinterest board full of
potential destinations. The Prix de l'Arc de Triomphe would be
front and centre.

"Could this finally be the year we go to the Breeders'
Cup?" Nate broke in. He'd obviously caught at least part of
their conversation.

"It could be," was all Liv said in response. Because no
matter how promising it all looked at the moment, that was
seven months away.

"We did all right this winter," Jo said, like she was giving
them a performance review.

Liv touched her can to Jo's in an informal toast. "More than
okay."

"More than fine," Nate quipped, citing the name of one of
his favourite Switchfoot songs.. "Put last year well and truly
behind us."

"And we're only a quarter of the way through," Jo added.

Can't Catch Me's injury had thankfully been mild, though
it earned him time off instead of a trip to Churchill Downs.
After a couple of quiet days, he'd returned to his old self —
worse, really, because he wasn't training. He'd been terrorizing
the crew since, and with Michel gone now, they drew straws
each morning to decide who had to walk him. His latest ultrasound was clean. He'd start training back in Ontario and they'd
focus on the Plate.

Kiss and Trop, the other three-year-olds they'd brought
with them, had yet to start but would be ready for the Woodbine meet. Dean had Reba in training there now, and his

reports on the filly were glowing. Emilie's dedication, all those cold dark mornings at the farm, looked to have paid off. The Canadian Oaks, Dean insisted. Not that she didn't trust his judgement, but Liv and Jo would see for themselves soon.

It was time to go home.

Nate didn't even remember last year's Sovereigns. They had gone, right? Sometime between his return to Ontario after the Winter From Hell. Before his past had come to visit, then blown up in tiny pieces around his Calgary family. *Horse of the year. Three-year-old filly. Outstanding jockey. Leading Owner.* All of it, all that accomplishment in one year, just a foggy recollection of Chique's brilliant sophomore season. This time around, the awards connected to Triple Stripe weren't as extensive, but he let it all soak into his pores. Embraced the good, commemorated the bad. The last six months had certainly gone a long way to smoothing out the rocks and bogs of the earlier ones.

Chique got her Horse of the Year title. Cory accepted the trophy for outstanding apprentice. Nate tried not to resent it when Dave Johnson reclaimed his outstanding jockey award. Part of him vowed to get it back this year; part of him didn't care about awards anymore. Besides, he'd ridden the Dubai World Cup winner; he'd take that over a title this time around.

He listened to Liv talking to the media about Jay. Yes, he was back at Woodbine with them. Yes, he was staying in training. No, they hadn't made a stud deal yet. Nor had they decided what was next on his dance card.

Nate fielded some more personal queries from colleagues. *Hélène is doing as well as can be expected, going through her last round of chemo. Roger is extending his leave to spend time with her, because life's too short, right? Chique's in foal to Mega-lodon and arrived back at the farm in King City this week.* Heaven help him. And *yeah, Michel and Sue had their baby. They thought about coming tonight, but decided it was too much. Uh, no, not expecting to follow their lead, sorry.*

Too many places to go.

CHAPTER TWENTY-FOUR

Oaks Day came made to order, the kind of early June weather that hadn't started to think about building the humidity and brewing thunderstorms so common later in the month. Reba stood politely for her bath, the suds scattering the mid-morning light to create tiny, colourful prisms. Had Faye slipped a hallucinogen into the cappuccino she'd dropped off a few moments ago? If not, there was definitely something in the air. Something good.

"Where's mine?" Nate, somehow looking presentable after breezing horses for the last three hours — helmet tossed, boots stashed, hair combed — sidled up next to her and reached for the cup.

Liv held it out of reach and dashed away comparisons, her own helmet-head of hair tucked under her navy Dubai World Cup ball cap. She tugged at its peak anyway, a little reminder of how amazing this year had been so far, and how there was no reason for that not to continue.

"I hid it in the office," she said. The rest of the crew had claimed theirs, but she wouldn't put it past any of them to snatch another if they thought it was extra. Or, truthfully, if they knew it was Nate's.

Emilie finished scraping water from the chestnut filly's coat and ran a sponge down all four legs. She dropped scraper and sponge into a bucket and took the shank from Jo.

"Coming in!" she called, before disappearing into the barn. Even though she didn't get that much time to spend with the filly now that Reba was at the track, what with the jobs she juggled and the volunteer work she still managed to fit in, she wasn't going to miss being a part of this day.

"All right, Michel, bring Camzilla out," Jo called. Jo had come up with that nickname all on her own.

No one enjoyed holding the big colt because he was so fit and full of himself. It was a nightmare to be on the other end of the shank — so Michel did it the majority of the time. Cam clattered out onto the apron, screaming like he thought he was the Black Stallion — except, of course, for not being black. Liv and Jo stood a safe distance away.

"I'm taking him for a roll," Michel said.

"Do you have to?" Jo's brow furrowed. "Today? When he's running in the Plate Trial?"

"He'll be fine." Michel dismissed Jo's concern and Liv didn't intercede. She wouldn't have trusted anyone else to do it, but Michel was good with the colt.

Nate returned with his coffee just as Michel led Cam to the newly created rolling pit on the lawn. "Just in time for the pregame show."

They'd fenced off the perimeter, at least, but if Cam put his mind to it, Liv didn't think he'd have any trouble hopping over the barrier. It wasn't very high, and the colt proved repeatedly he had springs. Michel kept a long loop in the shank, turning with Cam as he crouched, pivoting in the deep sand. Cam crumpled and launched himself onto his back, grinding the sand in before rolling right over, then flipping to the original side. Not every horse could do that so effortlessly. Chique came to mind.

"And, three, two, one..." Nate counted down, Liv laughing. Jo cringed.

Liv couldn't help thinking of Feste as she took in Cam's antics. Cam would be a favourite for the Trial, but a year ago, she'd been sure she'd be here with Feste. The bracelet of his tail hairs still encircled her wrist, rough against her fingers as she rotated it. She rarely took it off. Why? What had she learned? Loss could happen in an instant, so they were fortunate to be standing here with two promising three-year-olds to run today.

Cam scrambled to his feet, sand flying everywhere, and went straight up on his hind legs.

"I can't watch." Jo covered her eyes like she was avoiding a horror flick, peering through her fingers.

Michel stood almost lazily, holding the shank up and out of the way as the colt's flailing hooves struck the air. Cam returned to earth with a fire-breathing-dragon snort that set the entire line of horses on the shed into a succession of whinnies. Then the colt walked to the apron as calm as could be — or at least, his version of calm. Nate, of course, videoed the entire thing.

"Post that on your Instagram," he said, grinning at Liv, then sending her the video.

She did, with a tune for good measure, highlighting the part about *rage* in Fall Out Boy's "Champion." Then she took a moment to glance at the photos on the farm account. Emilie diligently kept it up to date. Liv had missed an image her sister had posted yesterday. She showed it to Nate.

"Pacino's doing great. He looks amazing," she said. The colt was so big and had so much bone, he looked almost like a Clydesdale cross. Racing might not be in his future — even with the surgery successfully stabilizing the vertebrae in his neck, he didn't scream speed and agility. Emilie would help him find his place.

"I've gotta go." He kissed her in parting. "See you all this afternoon."

They would be busy. Can't Catch Me first, in the Plate Trial, then little Reba, putting on her big girl bridle for the Oaks. The flashy little chestnut had only just broken her maiden three weeks ago, but bold was the theme this year and Reba deserved to be part of it.

The Woodbine Canadian Oaks didn't do the pink parade for breast cancer like its Kentucky counterpart, but the Triple Stripe contingent made their own tradition for Hélène, each of them wearing teal, to support ovarian cancer awareness. Everyone's idea of teal was just a little different, but it was fun to see the subtle variety as they gathered in the box to watch the race, a little sea of blue-green.

Nate had to wear the red, white and blue Triple Stripe silks, but if you looked closely, you could see the tiny teal ribbon at the back of his breeches. A third of the way down Reba's neck, Liv had braided one plait with matching yarn — just high enough Nate wouldn't need the tightly wound hairs for his hold in the gate. Even Paz was dressed up, teal pompoms in his mane bouncing along his crest as he escorted Reba through the post parade.

Liv wasn't nervous. Why wasn't she nervous? Maybe because it didn't matter, because no matter how Reba did, the family was together again, and whole. The barn crew watched from the apron, their own little teal pocket. Here in the seats, Dean, Will, and Faye joined them. Claude and Anne were here from Montreal for the weekend, sitting with Roger and Hélène, the pretty scarf around Hélène's head matching her dress. Her chemo was finished, but it would be a couple of months before her hair began growing back.

The pre-race buzz had been all about Galactic Dream, a filly sold at the Keeneland September sale as a yearling and previously only raced in the US. Her American connections probably thought this restricted race with its nice purse would be easy pickings, but it would be wrong to dismiss the local horses. Liv wasn't sure if Reba could beat the big US invader, but their filly would show up and run her heart out. Emilie squeezed her hand, damp palm betraying her nerves, and Liv squeezed back.

Ten fillies loaded into the gate set in front of the grandstand, an eighth of a mile from the wire. They burst out in a wave of verve and colour.

Nate let the speed go, settling Reba just off the rail in the second flight. This part of the race, first time past, was all about riders strategizing. Heading into the clubhouse turn, Reba was fifth and happy to be there.

The seconds ticking along the backstretch seemed so much longer, a waiting game of gauging pace. When it was honest like this, there was nothing to do but be patient and ready to make split-second decisions; capitalize on lapses in the judgement of others. Nothing seemed to happen until they reached the final turn.

Reba sneaked up the inside, her stride lively, ears pricked forward. Nate wove her stealthily through fillies and swept back down to the rail in the wake of a surging Galactic Dream as the field headed into the stretch. Galactic Dream looked frustratingly unbeatable with a huge, effortless stride. She rolled past the two fillies, valiantly leading the way to capture the lead for herself.

Reba ran hard up the rail, Nate driving with his hands, his stick waving alongside her neck before landing a quick strike on her quarters left-handed. And Reba dug in, ears pinned, creeping up until the sight of her was temporarily obscured by Galactic Dream's mass. Liv's heart was in her throat. Reba was a small filly, but that wasn't much of a hole. She prayed both fillies ran true.

"Come on, Reba!" Emilie screamed, jumping up and down as the filly's white nose poked out. Then her blazed face emerged, tiny, sweet Reba staring an enormous Galactic Dream in the eye and turning the larger filly away with each dip of her pretty head.

The official margin of victory was a neck. Maybe the purple and yellow of the blanket of flowers draped over Reba's neck clashed with chestnut and teal, but Liv could deal with that.

This time, she didn't try to escape the post-race interviews. She wanted the reporters to get the details right of the story behind this year's Oaks. She smiled at Hélène as Roger ushered his wife away from the winner's circle after the photo and presentation. None of the women in their crew had escaped Hélène's stern lecture on knowing the symptoms of the disease represented by their colour choice today, so often missed. Maybe Reba's triumph would contribute one small part to raising awareness.

Their stake party was a modest gathering; a warmup for the Queen's Plate, where the post-race festivities were part of the experience. The Plate was the day the backstretch let down its hair — at least as much as security would allow.

Roger assumed his usual position like he was in a cameo

role: bartender, monitoring the snatching of cans from the ice-filled muck bucket and pouring the requisite cheap sparkling wine. Now and then he glanced at Hélène, sitting at the picnic table with Claude and Anne. There was no masking the concern on his face — was she okay? Tired? Ready to go home? But Hélène smiled her beautiful smile and waved him off each time. This little celebration was for her. Reba's performance was a serendipitous bonus.

The bright chestnut filly looked pleased with herself, tearing at the lawn in front of the barn, one eye on the lounging humans. Marie was at the end of the shank. Liv had teased Jo about that development.

"Here I was worried about Elliot sweeping you off to Chicago, and you were just stealing his help. Nicely done."

"Right?"

It was Jo who had discovered Marie was actually Canadian. She'd gone to Payson with a friend, hoping to get a job with a Canadian outfit, but without a work visa, no one would hire her. Enter Elliot, who didn't care and typically paid his help with cash under the table. So quiet little Marie had worked illegally for four months and slept on the couch in her friend's rented trailer. Still waters and all that. Strike another one for crazy horse girls who defy common sense to pursue a passion.

Jo promised her a job at Woodbine, and now Marie was officially their swing groom, filling in on days off. On other days, Liv tried to make sure she got on a horse, or at least took Paz to the sand ring. If Marie wanted to do this, she might as well learn to do it right. She didn't want to be a jockey, so at least she was moderately sane.

Roger handed Liv a plastic glass of bubbles, and she touched it to those held by the small group around him. Jo, whose gaze drifted regularly to Marie and Reba. Emilie, who hadn't stopped grinning since her winter project dashed under the wire first in the country's premier contest for three-year-old fillies. And, of course, Nate.

"Congratulations," Roger said. Not that he hadn't hugged her immediately after the race. This was just his formal pronouncement.

Liv looked around the group. "Takes a village, right?" Even though it had been Liv's name as trainer in the program today and Nate's as rider, those could easily have been interchanged. By rights, Jo's should've been there too, followed by the whole crew. Including, in no small part, Emilie.

"Can't Catch Me ran well," Roger said. "The winner was tough."

"It's a curse to win the Trial anyway," Nate said. "When's the last time a Trial winner won the Plate?"

Not in recent times, for sure. Last year it had been Elemental, but Ride The Wave had beaten him in the Plate. The year before, Touch and Go, while Chique skipped the prep races. On the day of the big race, their filly overcame a disaster just out of the gate, rallying to grab the fifty sovereigns.

"So, Rog," Liv said slyly, "if both Reba and Cam run in the Plate, you might have to come back. Then I can ride Reba."

"Hey, wait!' Nate protested. "I won on her, I should get to decide if I ride her back."

"I might have to play the owner's daughter card on this one, Miller. Besides, Cam is more your kind of horse."

"You mean, crazy?" Jo quipped. "I agree."

Cory edged her way in beside Emilie. "I'll ride Reba. Not that we don't want you back, Rog, but, oh pretty please, give me a Plate mount?"

"I feel like I'm the victim of a conspiracy here." Nate crossed his arms and pressed his lips together.

"Oh, come on, Miller. No one's feeling sorry for you. You

won the Dubai World Cup. Three Queen's Plates in a row would be greedy, don't you think?" Liv commented.

"I agree," Cory said. "I guess Liv should get first choice, but it's only fair I ride the other one."

Roger laughed. "You've all been getting along so well. It might be best if I stay away lest a war break out." With that he excused himself to join Hélène and the elder Lachances.

"How come you haven't weighed in, Jo?" Nate asked.

"I'm saddling a horse either way, so matters not to me." She smiled, then caught Marie's eye. "You can put her in. Let's get our little pocket rocket done up."

Emilie insisted on doing that task, and Marie offered to help. Liv wiped off the bridle and put it away before joining Jo in front of the stall. Liv could almost feel the cool mud between her fingers as Marie mimicked Emilie, smoothing the grey clay over Reba's front legs. Dip the brown paper in the water bucket. Let the drips fall, then mould it to the poultice like a plaster cast. A layer of sheet cotton to soak up the excess and keep the pillow-like cottons dry. Then the thick Triple Crowns, and finally the linen bandage.

She remembered Geai schooling her as her inexperienced hands fumbled with the uncooperative white cotton. *Linen's not like those coloured nylon wraps. There's no stretch, so it's safer, but it's harder. You'll get it.* She'd taught her sister, and now Emilie supervised Marie, though Jo had approved of the young woman's bandaging skills, or she wouldn't be under their Oaks winner. Reliable help was hard to find, horsemanship a dying skill, but Marie was an adept student. Hopefully, she'd remain with the outfit for years to come.

Out on the lawn at the picnic table, Roger and Hélène prepared to depart, Roger helping Hélène to her feet. Liv broke away from her spot in front of the stall, because she couldn't let them leave without saying goodbye. It was so huge that Hélène had come.

Nate called a parting greeting from a few feet away, his arms already occupied. He held Sue's baby as naturally as he handled a foal, whereas the view gave Liv a queasy unease in the pit of her stomach. Not that she was against people having children, she just wasn't mother material herself.

"You looked quite at home there, Miller," she said once he'd given the child back and they waved at the Cloutiers' departing car. They wandered back to the shedrow.

"Ah. It's one thing to feel at home. It's another altogether to be responsible for taking them home, right?"

She wondered if the comment was for her benefit, or a true indication of how he felt. It was the tiny question mark she felt remained between them. "I'm sure they'll let you babysit any time you want."

"They'll have no shortage of babysitters," he said, both of them watching Faye gleefully snatch the baby from Sue's arms. "That is a side of Faye Taylor I've never seen."

"I would put money on her being next," Liv said wryly.

"That's quite a prediction. How much?"

"What?"

"How much money? Let's do this."

Liv just laughed at him before she turned back to Reba's stall, refusing to bet on her friend's reproductive future. It would be strange, Faye, with a kid. It would change the dynamic of their friendship again. Nate might be the unexpected buffer. *Uncle Nate.* She grinned at him. She loved those rare instances where it was obvious he had no idea why.

He was finally over his riding slump — winning a twelve million dollar race could do that to a guy — but Liv hoped Nate didn't define himself by his accomplishments any more than he'd scolded her for doing so. Cory still topped the standings, making the most of the remaining months of her apprentice allowance, so that coveted position might elude him for a while yet.

She'd neither anticipated nor been sure she wanted to tackle what circumstance had thrust upon her, but the truth of it all enveloped her in warmth and gratitude. Her name was recorded as conditioner of this year's Dubai World Cup — the first woman to claim that honour — but she could never accept the credit alone. This village — this family — made it happen.

Not long ago, family had meant little to her beyond Emilie and her parents, but the last six months had taught her it wasn't about blood. Everyone here was a part of something more enduring than any record or achievements. It had taken her an embarrassingly long time to figure out they were stronger together.

This here — all of it — was a good thing. An amazing thing. Chique had been the beginning, but this was not the end.

THANK YOU!

I hope you enjoyed *This Good Thing*. Thanks so much to everyone who emailed after Book Three — I used many of your comments to inspire Book Four. Your input really does matter. Let me know where you'd like to see the story go next! Email me anytime at linda@lindashantz.com

Reviews on your favourite retailer, as well as on BookBub and GoodReads are always appreciated. They feed authors, which lets us keep writing more books for you. It doesn't have to be long — pick some stars and write a few words.

If you'd like to keep in touch, sign up for my newsletter at lindashantz.com/writes for bonus chapters, updates, and more. Make sure you look for your confirmation email to be added. You can also follow me on BookBub.

I would be remiss if I didn't say a few words about ovarian cancer awareness. Symptoms are often vague and mistaken for other issues. If you're a woman experiencing any of these symptoms and they're new, persistent, or frequent, please consult with your doctor. Early detection is important!

• Bloating

- Abdominal pain or discomfort
- Fatigue
- Urinary symptoms
- Changes in bowel habits
- Difficulty eating
- Unexplained weight loss or weight gain
- Menstrual irregularities

Information source: https://ovariancanada.org/About-Ovarian-Cancer/Detection/Signs-Symptoms

ACKNOWLEDGMENTS

Special thanks go to my dear friend Juliet Harrison, who re-shared the details of her journey from ovarian cancer diagnosis through treatment and recovery. Any errors are my own. I'm especially grateful that eight years later, you're beating the odds.

Thanks to Nathalie Drolet, who planted the idea of the Dubai World Cup in my head, though I wasn't too sure about it. But, go big or go home, right? While I've been to Dubai with my artwork and had the honour of attending the race in 2007, I have not been there with a horse, so those details are mostly from my imagination!

As always, I'm indebted to my beta readers, Allison Litfin (for whom I must always leave at least one misplaced apostrophe), Bev Harvey, Nathalie Drolet, June Monteleone, Andrea Harrison and Dr. Kristen Frederick DVM. Extra thanks to Kristen for our discussions about the veterinary details.

I'm always grateful to Michelle Lopez, author and business accountability partner, who helps keeping me on task and is always supportive.

A particular shout-out this time around goes to one of the horses who inspired an equine character. Pacino is modelled after Henry, a horse who came to me for rehabilitation as a two-year-old. I'm so grateful for his owner's big heart as he lives out his days as a pasture ornament. His personality is as big as he is. Everyone loves Henry!

ABOUT THE AUTHOR

It was an eight-year-old me, frustrated that all the horse racing novels I read were about the Derby, not the Plate, who first put pencil to three-ring paper and started what would become this story. Needless to say, we've both grown up a bit since then.

I began working at the track before I finished high school, and after graduating the following January, took a hotwalking job at Payson Park in Florida. Once back at Woodbine, I started grooming and galloping. While the backstretch is exciting, I found I was more at home on the farm — prepping and breaking yearlings, nightwatching and foaling mares. Eventually I started my own small layup/broodmare facility, and in the last few years I've transitioned into retraining and rehoming. Somewhere along the way I did go back to school and get a degree. I should probably dust it off and frame it one day.

I live on a small farm in Ontario, Canada, with my off-track Thoroughbreds and a young Border Collie, and I'm probably better known for painting horses than writing about them — if you like my covers, check out my artwork at www. lindashantz.com

Author Photo courtesy of Ellen Schoeman Photography

Made in the USA
Coppell, TX
04 October 2023

22421472R00177